TRICKLOCK

Operation Powerful Vendetta

A Jake Tricklock Air Force Pararescue

Adventure

A book by

W I L L I A M F . S I N E

ISBN: 0990699706
ISBN 13: 9780990699705
Library of Congress Control Number: 2014916247
William F. Sine, Rio Rancho, NM

This is a work of fiction. Names, characters, businesses, places, events and incidents are either the products of the author's imagination or used in a fictitious manner. Any resemblance to actual persons, living or dead, or actual events is purely coincidental. The views expressed in this book are those of the author and do not necessarily reflect the official policy or position of the US Air Force, the Department of Defense, or the U.S. Government.

Chapter 1

TRICKLOCK

Air Force Pararescueman Jake Tricklock raced his truck down the taxiway to his awaiting helicopter. It was early morning but he could already see heat waves rising off the tarmac. The Philippine sun blazed hot, baking the concrete and driving steam off the verdant jungle. Tricklock parked the pickup and he and his teammate, Senior Airman Rob Evans, hopped out and grabbed their gear from the back of the truck. The pilots and flight engineer were already preparing the helicopter for flight. Minutes before, Tricklock received word that his crew had been tasked with a mission to extract an Army Special Forces team from deep within the jungle. Tricklock figured that this mission must be an emergency since they rarely flew these types of operations during daylight. The army team must be on the run, probably pursued by rebels. If that was the situation, the enemy would almost certainly outnumber the army patrol. In any case, Tricklock and his crew were prepared for the worst. They had to be. They were flying their MH-47E Chinook helicopter to an unfamiliar landing zone that was just a set of scribbled coordinates—a nondescript splotch on a map.

Moments later two massive helicopters powered into the humid air and slipped into a tactical flight formation. The twin rotor helicopters flew low and fast over dense triple canopy rain forest. Tricklock and Evans were on the lead helicopter while two other pararescuemen flew on the second chopper. While the helicopters raced above the trees, Tricklock and his teammate prepared the passenger compartment to receive the army patrol. They carefully positioned their medical gear near the suspended litters in case they picked up injured men. In only minutes, wounded soldier's lives could hang in the balance. When that happened, the pararescuemen and their medical expertise were expected to save the day. Tricklock was confident—pararescuemen, also known as PJs, were the best combat medics in the world. Although they were both newly assigned to their unit, Tricklock and Evans had received years of extensive training and possessed state of the art medical gear.

When the choppers neared their destination, the pilot contacted the American patrol on the radio. The pilot briefly quizzed the army team with prearranged questions designed to make sure they were not insurgents masquerading as Americans. After correctly answering the questions, the commando's patrol leader radioed that they had freed hostages with them and also some walking wounded. On the pilot's mark, the patrol popped a purple smoke grenade to identify the landing zone and show wind direction and velocity. Tricklock's lead helicopter swooped from the sky and flared hard at the last second. As the chopper settled into the remote jungle clearing, its whirling rotor blades whipped up gale force winds that flattened the high grasses. Tricklock and Evans jumped to the ground and rushed to meet the camouflaged men emerging from the tree line. While Tricklock's helicopter made the pickup, the second chopper circled overhead ready to come to the rescue if the other helicopter came under attack.

The army team looked beaten-up and exhausted. They half jogged, half limped towards the chopper. Some men supported wounded teammates between them, staggering with their buddy's arms draped round their necks for support. Although outwardly ragged, the expression in the men's eyes broadcast vitality and determination; their spirit burned strong. The patrol had placed their two freed hostages in the middle of their squad to more easily control and protect them. The former captives moved like walking dead. Tricklock and Evans positioned themselves so as to funnel the line of army men onboard the Chinook. In short order, the hostages and most of the Green Beret operators had entered the helo. Tricklock guessed the last man in line was probably their patrol leader—he hung slightly back, scanning the forest for threats and making sure that all his men got onboard.

Tricklock saw a bright flash at the jungle's edge and the patrol leader pitched forward. A split second later a geyser of crimson erupted from the soldier's thigh. Tricklock swung his rifle into play and unleashed a long burst of gunfire aimed where he had seen the flash of light. As he dashed zigzagging towards the fallen man, Tricklock yelled out the clock position of the gun flash into his radio while he continued to unleash short bursts of automatic gunfire into the jungle. He could hear the staccato cracks of return fire and as he reached the fallen soldier he could see the impact of enemy bullets ripping through the tall grass around him. Then suddenly, the roar of the Chinook's miniguns drowned out all other sound in the universe.

Tricklock struggled to lift the gun-shot sergeant, and then Evans was suddenly at his side. The two PJs supported the wounded commando between them and ran as fast as they could. Adrenaline pumped through the PJ's arteries, seeming to give them superhuman strength and speed. The helicopter's machineguns chopped up the jungle, keeping the attacker's heads down so they couldn't get a bead on the running PJs and their precious cargo. The six spinning barrels of the miniguns, modernized and perfected incarnations of Civil War era Gatling guns, fired 30 caliber high-powered rifle bullets at a rate of four thousand rounds per minute. While the helicopter's guns blazed, the attackers in the jungle were forced to cower behind thick tree trunks in order to survive the helicopter's blistering onslaught of machinegun fire. With supersonic chunks of lethal lead filling the air, the rebels could not leave cover for even an instant to aim and fire their weapons. The dense swarm of minigun bullets destroyed and deconstructed the rainforest. Jade specks of exploded vegetation floated thickly in the moist air like green confetti. The roar of the guns shook the forest, and saplings and stalks of bamboo sheared and splintered under the remorseless onslaught of hot bullets. When the PJs carrying the wounded soldier reached the helicopter, a gang of strong hands yanked them unceremoniously inside. A split second later the Chinook rose into the air, the nose dipped, and the helicopter accelerated to top speed, skimming the treetops that bordered the clearing.

During the flight back to base, Tricklock and Evans worked non-stop treating the wounded soldiers. They staunched deadly rivers of blood, started IVs, and administered powerful Ketamine pain medication to stoic warriors struggling keep it together despite their devastating wounds and excruciating pain. The patrol leader was lucky. The bullet had missed his femoral artery and the bone, but he was still in serious condition. With his leg splinted and bandaged, he sucked on a pain-killing fentanyl lollipop and surveyed his team. The two freed hostages were miraculously unhurt and sat quiet and unmoving. They were gaunt as zombies and appeared bewildered at their sudden change of fortune. Tricklock wondered how long they had been held captive in that vermin infested jungle. Sometimes the terrorists kept their victims for years. Liberation was not the usual outcome in these hostage situations, but this time the story had a rare happy ending.

An ambulance met the helicopter when it landed and hospital medics took custody of the injured. Every one of the Army Green Berets had survived. This was Tricklock's first taste of combat action and he was smitten. Tricklock had relished his first combat deployment to the Philippines, and in the PJ community, he began to earn a reputation as a fearless operator. He was amazed at how drastically his life had changed in the past couple of years. He had only recently graduated from the USAF Pararescue School and was now stationed at Kadena Air Base in Okinawa, Japan. After the terrorist attacks on September 11, 2001, the PJs on Okinawa went on war footing. In the following months while the world's attention was laser focused on the fighting in Afghanistan, the PJs from Okinawa were concentrating on combat actions in the Philippines.

When most Americans think of the Philippine Islands, if they think of them at all, they envision the large island of Luzon, the site of the capital city of Manila and the seat of government. Luzon is 99% Catholic, a legacy of historical Spanish colonial influences, but for decades the Philippine military has been fighting insurgents from the large island of Mindanao, which has been predominantly Muslim since the 15th century. The terrorist adversaries are primarily the Abu Sayyaf Group, Moro Islamic Liberation Front, and Jemaah Islamiyah. The American Joint Special Forces Task Force-Philippines assists the Philippine military in their fight against the terrorists, which is complicated by the fact that the country consists of 7000 islands.

In stark contrast to the deserts of Southwest Asia, lush tropical rainforests carpet the Philippines. Operation Enduring Freedom-Philippines is largely based out of Zamboanga Airport in the southern part of the islands. Joint Filipino and American training exercises called *African Lion* are an important part of the anti-terrorist operations. For years Islamic terrorists have carried out frequent kidnappings in the contested region and hold the innocent victims hostage for unreasonably large ransoms and for unconscionable spans of time. The Islamists use roadside bombs and ambushes to kill indiscriminately and have carried out assassinations across the entire region. Tricklock and his fellow airmen faced the same fanatical Islamists and the same ruthless tactics as coalition forces in Afghanistan, but they fought in steaming jungles instead of arid deserts.

In the Philippines Tricklock was frequently involved in covertly inserting and extracting Army Special Forces commando teams, sometimes referred to as Green Berets. Tricklock had trained with Army SF teams in the past and had great respect for their capabilities—they are very good at what they do. Typically the aviators flew their helicopters at night with all the aircraft lights turned off and set down in secretive jungle clearings. They were invisible night-raiders, and even the sound of their aircraft engines were muffled and dispersed by the thick jungle foliage. Tricklock and the rest of the aircrew wore night vision goggles that painted the night time landscape in bright monochromatic shades of emerald green. They would land their helicopter in hidden jungle clearings, and grim faced camouflaged men would quickly exit the chopper and melt into the tree line. The missions were always classified, but Tricklock knew that the teams were spying out terrorist bases and activities. Oftentimes the patrols were dispatched on search and destroy missions, but sometimes they would attempt "snatch and grab" rescue operations to free hostages. While in the Philippines Tricklock experienced the danger and excitement of combat missions, and he loved every minute. He had found his calling and resolved to dedicate his life to combat rescue and fighting terrorism.

When Tricklock thought back over the past three years he was amazed at the convoluted and adventure-filled journey that had taken him from small town USA, across the world to these battlefields in the primordial jungles of the tropics. As a U.S. Air Force Pararescueman, Jake Tricklock was an elite warrior. He was six feet two inches tall and had hair so black it had a bluish tint like comic book renderings of Superman. He kept his hair relatively short and brushed it straight back. With his chiseled features, confident demeanor, and aviator sunglasses, most people instantly guessed him to be Secret Service or military. Tricklock's steel gray eyes were as intense as those of a bird of prey, and seemed to darken or lighten with his moods. When he pinned you with his gaze it was hard to look away. Tricklock's eyes glinted with intelligence and humor, and if eyes are truly windows into a man's soul, then Tricklock's eyes revealed a soul possessed of immense vitality.

Most people called Jake Tricklock by his last name. Family lore had it that when his great grandfather Jakub emigrated from Czechoslovakia, his last name was Trcalek. But as so often happened in those days, an official at the European port of departure transliterated Trcalek as Tricklock onto the ship's register. At Ellis Island American officials used the ship's register to verify that immigrants had the means to pay for passage and were not stowaways. If an immigrant's name was missing from the register, he would be deported, and if a person's name was misspelled on the register, it was smart to accept the change and enter America without a fuss. Jakub was smart and for ever after, his family name was Tricklock.

On first meeting Tricklock, one instantly knew that this was not a person to take lightly. He had the hard muscles of someone who began exercising at a very early age and never stopped. He was clean shaven and had a square jaw that some thought was made of stone. That was because during boxing match-es his jaw seemed impervious to even the hardest punches. In fact, more than one of his opponents had broken his hand while delivering what he thought would be a perfect knockout punch. Not that it was easy to land a solid punch on Tricklock. He would probably have become a professional mixed martial arts cage fighter if he had not joined Air Force Pararescue.

Encouraged by his father, Jake took up karate and jujitsu when he was a teenager and proved to have an innate talent for martial arts. He was a natural at grappling and ground fighting and became a dominant force on his high school wrestling team. He was a prodigy and in a remarkably short time it was hard for Jake to find anyone who could challenge him in the ring. Since his father was a career Marine, Jake grew up around military bases and was always able to find good fighting clubs. These were the years when mixed martial arts were just beginning to become popular. Jake was too young to fight in professional matches, but the eventual possibility interested him. He also realized that if he was to seriously compete, then fighting would have to be his occupation. Part-time fighters never seemed to go far. Jake was also smart. With hardly any effort he achieved almost perfect grades in school, but he still thought that his best natural talent was fighting

Jake was not an angel—he had his share of run-ins with the law. He was guilty of all the usual teenage offenses: drinking, fighting, and skipping school. In the course of his adventures, he discovered he had a knack for escaping bad situations. While his friends were often nabbed in the act or shortly thereafter, the cops were never able to catch Jake. He was mystified by his friend's bumbling and lack of resourcefulness. It all seemed just common sense to Jake. If it hadn't been for his good upbringing he could have ended very differently. But his parents had instilled in him an enduring love for his country and strong moral values that eventually overwhelmed his immaturity.

When Jake graduated from high school he planned to follow in his father's footsteps and serve his country. He decided to join the military for a four year hitch. Ideally, he would live the stereotypical military experience, *see the world and have adventures while earning benefits for college.* Jake had no desire to kill people, so he planned to choose a specialty with a humanitarian focus. After his military hitch was up, he planned to attend college and pursue his life profession. He didn't know exactly what career that would be, but he would have four years to figure that out. Although his father had been a Marine, Tricklock decided he would march to a different drummer. He wanted to make his own mark, totally unique to his special talents. While researching special forces and unconventional warfare, Jake stumbled upon Air Force Pararescue. Intrigued, he read everything about pararescue that he could find. He learned that pararescue was as old as the U.S. Air Force and epitomized adventure, and patriotism—it seemed exactly what Jake was looking for. Pararescue seemed all action, danger, and excitement, requiring high altitude freefall parachuting, scuba diving, mountain climbing, field craft, and mastery of advanced weapons. The primary mission of pararescue is combat rescue, going behind enemy lines to save pilots forced to bail out of their jets. This often involves flying on a helicopter in the black of night, straight into the teeth of enemy air defenses. Pararescuemen, nicknamed PJs, are paramedics who specialize in providing medical care under the most difficult conditions, such as on a battlefield or in the back of a blacked-out helicopter dodging enemy gunfire.

Pararescue seemed like an extreme sport, and the life-saving aspects of the profession added intellectual and humanitarian dimensions that appealed to Jake. He could feel in his bones that pararescue was tailor-made for him. Jake learned that PJs are a highly decorated force with an amazing list of historical accomplishments. They are modern knights in shining armor who ride to the rescue on tricked-out helicopters instead of on barded and caparisoned destriers. Although other special operators are better known, such as Navy SEALS, Green Berets, and Marine Recon, the maroon berets of the PJs identify them as members of the most powerful commando rescue force in the world. Jake also learned of an ironic twist that cemented his decision to become a PJ. Near the end of the Vietnam War, USAF Pararescuemen had played a key role in evacuating the besieged Marines on Koh Tang Island, including his father Isaac.

Tricklock's high school sweetheart Barbara Ann visited while he was still in pararescue training. From the beginning, BA had made it clear that she did not approve of Tricklock's decision to join the Air Force. Her visit only reinforced her convictions; she detested everything military. A month after she left, she informed Tricklock that she was pregnant. He wanted to marry her, but she refused to get married unless he promised to leave the military. Even if he had wanted too, it was not that easy. He had a legal commitment to serve four years in the Air Force. Tricklock decided it would be better for all involved for him to finish his training and serve. He would be able to pay child support and planned to spend as much time as possible with his child. His son Simon was born in the first year of the 21st century while Tricklock was still in PJ training. Given BA's hostile attitude, Tricklock knew he would have a lifelong struggle to make his imprint as a father. Once he was established, he hoped that she would reconsider her stance.

Tricklock graduated at the top of his class and became one of the newest members of the official U.S. Air Force weapons system called Guardian Angel, the only Department of Defense agency dedicated to personnel rescue and recovery. Normally, weapon system status is reserved for aircraft, such as F-15s, but Guardian Angel is made up of human beings, PJs, combat rescue officers called CROs, and survival specialists. Weapon systems have the advantage of gaining certain priorities when it comes to money, which is always scarce in the military. Guardian Angel is an especially appropriate name for the weapon system, because guardian angels protect and also because a rescue angel forms the centerpiece of the silver emblem that adorns the distinctive pararescue maroon beret. The PJ motto is especially fitting, "That Others May Live."

Chapter 2

POWERFUL VENDETTA

Tricklock loved being stationed overseas. He had requested, and received, a follow-on assignment from Okinawa to England. The climate and culture in England is dramatically different than Okinawa's, but Tricklock loved culture shock and welcomed the change. He arrived at his new unit, the 321st Special Tactics Squadron on a gloomy and rainy fall day. His squadron was part of Air Force Special Operations Command. In his new unit he would be working closely with other special operators, such as USAF Combat Controllers. Combat controllers can direct airfield operations and manage airspace like air traffic controllers, but they can also call in airstrikes to blow up enemy fighters.

Tricklock quickly acclimated to his new home. It was a totally different environment than Okinawa. The weather was cool and rainy much of the time, but on the positive side there was no danger of typhoons. Tricklock felt like a time traveler, dwelling amid the old and the new. Randomly interspersed among contemporary structures was the architecture of bygone centuries. Ancient stone castles stood defiant, their weathered rock parapets colored by time and nature. Multi-hued patches of lichen decorated the rock fortifications with splashes of rust and lime. Dickensian pubs and eateries, built with medieval timber nestled among shiny new businesses. Thatch-roofed country cottages dotted the rural landscape, looking like illustrations from a book of fairy tales. Local pubs served delicious ales and simple food affectionately dubbed *pub grub*. Traditional menu items included country ham sliced thick and made into sandwiches with fresh baked bread and aged cheeses, breaded scampi, and savory meat pies. Tricklock's favorite meal was the cod and chips, battered, deep fried and plated with bright green peas.

During his first year in country, Tricklock's home was a small flat in an old row of houses set on a narrow lane. He was surrounded by history, even his local pub had been built before America was founded. Later on Tricklock moved into an old gamekeeper's lodge at the edge of a country estate. His nearest neighbor was a quarter of a mile away. When he gazed upon the bucolic landscape, he felt like landed gentry surveying his lands. The neatly manicured fields teemed with pheasant, and abundant deer bounded through the King's forest. During leisurely strolls down country lanes he would often encounter rabbits, hedgehogs, and other wild creatures. The fields resonated with birdsong and trilling insects. England felt like home, familiar at some deep ancestral level. All that Tricklock needed to make this a truly great assignment were some kick ass rescue missions.

Tricklock soon got his wish when he deployed to the Horn of Africa, commonly referred to as HOA. Tricklock was part of the combined joint task force operating under the auspices of the U.S. Africa Command. The task force's primary area of operations included the African countries of Sudan, Somalia, Djibouti, Ethiopia, Eritrea, Seychelles and Kenya. Anti-terrorism and piracy operations are the primary missions of Operation Enduring Freedom, Horn of Africa. The task force is based at Camp Lemonnier, a U.S. Expeditionary Naval Base located at the international airport in Djibouti. The camp, originally built by the French Foreign Legion, occupies two square kilometers. The main military housing complex is called CLUville and would not seem out of place as part of a moon base, because the apartments consist of long rows of prefabricated containerized living units—rectangular steel containers usually used to hold ship's cargo, converted into compact *cookie-cutter* living spaces for soldiers and airmen.

The base is home to approximately 1500 people including a robust contingent of special operators. Camp Lemonnier also shelters various aircraft including F-15 fighter jets, HC-130s, Navy P-3s, various models of helicopters, and Predator drones. During the day Tricklock and the other PJs pulled rescue alert at the task force compound. This kept them close to the center of activities and decision making. The compound also contained the intelligence shop which could provide essential information on any mission area. There are numerous opportunities for unique rescue missions in HOA. There have been operations to liberate ships from Somali pirates, missions to rescue civilians taken hostage by Islamists, and missions to snatch *high value targets*—important kingpins in the shadowy Islamist syndicate. Like cockroaches surviving and multiplying where they can, Islamist fighters relentlessly struggle to build a stronghold in this area of the planet and are the continuing focus of U.S. eradication operations.

Joint Special Operations Command usually has a monopoly on the really high-speed *James Bond* type missions, but sometimes conventional PJs get involved. In the public arena the most famous special units are Delta and Seal Team Six, but there are other special units that still dwell in the shadows. Tricklock eventually planned to try out for one of these secret units, but was having so much fun and combat action in the conventional arena that he just hadn't pursued membership. In the relatively small special operations community reputations spread, and some special units had actively recruited Tricklock on several occasions; many of his friends currently served in those units. So when the PJ attached to one of the special units working out of Africa was injured, he suggested that Tricklock could stand in for him. Tricklock was already in-country, and their unit had just been tasked with an extremely important mission. The special unit asked for Tricklock by name, and Tricklock's unit agreed to transfer him for the duration of the mission.

Tricklock was proficient in his parachuting, medical, and weapons skills and would be expected to seamlessly integrate into the team. His reputation had opened the door, but now he had to prove himself. When he was briefed on the details of the operation he was excited—jumping up and down excited! This was the type of mission he had always craved. Their mission mandate was to capture a very high level Islamist leader in the heart of his terrorist stronghold, Mogadishu, the capital city of Somalia. To remain undetected and capitalize on the element of surprise, his team would infiltrate by HAHO parachute jump.

HAHO is an acronym for High Altitude High Opening. During this type of jump, parachutists dive from the plane from as high as 30,000 feet and immediately open their parachutes. The team members form up in the sky and fly their canopies tens of thousands of feet above the ground, much like a formation of killer geese. A HAHO parachute drop is an elaborate way to infiltrate enemy territory and requires resources available only to the most powerful and wealthy nations. During this type of operation, a plane can offset as much as 40 miles from the parachutist's ultimate destination. Special computers on the aircraft calculate the best place for the jumpers to exit from the plane in order to use the prevailing winds to fly their parachutes to the desired landing spot many miles away.

There are numerous hardships that make this type of jump a remarkably complex and dangerous undertaking. The parachutists must defeat the effects of high altitude which can starve the brain of oxygen and make a person so confused he cannot add two plus two. Lack of oxygen will eventually lead to unconsciousness and death. Jumpers must breathe with a mask and small oxygen bottle strapped to their thigh. Without oxygen, a human being's *time of useful consciousness* at 30,000 feet is only one to three minutes. Other dangers of altitude include decompression sickness, commonly known as *the bends,* and extreme cold. The average temperature at 30,000 feet is minus 50 degrees and requires jumpers to use special high-tech clothing to stay warm. Teams usually parachute at night in order to stay invisible and as stealthy as night owls. Jumpers also wear the latest generation of night vision goggles which enables them to see on the darkest nights. They navigate with special GPS units and talk to each other through hands free radios that transmit to their helmet ear-pieces.

One of the reasons that the special team picked Tricklock was because he was an experienced tandem parachute jumper. Tandem jumpers can parachute with another person attached to the front of their parachute harness. This is the type of tandem jump that is available at most civilian skydiving clubs. But a military tandem jumper can skydive with an interpreter or a specially trained K-9 war-dog, or he can jump with up to 400 pounds of gear crammed in a barrel that dangles below him on a tether. The contents of the barrel are only limited by imagination.

After his bosses relieved Tricklock of his normal duties and lent him to the special unit, he immediately joined the team for train-up, planning, and rehearsal. Navy SEALs and Army Special Forces formed the bulk of the team, with a SEAL acting as team leader. Tricklock was the only air force guy on the team. He didn't know any of the other operators, but after talking with the guys they soon discovered they had some mutual friends. After some time on the shooting range, a few iterations in the kill house, and some hardcore exercise sessions, Tricklock began to establish his bona fides with the rest of the team. The team leader was named Jack Spenser, but everyone called him Jack Man—he was a proven badass. He was older, more experienced, and much higher ranking than Tricklock, but Jack Man and Tricklock immediately hit it off, competing in cross fit workouts and squaring off during combatives sparring sessions. Jack Man was impressed with Tricklock, having rarely met his match in mixed martial arts. Tricklock was also impressed, conceding that Jack Man had the edge in shooting skills and tactical experience.

Tricklock and a SEAL were slated to jump with tethered barrels containing hundreds of pounds of crucial gear. The team had sheaves of photos, video and other intelligence information to absorb. They memorized numerous details of the operation including descriptions of their objective so they could positively verify their human target by sight. They also did a few practice HAHO jumps to shake off any rust and to fine tune team dynamics. They started with daytime jumps and ended with a night jump that mirrored their actual mission drop. When Jack Man first briefed him, Tricklock experienced goose bumps and chills. This was the type of mission that he yearned—an operation he knew that very few people on earth could pull off. The fact that if successful, it would be a significant gut punch to one of America's most implacable enemies was extra gravy for the feast.

For all intents and purposes, al-Shabaab is *al Qaeda in Somalia*, and was the predominant ruling power in Mogadishu until Ethiopian and

Somali forces joined forces to fight them. This African alliance reclaimed most of the capital city, dealing the terrorist organization a terrible blow. The focus of Tricklock's mission was a top al Qaeda commander whose mission was to reconstitute and re-focus the al-Shabaab forces in Somalia. Marwan Rashid had a reputation as a brilliant tactician and strategist responsible for numerous successful attacks on Western targets, including a U.S. outpost where nine Americans had been killed. Al Qaeda leadership hoped that Rashid could re-constitute Al Shabaab and reverse the terrorist group's recent setbacks. This mission was aimed at capturing Rashid and short circuiting al Qaeda's plans to regain dominance and destabilize the fragile Somali government. They also hoped to interrogate Rashid and pry some al Qaeda's secrets from him.

The CIA had information from deeply embedded informants that Rashid had convened a high level strategy session in a safe house in Mogadishu. Many prominent Islamist figures were slated to attend. This imminent gathering of evil men was very clandestine and the location was sure to be heavily guarded. These precautions were primarily aimed at foiling any possible interference from Somali government forces. An advantage for Tricklock's team was that the terrorists felt relatively secure in the midst of their stronghold—they probably would not expect an attack from American special forces in the heart of their territory. Tricklock's team knew the location of the meeting; they only awaited final word from intelligence sources as to the exact date and time. A few days later word came down. The mission was a go!

Jack Man chose HAHO as the method of infiltration for a number of reasons. The target location was near the beach, but any U.S. warship entering Somali waters would be a giant beacon, drawing a huge amount of attention. Because of that, Jack Man immediately dismissed plans to launch the team from a warship. Any attempt to infiltrate by boat from far out at sea also ran the real risk of encountering one of the many well-armed Somali pirate ships, making that course of action a non-starter. To infiltrate from the landward side would require the team to travel undetected for miles through a populated and highly hostile city, definitely not a viable course of action—that left HAHO parachute infiltration.

During the beginning phases of the parachute drop the plane is so high and so far away that even the most eagle-eyed bad guys will be totally unaware of their imminent danger. If they aren't backlit by bright moonlight, the parachutists will be invisible in the night sky. Like a predatory owl diving silently on an unsuspecting mouse, they will strike with devastating power and amazing precision. HAHO is a supremely effective method of infiltration if it's done properly, but it's a very difficult skill to master. Only the *best of the best* commandos backed by the full resources and might of a military superpower are able to successfully carry out a precision parachute operation in the dead of night.

Tricklock sat on the uncomfortable red canvas troop seats of the MC-130 breathing oxygen and awaiting commands from his team leader. All the planning, rehearsals, and equipment checks were accomplished. Tricklock was living in the moment. He was like a championship thoroughbred, high strung and straining to burst from the starting gate. He was vibrating with pent up energy, ready to begin the mission. His only fear was that a sudden development would cause the mission to scrub or postpone. That possibility was all too common in military operations of this kind. Terrorist commanders can change their plans in the blink of an eye. They are notoriously twitchy and paranoid—and they have good reason to be wary. Americans are constantly killing al Qaeda's best and brightest when they least expect it using ingenious methods, such as hellfire missile strikes launched from CIA predator drones, and even exploding goats. Tricklock relished the thought of an exploding goat taking out a terrorist.

For this mission the jump altitude would be 30,000 feet. The plan was to fly their parachutes for 25 miles, eventually landing in the ocean about a mile off the coast. They were not attacking the safe house where the actual meeting was to be held. They planned to hit a dwelling where Rashid was to spend the night while he waited for the meeting the next day. Tricklock's team totaled six operators and they all breathed off a large green oxygen bottle while they waited for the crucial 20 minute time call. That call would begin the sequence of events that would culminate in their diving out the back of the plane. The team was flying stealthily through the night in an MC-130J Commando II the latest generation of the Combat talon II aircraft. The loadmaster in the cargo compartment flipped a switch—hydraulic systems whined, and the plane's aft ramp and door opened like a giant clamshell.

The temperature suddenly plummeted, and condensation fog coalesced around the jumpers as sub-zero air swirled, momentarily chilling them to the bone. The city of Mogadishu, known as Xamar to the locals, nestled against pristine beaches lapped by waves from the Indian Ocean. The open ramp of the plane framed a dead black square of night sky. The jet-black night did not look so dark and formidable to the jumpers. Their night vision goggles turned the darkness into sparkling shades of green. The jumpmaster passed the two minute call, and the team formed a single file arranged in the order they would exit the plane.

A short time later, Jack Man held up his forefinger, signaling one minute to jump. The team shuffled close to the edge of the ramp, the man closest to the edge teetering on the threshold of nothingness.

When the jump lights turned green, Jack Man pointed out to space and yelled, "Go!"

The jumpers began leaping off the ramp at one second intervals. When Tricklock dove from the plane he was immediately engulfed by empty space and subzero temperatures. When he stabilized and deployed his parachute he was already falling at 125 miles per hour. After his chute opened he glanced up to check his canopy and then chimed in with his tactical call sign. Tricklock's actions were repeated by all the team members, and the team leader heard all his men check in on inter-team radio. Jack Man was the team leader in overall command, but they would all follow the man picked to be navigator. Everyone's parachute was open and they were flying at 27,000 feet. All the jumpers converged on the navigator's position putting him at the center. The team maneuvered into formation while the navigator set course for Mogadishu.

Tricklock's heart was just slowing back to normal after the adrenaline filled moments leading up to and following his dive from the plane. Everything had gone smooth as silk, and he now occupied his planned position in the formation. Through his night vision goggles Tricklock could clearly see his teammates and despite the barrel hanging beneath him on a tether, he was easily able to maintain his position in the group. The navigator followed his GPS bearing and forged ahead. The other jumpers mimicked the navigators every turn. Over open-ocean there are no geographical features or landmarks. The team had to have total faith and trust in their gear—it was an eerie feeling.

The commando team flew their parachute formation silently towards Mogadishu. Colored pale green by the night vision goggles, dim moonlight filtered through high clouds and glinted off the glassine sea far below. They flew their parachutes with the wind at their back. With the 25 knot forward airspeed of their parachute canopies added onto the wind velocity, they cruised at more than 40 miles per hour. In addition to following the GPS bearing, Jack Man closely monitored their altitude and elapsed time. Their flight plan had benchmarks of time and altitude. There are numerous techniques a jumper can use to slow or speed-up his parachute's descent rate, and Jack Man coordinated the team to match their planned benchmarks as closely as possible. The parachutists had to make constant adjustments, reacting to their team leader's commands and manipulating their parachutes to stay in formation. Time passed quickly and soon Tricklock could see the twinkling green lights of the city and the pale shoreline. Tricklock felt like he was about to visit the Emerald City in the Land of Oz. Maybe the wizard would give him the gift of a terrorist commander!

They were on course and flying at the proper altitude, so far so good. Rashid was supposed to be sleeping at a house close to the water in an affluent neighborhood. This was one of the factors that had made this mission possible. The accessible location of the house made it possible to plan a realistic infiltration and exfiltration scheme. The team steered to land in the ocean a mile from the beach. This was relatively close to shore, but they would be still be invisible to any nocturnal beach goers who happened to be watching the heavens. Once they landed in the sea, they would travel to GPS coordinates at a spot on the beach that provided a suitable area to leave the water unobserved. That location was a perfect springboard to launch their assault on Rashid's lair. At a predetermined time, their asset on the ground would turn on an infrared strobe light placed at a spot off the beach and near a concealing grove of trees. The flashing strobe would be clearly visible to anyone wearing night vision goggles but invisible to the naked eye.

Tricklock's team landed in a tight group, gently splashing into the calm, coffee colored sea. Once in the water Tricklock freed the barrel from his harness and then helped the rest of the team organize their gear. First they unpacked the two tethered barrels. Each barrel contained a tightly rolled Zodiac raft, powerful outboard engine, and rubber bladders full of fuel. Each fifteen and a half foot boat weighed 265 pounds. With engines, fuel, and other gear, the tandem bundles had been packed at their max weight limit of 400 pounds. The team used the remaining air in their HAHO oxygen bottles to inflate the boats. Next they mounted the engines onto the boat transoms and hooked up the fuel bladders. Before leaving the area, the team placed their parachutes and disposable gear into the now empty containers, then flooded and sank the barrels.

Tricklock and the other commandos clambered into the boats, tied–in, and organized their equipment. They started both engines and headed towards their infiltration point on the beach. They switched to paddles when they got close and needed to be silent. Viewed through their goggles, the sandy beach was a lime green sparkling line in the distance. Still heading towards their coordinates, they soon made out the periodic flash of the infrared strobe. The strobe light was situated near an oasis of trees on a deserted stretch of sand. The team had their first bit of good luck—the beach was completely deserted. Under the cover of darkness and keeping as low a profile as possible, they hefted the boats onto their shoulders, jogged across the beach, and hid the craft in the concealing grove of trees. They carefully camouflaged their boats; they would need them later for their get-away. Jack Man sent two men with palm fronds to carefully erase their tracks in the sand, and then it was time to go after Rashid.

Their agent on the ground had mapped-out a clandestine path to the house. Tricklock and the rest of the team had already run the exact route, except they had done it in 3d virtual reality as part of their train-up. They moved quickly and quietly through deserted back alleys keeping to the shadows. The ninjas of old would have been amazed and envious of their modern-day counterparts with their state of the art camouflage, night vision goggles, and high-tech weapons. Blazing speed was essential. The team traveled super light, wearing only wafer thin plate armor and slim tactical vests. They carried only their weapons and instead of combat boots, they wore running shoes and moved *fast*!

When they arrived at the target house, they immediately recognized the silhouette. Viewed through their NVGs, the blacked-out building loomed dark as hate, a sinister edifice surrounded by shimmering emerald sparkles. Due to repeated rehearsals, its familiar shape and angular lines were indelibly etched onto each team member's gray matter. They rechecked their silenced 40 caliber Glock pistols and formed a single file line called a stack, at the rear entrance of the house. For this mission they had modified their room clearing procedures. They were in the heart of a populous city, surrounded by enemies. They intended to carry out this operation as silently as possible. They would not use violent breaching techniques or loud flash-bang grenades. They quickly picked the primitive door lock and entered a narrow hallway filled with dense shadows.

They moved noiselessly in a predetermined and methodical pattern, their complex choreography a mute testament to their tactical skill and many hours of rehearsals. They cleared rooms as they went, making sure not to leave any enemies in their rear. Eventually they arrived at a closed door, behind which lay a living area and bedrooms which hopefully housed Rashid and maybe only a few trusted bodyguards. Once again they formed a stack—this door was unlocked, and they surged through the entrance smooth as panthers, each man clearing his zone of responsibility. Team members killed two men in the first seconds. They were hard men who despite being taken unawares died scrambling for their weapons. The team's silenced pistols flashed lightning and dealt death. The sound of the slamming metal slides of their Glocks sounded shockingly loud in the stillness, but a person standing just outside the house would have heard nothing. Tricklock was the last man into the room, and the rest of his team was already clearing the final two bedrooms that led off from the common area. He could hear pistol slides racking, cries of surprise cut short, and bodies thudding onto the floor. The enemy bodyguards were experienced fighters. Even caught totally by surprise, they had almost been able to get their weapons into play—almost but not quite. Only one man had managed to rip off a short burst from his rifle before Tricklock's team cut him down. The bullets missed Tricklock's teammates, but the sound was deafening. Hopefully the brief roar of the rifle would not draw immediate enemy reinforcements.

Every mission carried the potential for disaster, but so far no one on the team had been injured. Tricklock entered the last bedroom in time to see Rashid being silenced and secured. His mouth was taped, his hands flexicuffed behind him, and a hood placed over his head. Before the hood covered his face, Tricklock was able get a quick look at Rashid's eyes. The terrorist commander's eyes were wide and disbelieving, his pupils dilated. And then they were on the move. Two SEALs grabbed Rashid under his armpits and ran with the terrorist suspended between them. Rashid's legs wind-milled as he was forced to run between his captors.

Travelling their planned return route, the Americans sprinted past dark buildings and through dim alleys. Rounding a bend they encountered a group of men bristling with AK-47 rifles and rocket propelled grenades. The men were probably responding to the sounds of the earlier gunfire at Rashid's house and had run right into the path of Tricklock's team. Tricklock could tell they were not government forces by their garb—they weren't wearing uniforms. Each man dressed as he pleased, and their attire lacked the standardization common to military units. Their night vision goggles gave Tricklock's team a split second advantage over the militiamen.

Jack Man yelled, "Contact front!" and the Americans opened fire while spreading their formation and continuing to move forward. Caught by surprise, half of the enemy force went down from gunshot wounds in the first seconds. The rifle bursts sounded like staccato cracks of thunder and muzzle flashes lit the scene like strokes of lightning, momentarily overwhelming the night vision goggles. Tricklock dropped to the ground when he caught a brief glimpse of a fighter aiming his rocket propelled grenade. The grenade whooshed mere feet above his head and exploded on the side of a building showering brick and glass. Tricklock rolled to his left and dashed forward, only to be flung through the air by another explosion. He came up firing and saw his target go down with half of his head a distorted mess.

For a time, a rapid series of powerful concussions and automatic machine gun fire rocked and echoed through the alley ways. The cacophony of noise, screams, and explosions abruptly stopped. In an instant darkness and quiet returned to the narrow street. Jack Man called out to the team and everyone checked in with their medical condition and ammunition status. Tricklock and two others had sustained moderately serious wounds. Tricklock jammed a roll of gauze into the hole in his calf and tightly wrapped over it with an elastic bandage. Then he attended to the other wounded, using tourniquets and pressure bandages to staunch bleeding. He gave shots to dull pain and made quick, temporary fixes that would allow the men to continue the mission. In only a few minutes, Tricklock had everyone able to move and fight, including himself. The team took up a brisk-paced run and continued on towards their hidden boats. Luckily Rashid, their high value target, was unhurt and the mission could still succeed. From this point on, speed would be their most effective weapon. Their firefight had almost certainly attracted the unwanted attentions of dangerous men. His team had just whacked a huge Islamist hornet's nest, and they had to get out of there fast!

Tricklock felt the effects of blood loss and incipient shock. He reached deep inside himself, tapping into his vast reserves of willpower and physical strength. He ran hard and fast, ignoring the intense pain in his leg and managed to keep pace with the rest of his team. He had taken a bullet or shrapnel in his right lower leg, which was blood slicked and could barely, support his weight. An icy numbness slowly crept upwards from his wound. Adrenaline laced blood coursed through Tricklock's arteries and he moved with determination born of his pride, and his dread of the consequences of failure. Tricklock pushed his discomfort to the back of his mind and concentrated on moving with the team. After what seemed like forever, they arrived at their boats. Tricklock was functioning in a haze of pain, shock, and unsteadiness, but one would never have guessed his condition by talking to him. He appeared calm and together and continued to do his job flawlessly despite his inner turmoil and pain. Now that they had arrived at the Zodiacs it no longer mattered if Rashid was dead weight, so Jack Man allowed Tricklock to inject their captive with a potent sedative to keep him quiet and compliant.

The commandos shouldered the two Zodiacs and ran across the beach towards the sea. After erasing their tracks from the sand, they propelled the boats through the curling waves. Once past the surf break, they scrambled into the glistening black boats and hurriedly paddled out to sea. Luckily, there were no signs of enemy pursuit. When they were out of earshot from the beach they started the boat engines and gunned them to full throttle. The team crouched behind the gunwales to keep a low profile and streaked towards their exfiltration point five miles off the coast. Before they had started, Tricklock had the other wounded men moved to his boat so he could more completely treat their injuries on the way to their pickup site. Fortunately no one had any immediate life threatening wounds. The two boats cruised to a set of GPS coordinates, a nondescript piece of open ocean, where if all went well special ops helicopters would scoop them up from the sea. While the team had been in the midst of their mission, two twin rotor CH-47s were synchronizing their flight schedule to the commando team's mission timeline. The helicopters lifted off and after flying over open-water in the dark of night, they rendezvoused with an HC-130 at 1,500 feet to take on gas via aerial refueling. An hour before dawn, the choppers made contact with the commandos driving the two Zodiac boats. The pilot's authenticated the team and rolled into their extraction sequence.

If the sea had been turbulent, the team would have sunk their boats and used a Fast Rope Insertion/Extraction System to escape the area. Fortunately, the ocean was smooth as a mirror, which allowed them to stay with their primary pickup plan. The helicopters lowered their aft ramps and descended right down to the surface of the sea. The chopper's rotors blurred overhead and the powerful engines strained to levitate the ponderous bulk of the mechanical behemoths. The helicopter's aft ramps gently kissed the face of the sea then dipped slightly below the surface. Pungent sea water flooded into the chopper's cargo compartments, but only a few inches deep. The pilots kept their helicopters moving forward at a crawl, with just enough forward momentum for the pilots to keep positive control during this delicate and dangerous procedure. Inside the helicopters, the back-end crewmen stood ankle deep in sloshing seawater. The spicy smells of salty ocean water filled their nostrils. They constantly updated the pilot on conditions in the back of the aircraft. An ordinary pilot would never think of attempting this maneuver, but these were experienced special operations pilots who trained to accomplish these daring and near impossible aviation feats.

Moments later, two Zodiacs hurtled out of the dark. At first they appeared to be traveling too fast. The speeding boats generated bow waves that agitated and sluiced in the closed space of the helicopters. The boat drivers skillfully and boldly sped their Zodiacs into the cramped confines of the choppers cargo compartments. They drove their boats with just enough speed to propel them fully into the helicopters, but not so fast that they would crash into the backside of the cockpits. Immediately after the boats scraped to an abrupt halt on the aircraft's aluminum floor, everyone scrambled out and dragged the boats forward so the ramps could close.

While the crew tied down the boats and organized for the flight, the helicopters majestically lifted off the sea. Peering through their night vision goggles, the team watched as a shimmering waterfall of sea water drained from the helicopter's cargo compartments in coruscated torrents of luminescent green. Suddenly relieved of their ponderous burden of hundreds of gallons of seawater, the two helicopters rapidly gained speed and altitude. The choppers smoothly slid into a tactical formation and raced towards their aerial refueling coordinates. The aircraft left behind no evidence of their presence. Where moments before two powerful helicopters had whipped sea water into foam and retrieved two commando teams, only soft salt breezes blew across a placid expanse of olive colored sea.

While Tricklock gained experience and rose through the pararescue ranks, a continent away an ambitious young Egyptian named Khaled was climbing meteorically through the ranks of al Qaeda. The top terrorist leaders had embraced Khaled's bold plans to carry the fight to the West in a new and unexpected way. Around the world, and especially near military bases that hosted American and British forces, the terrorist organization began to build and consolidate intelligence networks to counter the spy organizations of America and her allies. They also set up a world wide web of sleeper cells to carry out sabotage missions and assassinations. Ironically, the Americans had assumed all along that al Qaeda had deep cover operatives living and working in the United States, much like the old Soviet Union had maintained during the cold war. Terrorist sleeper cells were even a staple of American spy novels. Al Qaeda certainly had sympathizers in America, but no extensive network of undercover assassins. Khaled resolved to help America realize its worst fears; he would form al Qaeda hit squads in the United States and use them to kill American commandos. He named his initiative *Operation Powerful Vendetta*.

The United States, Great Britain, and Israel use their intelligence services to spy-out al Qaeda and Taliban leaders, and then they dispatch drones or highly trained commandos to assassinate or capture the terrorist commanders. In the past, al Qaeda carried out spectacular attacks on the West, such as the destruction of the world trade centers which took years to plan and execute. Since the beginning of America's *War on Terror*, such complex operations were becoming increasingly difficult, if not impossible, to organize. Khaled proposed taking a page from their enemy's playbook to turn the tables on the United States and her allies. He insisted that al Qaeda improve their own intelligence service and use assassins to track and kill Americans. Although America's generals and commanders were often too well protected to target, he thought that al Qaeda could be successful going after the actual commandos and field commanders. It was an unexpected tactic that should be highly effective. Sometimes American grassroots operators even advertised their accomplishments and medals in their hometown newspapers, not even considering that they and their families might be targets of retaliation and revenge. Khaled smiled when he imagined the reaction of the American public after one of his assassination squads killed a Navy SEAL and his family in their hometown. Al Qaeda would proudly claim responsibility for murdering local American heroes and their loved ones. The executions would be potent proof that even the lowest ranking special operators were not immune from al Qaeda's retaliation. Khaled thought that such killings would send shockwaves through America's special operations community.

At every American overseas base, local nationals make up a large proportion of the workforce. From cooks in the cafeteria to janitors in the most sensitive buildings, a system exists that is ripe for terrorist exploitation and infiltration. At Khaled's urging, al Qaeda began to build their web of informants in earnest. Khaled wanted to emulate the cold war communist tactic of targeted assassinations but on a global scale. He had in mind operations like those conducted by the communist New People's Army (NPA) in the Philippines. In April of 1989 they ambushed and killed Colonel Nick Rowe, a famous escaped Vietnam POW and important founder of American special operations training. The NPA placed Col Rowe under surveillance and noticed a pattern to his movements. They attacked his car when he was going to work, killing him with a shot to the head. But Khaled also wanted to carry the fight against the actual commandos who raided against al Qaeda, and he didn't want his hits to be few and far between. When it came to al Qaida attacks, Khaled planned to break the mold. He wanted the assassinations to be a frequent and ongoing operation, an almost monthly occurrence.

Khaled thought that by assassinating American special operators, the very same soldiers who were killing al Qaeda's leaders, he would force the Americans to spend a lot of blood and treasure to counter the new tactic. Al Qaeda's top leaders gave Khaled the go-ahead. Over the following months Khaled's network of spies and assassins grew rapidly and collected prodigious amounts of information. The internet with its high tech search engines was an amazing resource. Khaled compiled lists of American special operators who had been in the news, or had publically boasted of their success against al Qaeda and the Taliban. Among the names of potential targets that made it into the terrorist's Powerful Vendetta database was an American pararescueman named Jake Tricklock.

Chapter 3

MARKED FOR DEATH

Helmand Valley Afghanistan, September 2013: Tricklock was enjoying his deployment to Camp Bastion. That was because he was saving lives and making a difference—he felt like he was fulfilling his destiny and doing the job he was born to do. It was dangerous but exciting work. His most recent mission was a case in point. After scrambling on a rescue mission, his Pave Hawk helicopter and crew flew to a small village of squat dwellings made of crude bricks. On this mission, Tricklock's team member was his friend Staff Sergeant Tommy Mason. Their mission was to rescue an Afghan soldier who had fallen into an empty well during a night patrol. While the lead helicopter circled above, Tricklock's aircraft landed and he and Tommy hopped down from the helicopter. Where the soles of their combat boots touched the ground, arid puffs of fine dust swirled around their legs. The helicopter lifted off to take up an orbit in tandem with the other chopper while Tricklock and his team member did their job. With both helicopters airborne the two PJs were suddenly wrapped in silence. A uniformed Afghan soldier warily approached and guided them to a nearby hole in the ground. Five other Afghan soldiers spread out to form a loose security perimeter to guard the PJs while they worked. PJs are Jacks of all Trades, expert practitioners of all things rescue. Tricklock beamed a powerful light into the depths of the well and could see a man lying motionless on dry rocky earth about forty feet down. There were no trees or supporting structures around the pit on which to attach a rope. Hell, there wasn't even a fence or sign to warn people of the deep hole in the ground. Tricklock told Tommy to pound two duckbills into the ground. A duckbill is a strong metal rod and cable that can be hammered into the earth to make a strong anchor to hook a rope too when there are no trees or other strong attachment points. While Tommy set the duckbills, Tricklock attached a device to a cord and lowered it to the bottom of the well to electronically sniff the air. If the stagnant air was poison, it would be suicide to descend without a small tank of compressed breathing air. The air in the well tested pure. The soldier's unconsciousness was probably due to his forty foot tumble and not to lethal vapors.

Before he left the helicopter Tricklock had grabbed the rope bag which contained a black 200 foot rappel rope. Slightly less than half an inch thick, this high-tech rope can suspend up to 7,500 pounds. Tricklock also grabbed a small gear kit containing some pulleys, carabiners, and slings. PJs always bring a rappel rope on the helicopter. If the aircraft can't land because the ground is strewn with boulders or the ground slopes at a steep angle, then the helicopter can hover and the PJs will rappel to the ground. Tricklock secured one end of the rope to the duckbill anchor points and the other end to Tommy's harness. This whole procedure took only a few minutes.

Tricklock slowly lowered Tommy into the hole, carefully controlling his descent with a special friction device. Tommy descended into the gloom carrying his rifle, medical gear, and a small portable litter. Once his feet hit bottom, he looked up to see Tricklock framed in the sun lit entrance to the pit. Tommy quickly examined the prostrate Afghan, systematically checking his pulse and breathing. While Tommy worked on his patient, Tricklock began to convert his rope setup into a system, much like a block and tackle, that he could use to haul both Tommy and the victim out of the well. Tricklock stopped what he was doing when he heard Tommy yelling. Tricklock leaned over the edge and peered into the hole.

Tommy hollered up to Tricklock, "This guy's dead."

Tricklock shouted back, "I'm almost ready to haul you both up."

There was urgency in Tommy's reply, "This guy didn't fall—he's been shot!"

Tricklock felt the hair rise on the nape of his neck and alarm bells clanged in his brain. The implication of Tommy's discovery was staggering—this could be a trap. He quickly looked up to scan his surroundings. Two wide-eyed Afghan guards nervously squirmed and fidgeted in their security positions, but two other guards were sprinting away towards the nearby mud brick huts. Heavy machine gun fire suddenly erupted from the nearby structures. The deafening roar was deeper and more ominous than an assault rifle. Tricklock immediately identified it as a 12.7mm, Russian DSHK. This gun is bad news. It's twice as powerful as the American Browning M2, 50 caliber machine gun and is capable of shooting down helicopters and shredding lightly armored vehicles. Tricklock couldn't believe it! What was a DSHK doing in this tiny shithole of a village?

The DSHK gunner began to walk his bullets towards Tricklock's position. Where the powerful rounds impacted the ground they kicked up geysers of yellow clay. The Russian gun's powerful bullets nearly ripped one of the guards in half, lifting him off his feet and spattering his bloody remains across the dirt. Tricklock dived into the well a split second before a fusillade of screaming hot lead would have torn him into pieces. He frantically clutched at the rappel rope as he fell and finally managed to clamp his grip on the thin line to slow his fall. The rope slid through his gloved hands charring and smoking the leather. His shoulders strained near to bursting, but his years of special operations training had forged his muscles hard as steel and his joints held together. When his iron grip finally prevailed, he jerked to a wrenching stop. Tricklock had the strength of desperation as he lowered himself down the rope hand under hand. In a matter of seconds he reached the bottom of the well and frantically scraped off his smoldering gloves.

"What the hell is going on?" yelled Tommy.

Tricklock snapped back, "We're under attack! Get your rifle up! I'm radioing the chopper.

Pedro one four, we're taking fire from the village and at least one guard is dead. We're both trapped in the well. Keep your distance, they have a DSHK!"

The Pedro immediately responded, "Roger thanks for the safety tip. We're on it."

When they next heard from the Pedro, Tricklock recognized the voice of Lieutenant Thomas, his combat rescue officer, or CRO. The Lieutenant explained to Tricklock that they had an inbound Apache attack helicopter only a few minutes out. The Apache would have to destroy the DSHK before the Pedros could attempt to pull the PJs out of the well. Until then Tricklock and Tommy were on their own.

The crashing din of the gunfire up-top abruptly stopped. The PJs were trapped in their hole and blind to what was happening topside. Tricklock nudged Tommy to stay on-guard—they squished against the side of the well trying to stay small. Suddenly a Taliban fighter appeared above and sprayed AK-47 rounds down into the well. The soldier was wary, and his un-aimed fire was hurried and off target. The Kalashnikov's bullets churned up the earth next to Tommy before Tricklock unleashed a short burst of high velocity rifle bullets into the attacker's chest. Due to the upward angle of Tricklock's shots, his rounds ricocheted off the soldier's armored chest plate and deflected up into his bearded chin. In an instant the bullets demolished the attacker's face and blood and teeth showered down upon the PJs. Dead on his feet, the Afghan dropped his rifle and tumbled forward into the well. Trapped in the narrow confines of the shaft, the PJs scrambled to dodge clear. The falling Afghan thudded wetly onto the other dead Afghan narrowly missing the PJs, but his AK-47 slammed into Tommy's shoulder. The 10 pound rifle fell from a height of 40 feet and generated more than 1500 pounds of force. The rifle knocked Tommy to the ground as if he were poleaxed. Tommy miraculously remained conscious, but he writhed in agony. His shoulder and collarbone were almost certainly broken and his right arm flopped alarmingly at his side.

Tricklock did his best to help Tommy. He put Tommy's arm in a sling and strapped it with an elastic bandage while keeping one eye focused up-top looking for other attackers. A short time later the PJs heard all hell break loose. The Apache had arrived angry and immediately began firing its 30mm chain gun and unleashing its Hellfire missiles. The weapons pulverized the buildings that sheltered the Taliban DSHK and turned the brick structures into jumbled piles of dust and rubble. To Tricklock and Tommy, it sounded like the Apache was tearing apart the planet. To the Taliban it felt like the end of the world, and for them it actually *was* judgment day. Afterwards, Tricklock could still hear sporadic small weapons fire, but it was obvious that the Apache had destroyed the DSHK. The attack helicopter mopped up the remaining small pockets of resistance and loitered on scene looking for targets of opportunity. With the main threat destroyed, the Pedros began their run-in to pick up the PJs.

After the Apache had rained down its unique brand of destruction, Tricklock had injected Tommy with a generous dose of pain meds and finished the sling and swathe splint on his damaged arm and shoulder.

Shortly after the Apache finished sterilizing the village, Pedro 13 radioed, "PJs, we're going to lower our rappel rope into the well. Tie in and we'll lift you out."

Tricklock responded, "Roger Pedro one three. Be advised that Tommy has a broken shoulder. We are standing by for extraction."

A short time later the hovering Pedro blotted out the sun above the well, and a flight engineer lowered one end of a rappel rope into the pit. Tricklock quickly tied two loops a few feet apart, and he clipped Tommy and then himself onto the loops. Tricklock yelled instructions into his radio and the hovering chopper lifted vertically into the air, until he and Tommy were clear of the well. The helicopter continued to ascend and gradually transitioned into flight. The two PJs dangled below the helicopter, fluttering in the wind generated by the helicopter's forward motion. Tricklock was attached to the upper rope loop and controlled Tommy with his legs. He used his spread arms to stabilize them against the force of the wind caused by the choppers forward flight speed.

When they were miles clear of the hostile village, Pedro 13 slowly lowered Tricklock and Tommy to the ground. The PJs unclipped from the rope, and the chopper landed off to the side. Pedro 14 soon joined them, and after a brief gathering with man-hugs all around, they returned to the choppers. The pain medication had fortified Tommy and he was able to board his helicopter supported between Tricklock and Lieutenant Thomas. The crews returned to base feeling very fortunate to have survived the ambush.

A few weeks earlier, Tricklock had deployed to Afghanistan from his home base in New Mexico. For the past couple of years, he had been assigned to the

Guardian Angel Training Center on Kirtland Air Force Base. Kirtland borders the Southern edge of Albuquerque, the most populous city in New Mexico and home to about nine hundred thousand people. On the east, the city bumps up against the burnished pink granite of the Sandia Mountains. An Indian reservation borders the city to the north, and the legendary Rio Grande River flows southward through the city. The *Duke City* actually straddles the river, nestling in the Rio Grande Valley. Albuquerque's streets are laid out in a neat grid, like a giant chess board. The land gradually slopes up on the West side of the river forming the West Mesa. At the Northwest edge of Albuquerque, the city morphs into the rapidly growing community of Rio Rancho. This is where Tricklock rented a house, although Rio Rancho is a 25 mile drive from the PJ School.

His neighborhood in Rio Rancho reminded Tricklock of a medieval forti-fied village. In the distance, he could see other small sub-divisions perched on hilltops. Like his neighborhood, they were completely surrounded by sand colored cement block walls. In his community every back yard was enclosed by masonry walls. If another country ever invaded, the people could actually organize and defend their subdivisions. Tricklock guessed that the real reason for the brick walls was protection from high winds. Every spring the breez-es build, whipping sand and tumbleweeds across the open spaces. The walls break the wind and protect the stucco houses. Tricklock's yard was gravel and stone planted with native trees and cacti. His yard was home to desert willows, western red buds, lilac chaste trees, Mexican elders, Russian sage, agave cac-tus, and chitalpa trees. Red yucca and large tufts of various decorative grasses also dotted Tricklock's land. Instead of artificially maintaining a grass lawn in the middle of a desert, he practiced xeriscaping, a landscaping technique that uses gravel, stone, and drought resistant vegetation. His yard looked natural and required very little up-keep.

Sage, low-scrub, and stunted trees grow in the open fields between dwell-ings. In the early morning hours, coyotes lope brazenly through neighborhoods in search of rabbits and stray pets. Occasionally a roadrunner will dart across the street, usually with a lizard or snake dangling from its beak. Quail walk single file through the sage while hummingbirds float effortlessly, sipping nectar from wild blossoms. Except for the green-leafed trees and bright flowers in neighborhood yards, the high desert is colored in subdued shades of brown, rust, and purple. The great exception is the fertile green area that extends outward from the banks of the Rio Grande River. Called the Bosque, it is dominated by giant gnarled cottonwood trees. The high desert climate is a big change from the humid, green Midwest. No mowing the yard and working the weed whacker, and best of all no mosquitos to spoil evening grilling on the patio.

Tricklock was an avid outdoorsman and New Mexico offered a veritable smorgasbord of exceptional adventures. The state is famous for its world class hunting—elk, deer, sheep, bear, and mountain lions are plentiful. Bobcats, coyote, fox, and wild turkeys also thrive in the wild areas. Anglers can fish pristine, gurgling brooks in the northern mountains while enjoying breathtaking wilderness scenery. But Tricklock most liked living in New Mexico, because his parents Isaac and Alice had their home only a few hours' drive from Rio Rancho. They had a small spread on the edge of the Pecos Wilderness, northeast of Santa Fe.

Tricklock settled into a routine of work with weekends dedicated to outdoor adventuring. Occasionally he traveled to Florida to teach water parachuting to students, or went to Zuni Canyon near Grants to teach land navigation or to Box Canyon near Socorro to instruct mountain rescue. When he wasn't actively teaching he worked with the other instructors to keep the course up to date and cutting edge. It is important for the PJ curriculum to keep pace with advancements at the operational units. The enemy threat keeps evolving and advancements in PJ equipment, tactics, techniques, and procedures must keep pace. The school has to prepare PJ and CRO students for life in the real-world rescue squadrons and special tactics teams. A couple of years into his assignment at the Guardian Angel Training Center, Tricklock received orders to deploy to Camp Bastion, Afghanistan for six months. He would augment the 38th Rescue Squadron, and fly as a team leader on HH-60 Pave Hawk helicopters. Tricklock was about to get a crack at rescue missions in Afghanistan, and he was stoked!

Tricklock was excited to deploy to Afghanistan, because there are a lot of rescue missions flying out of Camp Bastion. At bastion, it's not unusual for a PJ to have hundreds of rescue missions during a single deployment. Camp Bastion is a British military base in Southwest Afghanistan's Helmand Province, the largest of the country's thirty four provinces. The base is northwest of Lashkar Gah, the capital of the province. Camp Bastion forms a rectangle four miles long and two miles wide stuck smack dab in the middle of nowhere, baking in a featureless desert far from population centers. The remote location isolates and helps protect the base which supports more than 30,000 coalition troops. Helmand province produces most of the world's supply of opium and is a known Taliban stronghold. The local population is more than 90% ethnic Pashtun. Pashtuns are the most dominant and powerful ethnic group in Afghanistan and are considered the original, true Afghans. Helmand is a dangerous place. In addition to Taliban and al Qaeda terrorists, there are many tribal groups warring for domination of the lucrative opium trade.

Camp Bastion has an airfield with a long runway that can handle any type or size of aircraft. The airdrome supports hundreds of planes per day and is one of the busiest airfields in the world. There are CV-22 Ospreys, Harrier jump-jets, Tornados, F-16 Falcons, F-84 Thunder jets, and other NATO aircraft. There are helicopters of all kinds including Pave Hawks, Chinooks, and Apache and Kiowa attack helicopters. Massive cargo planes continuously ferry supplies and personnel to and from the base. Camp Bastion is the coalition's logistics hub of Helmand, province.

Camp Bastion has a fully equipped field hospital that is one of the busiest medical centers in the country, handling NATO battlefield casualties and local nationals injured in various ways. When it comes to saving service member's lives, this hospital may be the best in the history of human warfare. The hospital is designated a Role 3 hospital which means it can handle any medical situation no matter how extreme. This medical center routinely deals with horrendous wounds such as, double or triple amputations, third degree burns, gunshots, and blast injuries. In fact, only the very best stateside hospitals can approach the lifesaving expertise available at the Bastion hospital. Amazing doctors from numerous countries work around the clock. If rescuers can deliver a casualty within an hour after his injury, known as the *golden hour*, then doctors at the hospital will be able to save the person's life 98% of the time.

Many of Tricklock's former teammates were now stationed at the 38th Rescue Squadron based out of Moody Air Force Base in Georgia. They all greeted him effusively when he arrived at Camp Bastion. Tricklock knew most of the PJs and CROs he would be flying with during this deployment. This was a good thing, because he was always nervous when flying with unfamiliar team members. It took some time to discover a person's strengths and weaknesses, their sense of humor, and their eccentricities. Of course those feelings go both ways. A team member, who is unfamiliar with his team leader, will be leery until he gets a feel for the team leader's skill and methods. Tricklock was glad to be flying with men he knew well.

One very positive aspect of this deployment was that Tricklock would be spending it with his good friend Tank. Tank's real name was Tim Miller, and he and Tricklock had known each other for some years. Their friendship was strong, and they had shared many adventures around the world. They had met years earlier during a massive military exercise in Nevada. Later on they had been stationed together overseas, and Tricklock and Tank became as close as brothers. Tank was now an experienced element leader. Seeing Tank again brought back a lot of memories. Tricklock chuckled to his self when he thought back to their first meeting.

At the end of a large military exercise near Las Vegas, participating PJs from around the world agreed to rendezvous for dinner. Soon there were more than twenty PJs feasting, drinking, telling war stories, and exaggerating their heroic exploits. Afterwards, they took over a nearby bar called *The Rotor Head* that was furnished with pool tables and a quality juke box that had a good selection of rock and country music. The owner was a retired HH-60 gunner named Gus, who had served with a lot of PJs. Tricklock knew that as long as the PJs didn't smash up the furniture and destroy the bar, they wouldn't have to worry about Gus calling the cops. Cops at a PJ party are always a buzz-kill since they unrealistically expect civilized and respectful behavior. As an added bonus, Gus was competing with a nearby Hooters restaurant, so he had employed a bevy of scantily clad waitresses. Gus reminded the PJs that his girls liked big tips and having fun, with a strong emphasis on big tips.

It was at this party that Tricklock met a young PJ named Tim Miller, nicknamed Tank. Tank was shorter than Tricklock but had massive arms and was about three feet across at the shoulders. His thighs were as big around as sturdy tree trunks, and his neck was thick to the point of being nonexistent. Even his muscles had muscles—he was built like a tank. When he was happy, Tank was the friendliest, most jolly man in the world, impossible not to like. A quick mind and a great sense of humor rounded out his personality. Tank's most recent claim to fame was that during his last four consecutive PJ training trips he had knocked someone out in a bar fight. For some inexplicable reason, bar room Neanderthals seemed drawn to Tank. Tricklock didn't get it. Tank was the last person he would choose to antagonize. Tricklock had never met him before, but he knew Tank by reputation—a good PJ operator. Tank was Tricklock's kind of guy.

Tricklock and Tank were kindred spirits and immediately hit it off. They were soon joking around like they had known each other for years. They were having a terrific time drinking and telling war stories.

"So," Tank asked, "what's the deal with the cane?"

"Well," explained Tricklock, "a good hickory cane is an awesome weapon, *and* you can take one anywhere—on a plane, even into a bar. Stick fighting is a bad ass martial art. I made this particular cane especially for fighting. In fact I have a collection of fighting canes. A stout cane also comes in handy when you're out walking and come across a loose junkyard dog or an escaped zoo lion. In the case of the lion you can break the knee of someone close by and then beat feet. Lions will always go for injured prey, just like sharks after blood."

Tank said, "Sweet. At first I thought you might be a gimp."

Tank went on, "Like in that movie."

Tricklock almost choked on his beer, "Hardly, I just like to be prepared. It's the Boy Scout in me."

Later when Tank got up to use the restroom, Tricklock chided him, "Remember Tank, this bar has rules against dragging women by the hair."

Tank fired back with a dig of his own, "Don't worry about me. Just pray that while you're away from home, no one gives your girlfriend her first orgasm."

Tank returned just in time for stupid human PJ tricks. At the center of attention were two PJs named Chris and Dave. They were competing to see who could jump the highest from a standing start. During cross fit workouts, guys are always jumping on taller and taller stools as part of the workout. Chris and Dave had easily leaped onto the highest bar stools, then the pool table. Now they were stacking objects to get a higher platform. The unstable stack was now chest height, and as usual safety was not a consideration during these competitions. Tricklock was watching the spectacle and chatting with a cute waitress named Tammy when he heard a door slam open. He looked over to see a bunch of guys march into the bar like they owned it. The men had long hair and beards and wore jean jackets and lots of leather. They were stereotypical bikers.

The new arrivals fanned out across the bar, and a couple of them claimed a pool table. The biggest biker swept the bar with his eyes, noting all the PJs with undisguised displeasure. He had a huge black beard and close set black eyes. He was over six feet tall and had a large biker belly. He was a large brutish character who reminded Tricklock of Bluto, Popeye the Sailor's nemesis. His visible skin was decorated with lurid tattoos, and he wore a large golden hoop earring in his left earlobe. He swaggered straight over to where Tricklock stood talking to Tammy. Hostility radiated from the biker like heat waves off a sunbaked sidewalk. Tammy nervously greeted him, "Hey Cue Stick. What's up? You want a beer or something?"

Cue Stick stared at Tricklock and scowled, "Who's this?"

"My name's Tricklock, how's it going?"

Cue Stick snarled, "Stay the fuck away from my girl!"

Tricklock's demeanor subtly changed—he said, "I didn't know Tammy was your girl."

Cue Stick smirked, "All these girls are my girls. And this is my bar too."

"Ah, I see." said Tricklock.

He left and walked over to where Tank casually leaned against the bar. Tank had followed his friend's exchange with the biker with growing interest. Cue Stick glared at Tricklock for a second, walked over to his buddies, and began talking earnestly, occasionally motioning in Tricklock's direction.

Tank laughed, "I think you made a friend. You're just so fucking likable."

Tricklock shrugged, "I can see where this is going. Give the guys a heads up."

Tricklock walked back over to Tammy who looked worried, "Hey Tammy. Why is that guy called Cue Stick?"

Tammy answered, keeping her voice low and conspiratorial, "He's bad news, famous for cracking heads with a pool stick—that's his claim to fame. These guys are local bikers and have been giving Gus a big headache. They're starting to drive our regular customers away."

Tricklock followed up, "Does Cue Stick and his boys know any boxing or martial arts?"

"I don't think so. But he's a pretty badass street fighter." she answered.

Tricklock had been watching Cue Stick out of the corner of his eye and saw him approaching, pool stick in hand. The biker's friends were spreading out into what they thought was a good tactical position. Tricklock smiled to himself and nonchalantly turned to face Cue Stick. Tricklock was done with playing games.

Cue Stick blustered, "I told you to stay away from my girl asshole."

Tammy stepped between them, "Come on Cue Stick, we don't need any trouble in here."

Cue Stick blurted, "Fuck off and get outta my way!"

He moved to shove Tammy but his hand never reached her. Tricklock had casually reached out and intercepted Cue Stick's arm. He twisted the biker's wrist, dropping him to his knees with seeming effortlessness, and then with a gentle shove Tricklock sent Cue Stick reeling backwards to sprawl unceremoniously onto his ass.

Tricklock casually remarked, "You shouldn't pick on girls. Only pussies hit women. Yep, I can definitely see it now—you're a big pussy. You and your pussy friends should probably leave now before you get hurt. Oh, and you should probably never come back."

Cue Stick scrambled to his feet rubbing his sore wrist. His face was flushed red from embarrassment and rage—he trembled with pent-up fury.

His beady eyes darkened with hate and spittle flew from his mouth when he sputtered, "You're a dead man!"

With impressive quickness, he swung his pool stick like a major league batter, but with violence and evil intentions. Tricklock held the crook of his cane in his left hand with the shaft running down his forearm. He stepped back with his right foot while simultaneously raising his left arm into the arc of the pool stick. Cue Stick's two handed swing was powerful and would have broken even the strongest man's arm. The pool stick struck Tricklock's forearm, but his arm was protected by the length of his cane, and the pool cue shattered with a thunderous crack. The thick part of the broken stick flew across the room and smashed into the bar.

Tricklock stood unharmed and disdainful. Cue Stick's eyes widened and his mouth gaped open in astonishment. Before he could form a coherent thought, Tricklock slipped the crook of his cane behind the biker's neck and yanked his head forward, straight into an elbow smash that pulped his nose and sent bright red blood splashing onto the front of the biker's sweat-stained tee shirt. In a motion almost too fast to follow, Tricklock disengaged his cane from the biker's neck, hooked Cue Stick's ankle and violently jerked upwards. The stunned biker hovered in mid-air for a brief instant before he thudded to the tile floor. Cue Stick screamed in agony, momentarily paralyzed by his shattered tailbone.

Tricklock glanced around to see how the rest of the brawl was going. Chairs were being smashed onto backs and men grappled and scrabbled for an advantage. The bikers didn't seem to know much about technical fighting, and mostly tried to throw beer bottles and chairs to gain an advantage. The PJs were handing the bikers their asses. The PJs they broke knees with kicks and noses with punches. Joints cracked and ligaments tore away from the bone.

Cue Stick was on his hands and knees about to rise when Tank calmly offered sage advice, "Stay down man—do not try to get up."

Cue Stick ignored Tank's helpful tip on how to stay conscious and struggled to gain his feet. Tank kicked Cue Stick's face so hard that the biker lifted into the air and landed flat on his back unconscious. Tank checked him out to make sure he was still breathing. After all, Tank was a paramedic and was dedicated to preserving life, even the life of a dirtbag.

Tricklock saw movement out of the corner of his eye and parried a knife thrust like a matador deftly avoiding the charge of an infuriated bull. He brought his cane down hard on the thug's forearm, snapping the bone and forcing him to drop his knife. Tricklock stepped behind and applied a choke hold that put down the flailing biker like a Vulcan nerve pinch. Suddenly the fight was over. The bikers who were still conscious fled the bar like little girls running away from giant spiders. The others lay scattered, either knocked out or nursing broken bones and dislocations.

Tricklock whistled to get everyone's attention, "Time to find a different bar guys. Let's go."

Tricklock handed Gus a thick wad of bills to pay for damages. Gus said he would stonewall the cops. These bikers were always getting into trouble and were well known to the police. Tricklock suggested that maybe Army Rangers did all this.

Gus laughed, "That's a great cover story, but you guys should probably continue your festivities on the other side of town. Take care."

Later on in another watering hole across town, Tank and Tricklock continued their conversation over beers.

Tank grinned, "Damn Tricklock, you are Mr. Jujitsu! That was a nice move on that guy with the knife. I'm just glad you didn't grab me by mistake and get me in one of those rear naked butt fuck holds!"

Tricklock retorted, "It's called a rear naked choke hold, but I get your perverted meaning and you're not my type. By the way, that was a nice face kick. I think that might have left a mark on Mr. Cue Stick."

They looked at each other for a second, and then burst into laughter that didn't stop until they were interrupted by a PJ extravaganza. A naked PJ streaked through the bar, appearing to have a giant flame shooting out of his butt; everyone enthusiastically cheered his performance.

"Is that one of your guys Tricklock?"

"Yep, that's Steve. It looks like he used about ten feet of toilet paper. You tuck one end in your butt-crack, light the other end, and run. It's called the *Flaming Asshole*—very mature."

Tank nodded his head appreciatively, "Nice."

Now flash forward a few years and a hundred adventures later and Tricklock and Tank were together again in Afghanistan, but this time they wore their war faces. A week ago Tank had a close call during a rescue mission. Tank and his team member had picked up a young Afghan who had a severely infected leg wound. The victim's older brother was his escort. Tank's team member patted down the escort and cleared him onto the helicopter. When they delivered the patient to the hospital, security conducted another routine search of the escort and discovered a grenade hidden in his man-dress. Somehow the PJ had missed finding the grenade during the initial pat-down. Luckily, the Afghan didn't have any bad intentions. In his reality it was just normal for a man to carry around a live hand grenade.

When an Afghan villager needs medical treatment there are a couple of ways to arrange an evacuation. One way is for an emissary from the village to carefully approach a coalition patrol operating in the area. Patrols are often British, because the Brits are primarily responsible for the force protection of Camp Bastion and patrol a 600 kilometer area around the base. Marines also patrol around Bastion. Sometimes soldiers patrol on foot and sometimes in vehicles. An interpreter, called a *terp*, accompanies each patrol. Terps working with Americans keep their identities secret and their faces concealed so the Taliban can't target them later for torture and death. The village messenger explains the nature of the medical emergency, and the terp translates. The patrol radios the situation into the Tactical Operations Center, who then assigns the mission to one of the helicopter rescue or medevac units. The patrol will pass medical information over the radio and wait for the helicopters to arrive. They will also prepare a helicopter landing zone and sweep it for landmines. The soldiers mark the landing zone with a brightly colored magenta signal panel easily visible from the air, or they will pop a colored smoke grenade which will pinpoint the landing area and simultaneously show the wind direction. When a flight of two helicopters arrives on scene the trail aircraft carrying two PJs will usually land while the other helicopter circles above with its machine guns trained on the surrounding area, keeping a protective birds-eye view of the operation.

Security suffers a bit due to the humanitarian policy of letting one family member travel with their sick or injured relative. After the helicopter lands the PJs quickly exit the helicopter and move to the patient's location. The PJs carefully search the escort for weapons. The team leader keeps his head on a swivel and provides 360 degree security while the PJ team member rapidly assesses the patient. A couple of minutes later, the PJs walk the patient and escort to the helicopter and load them onboard. If the patient can't walk, the patrol will strap them onto a collapsible pole litter.

Once onboard the helicopter, Afghans are often struck with childlike wonder. It's like a switch suddenly flips in their heads and they realize they are flying through the sky in a big metal bird. Both the PJs and the Afghans suddenly experience the vast cultural gulf between them. The PJs try to amuse an injured child with a chemical light stick, only to discover that the parent is upset because he also wants a light stick. Or the PJ passes the Afghans some foam earplugs to protect their ears from the deafening whine of the helicopter engines only to watch them pop the plugs into their mouths and start to chew. The villagers are from another world and another time. They are often unfamiliar with even the most taken-for-granted everyday knowledge of Western society.

Chapter 4

AMBUSH

Tricklock snapped awake. It took him a second to get his bearings, but then his mind focused. His beeper had gone off. Scramble, scramble! He had been sleeping almost fully dressed and was ready in seconds. Tricklock and the other crewmembers raced to the flight line to fire up the helicopters. The Tactical Operations Center passed down medical information and details on the situation. Their mission was to fly to a location near a walled-compound about thirty minutes from Bastion. Local Afghan nationals had reported that they had a child who had been injured the day before during a coalition firefight with the Taliban. The child had taken shrapnel or perhaps a bullet in the leg. This incident fell within the *Medical Rules of Engagement*, which stated that only civilians injured as a result of coalition action were eligible for medical evacuation. Tricklock wished the Afghans had not waited to seek treatment for the child. Infection probably now exacerbated the child's medical condition.

Tricklock was acting as a PJ element leader and Tank was his team member on this alert cycle. Tank might look like a caveman, but looks can be deceiving. Tank was an exceptional medic who loved the challenge and intricacies of emergency medicine. At his PJ unit he was known as the Sherlock Holmes of emergency medicine. Tank delighted in using his impeccable logic to solve medical mysteries. During practice medical exercises at the unit, evaluators simulated complicated situations using volunteers as patients. Using Hollywood style makeup called *moulage*, they created masterpieces of medical ruination complete with squirting blood and sliced-open bellies with exposed intestines that writhed like a nest of giant pinkish gray worms. When a PJ arrives at a victim's side, his goal is to quickly determine what injuries will kill his patient first. A PJ will quickly resolve the most urgent life threatening condition and then move on to the next most lethal conditions, treating them in turn. The PJ will resolve his patient's injuries in a logical sequence, from the most serious wounds to the least harmful, until the patient is out of danger. Tank was a master of logic, and all the other PJs acknowledged him as the best medic on the team.

Tricklock felt fortunate to have his good friend Tank as his team member and primary medic. Although Tricklock was good at medicine, it was not his favorite discipline. Tricklock lived for the rescue. If the "God of Rescue" gave Tricklock a choice between hoisting down from a hovering helicopter at night onto a ship tossing on twenty foot ocean swells to retrieve a casualty, or performing all the medical treatment once the patient was hoisted aboard the helicopter, Tricklock would choose to do the rescue every time. In Tricklock's mind the only real choice was the rescue, anyone who would choose otherwise should not be a PJ—they should be doctors or ambulance paramedics. Although, others often refer to PJs as combat medics, PJs are technically not medics. They are rescue specialists who can also do medicine. They carry rifles, and by the rules of the Geneva Conventions, they are considered combatants.

As they waited on the tarmac with rotors turning, miles away soldiers at the scene were already clearing a landing zone and preparing the child for transport. The boy's father was slated to accompany his son on the chopper ride to Bastion. The two Pedros were poised to take off.

Then in their headsets came the eagerly anticipated words, "Go Pedros!"

The two HH-60 helicopters lifted off into the oppressive morning heat and banked towards their destination. The helicopters were equipped with 50 caliber machine guns in the left and right windows just forward of the sliding side-doors.

The GAU-21, 50 caliber machine gun has a cyclic rate of 1000 rounds per minute, and each bullet weighs a whopping 1.7 ounces. The massive bullet travels at Mach 3.8 or 2,900 feet per second, and impacts with incredible energy. To fully appreciate the amazing power of the 50 caliber round, one has only to compare its impressive kinetic energy to that of the venerable Colt 45 pistol bullet. Although widely acclaimed as a devastating man stopper, a pistol firing a 45 ACP cartridge only delivers a meager 327 foot pounds of energy on impact. A 50 caliber bullet delivers a devastating 14,000 foot pounds of energy.

As soon as the two Pave Hawks were clear of inhabited areas, the gunners and flight engineers test fired their weapons. The satisfying roar of the machine guns was exhilarating—it gave Tricklock goose bumps. He felt his adrenaline surge and took a deep breath. He felt all sharpened up and ready for the ultra-rescue. The only thing missing was strident battle music, such as *The Flight of the Valkyries*.

On this mission their helicopter was a bit crowded. A video journalist named Dave Jasper was embedded with the PJs at Bastion and was going along for the ride. Dave hailed from Alabama and had a lazy southern drawl and droll sense of humor. Luckily for Dave, he was not a large man. He was lucky because the cabin of the Pave Hawk is extremely cramped. Dave was slightly built and had a knack for staying out of the way and remaining almost invisible—he was an unobtrusive ghost journalist. Dave came to the unit with a solid reputation and was very deferential to the PJs and flight crews. Tricklock had immediately liked Dave and thought he would do well. But even though the patient was a small child, with the aircrew, escort, and Dave along for the ride the back of the helicopter was going to be very congested indeed.

After a short flight, the compound appeared off in the distance. A sand-colored stone wall enclosed a cluster of dun-colored brick houses. Squat and prosaic, the structures formed a mini-fort sprung up seemingly in the middle of nowhere. Far from the green zone, the fertile region near the river, it was hard to fathom why anyone would choose to build at this godforsaken location. The walled compound blended into its barren surroundings. The architecture was minimalist, stark, and angular. The Spartan structures and grounds were monochromatic. They were colored beige, rust, tan, khaki, fawn, copper, ochre, taupe, wheat, dun, sand, russet, and toast—all words that describe bland, mind-numbing shades of brown. The mud brick walls baked in the harsh sun and cast sepia shadows where gaunt dogs huddled. The glaring sun heated the bricks and stone and rippled the air. Pallid, sun bleached vehicles were parked a couple of hundred yards from the compound. A knot of curious Afghans had gathered, their brightly colored clothing was a lurid splash on the insipid surroundings.

The helicopters flew over the landing zone for a reconnaissance pass while the pilot talked on the radio to the landing zone controller who confirmed that soldiers had swept the barren earth for land mines. The plan was for Tricklock's helicopter to land and pick up the patient while the other chopper circled overhead providing over-watch security with its machine guns. On cue, a soldier popped a smoke grenade and tossed it on the ground. The billowing purple smoke wafted upward, identifying the landing zone and showing the wind's direction and velocity. The Pave Hawk banked into the light wind and began its approach to landing. The terrain was flat with no obvious obstacles. The surface of the landing zone was level but and sandy, so the pilot expected a brown-out close to the ground. A brown-out occurs when a helicopter's rotor wash raises a cloud of dust just before touchdown, obscuring the pilot's vision like a mini-sandstorm. The pilot slowly brought the chopper down, flaring at the last moment. As expected, powdery soil billowed upwards around the cockpit, but by then the chopper hovered only a few feet above the ground. The pilot smoothly settled his aircraft onto solid ground and reduced power. The thick brown cloud slowly settled back to earth affording the crew a clear view of their surroundings.

As soon as the helicopter touched down the PJs were on the move. They unplugged from the aircraft intercom system and hopped out the door. As the team leader, Tricklock jumped out first and kept his eyes peeled for threats. Tank closely followed on Tricklock's heels. During the landing, curious Afghan spectators huddled in a group a couple hundred yards off the nose of the air-craft. As the Pave Hawk touched down, the people instinctively turned their backs to avoid the whirlwind of stinging sand. When the helicopter reduced power and the fury of its rotor wash abated, the crowd moved en-masse to a position 100 yards away and directly across from the right door of the chop-per. Something about the way the crowd moved struck Tricklock as strange. They flowed like a school of *land fish*. They were not threatening; they just all seemed to move purposely at the same time. This was a fleeting impression that played across the retina of his mind's eye. Tricklock wasn't exactly sure why, but he felt uneasy.

A couple of Afghan soldiers acted as guards and crowd control. A young boy on a litter lay on the ground near the guards and curious onlookers. As usual there was a confusing knot of people milling around the patient. Two older men bent over the child. One of the men was probably the family member who would accompany the boy, and the other man was most likely the interpreter. Tank forged ahead, making a beeline for the patient. Tricklock followed, lagging behind and keeping separation. He could see a few other soldiers taking up security positions. The security perimeter was very thin and sparse. Overhead the other Pedro flew in a giant circle providing backup for the grounded chopper. Tank reached the patient and immediately began his medical protocols. While Tank worked, the terp translated Tank's questions about the patient's medical history. The PJs planned to do a rapid medical exam and quickly move the patient to the helicopter. While Tank finished with the patient, Tricklock carefully searched the relative who was supposed to be the escort. Afterwards, Tricklock switched his attention to the crowd. A dry hot wind flapped the spectator's robes as they huddled round. Tricklock scanned the crowd looking for strange-ities, things that were out of the norm. For a second Tricklock locked eyes with an intense, furtive man who quickly looked away.

Tricklock whispered under his breath, "Was that my imagination or did that just happen?"

The man looked suspicious, but *all* unknown Afghans were unpredictable and suspect. They were not to be trusted; that was one of the reasons that these missions were so dangerous. Tricklock experienced another moment of unease—something didn't feel right. The crowd's movements and *look* seemed slightly off. The chords of their social interactions seemed to be slightly out of tune. There didn't appear to be any obvious threat, but that didn't mean there wasn't a danger. Tricklock realized he was feeling unusually on-edge and resolved to stay calm but alert. The terp motioned to Tricklock and then pointed to a nearby man.

Everyone had to yell to be heard over the helicopter noise, but in passable English the man said, "My name is Gorg."

He seemed to be about 30 years old and did not look malnourished-thin as did most of the other locals. In fact, he appeared to have some bulk and actual muscle under his man-dress. But what impressed Tricklock most were Gorg's arresting eyes. They were not the eyes of a dullard, but rather the clear and penetrating eyes of an intelligent man. Gorg motioned towards the child's escort whom Tricklock had just searched.

Gorg told Tricklock, "God works in mysterious ways. Today my brother Abdel is shahid."

Tricklock glanced over at Abdel, and when he turned back to ask what the hell a *shahid* was, Gorg had melted back into the crowd like an Afghan ninja.

Tricklock muttered, "What the fuck was that all about? Just what I don't need, a cryptic Muslim saying to ponder."

Tricklock glanced over at Tank in time to see him give a thumbs-up, indicating he was ready to leave. Med checks were complete. Tank motioned for the Afghan guards to pick up the litter and carry it across the intervening 100 meters to the helicopter. They would load through the sliding right-side door, which was locked open. To the uninitiated, the interior of the Pave Hawk looked to be a cluttered jumble of electrical cords, nylon webbing, metal tubing, and mysterious objects. On board the chopper, Dave was in videographer heaven. He crouched unobtrusively near the back edge of the door and filmed the action with his high-tech digital video camera. Just forward of the door, the formidable barrel of the flight engineer's 50 caliber machine gun thrust menacingly out the open hatch. The PJs approached the idling helicopter accompanied by litter bearers carrying the patient. Their M-4 rifles with single point slings were slung off to the side and pointed down.

Tricklock talked on his radio, updating the pilot on their progress. "So far, so good." he thought.

Tricklock estimated they would be ready to leave the area in a couple of minutes. As Tank and the litter patient neared the open door, Tricklock peeled off and held well back, positioning himself between the crowd and the helicopter. For some reason he couldn't explain, he felt like he needed to keep his distance from the helicopter and stay on guard until the patient was completely loaded and the chopper was ready to take off. Normally, he would be boarding with his team. Tricklock stood 50 meters from the helicopter and faced the crowd. Only one coalition guard remained in position near the spectators. Tricklock glanced back at the helo. Tank was surrounded by a jumbled knot of people in the process of pushing the litter onboard. Their task complete, the Afghans who had helped to carry the child to the helicopter, began walking back towards the crowd. Still Tricklock hung back. During this entire operation he had felt disturbances in the *force*, subtle differences from other missions he had accomplished. Slight anomalies compounded, nibbling at Tricklock's gray matter. Comprehension struggled to emerge from his subconscious like a chick fighting to peck free from its imprisoning egg shell.

Just when Tricklock was about to dismiss his unease as due to an overly active imagination, a man burst from the crowd and sprinted off parallel to the helicopter. Some of the Afghan guards saw the man running and dashed to intercept. The last remaining guard responsible for crowd control abandoned his post and also ran to head off the suspicious runner. When Tricklock looked back at the helicopter, he was shocked to see Tank fighting with Abdel the escort who had suddenly tried to snatch Tank's rifle. Physically frozen in a moment of time, Tricklock's mind raced to come up with the most effective way to react. Reality seemed to swirl around Tricklock, offering a myriad of potential outcomes, all dependent on his actions. He tore his gaze away from the commotion near the chopper and turned his attention back to the crowd. Gorg, the intense young man who had made the mysterious *shahid* comment, was confidently striding towards Tricklock and the helicopter. Because of the confusion and commotion caused by the running man, Gorg's calm deliberate stride did not immediately attract attention.

Tricklock raised his rifle and yelled, "Halt!"

Gorg just smiled and kept walking. Tricklock glanced back at the chopper just in time to see Tank butt-stroke Abdel. Abdel's face exploded in a spout of crimson, forcing him to abandon his struggle for Tank's rifle. Tank followed up by slamming his stunned attacker to the ground and stomping on his voice box.

The flight engineer saw Gorg approaching, but he couldn't fire his machine gun because Tricklock was smack-dab in the middle of his line of fire. There was also a crowd of possibly innocent people standing directly behind Gorg who would most certainly be shredded by the hail of 50 caliber bullets. Gorg had shrewdly positioned himself directly in front of the knot of onlookers made up of curious men, women, and children. Tricklock raised his rifle, realizing that if he fired his M-4 he might hit an innocent standing behind Gorg, but Tricklock didn't hesitate. Time slowed, and Tricklock's mind raced with terrible clarity as he charged at Gorg.

In one revelatory instant, all the recent discomfiting irregularities coalesced into a frightening truth—Tricklock now understood Gorg's plan. The un-natural movement of the crowd that had piqued Tricklock's attention had been due to strategically placed Taliban soldiers who shepherded the compliant group of Afghan onlookers into a position directly opposite the helicopter's right door. This placed the innocent villagers in the helicopter gunner's line of fire, sowing doubt and causing hesitation. The running man and the attack on Tank were diversions to draw everyone's attention away from Gorg as he casually strolled towards the helicopter. The plan was ingenious and revealed the insurgent planner's detailed knowledge of the Pedro's normal rescue procedures. While running at full speed, Tricklock fluidly aimed and fired his weapon, slamming two rounds into the Gorg's chest. Tricklock saw his bullets impact over Gorg's heart, and the terrorist stumbled back, his eyes gone popeyed. But inexplicably the terrorist did not go down. As Tricklock dashed forward he could see that Gorg held a frag grenade in his right hand.

Tricklock's sudden assault had caught Gorg off guard. He had studied the rescue helicopter's operating procedures and had not expected anyone to be in a position to intercept him so far away from the aircraft. If the PJs had followed their normal practices, Tricklock would have been close to the helicopter and preoccupied with loading the patient. Gorg felt the bullets impact his chest like sledgehammer blows, but he was protected. The bullets did not harm him, but the charging infidel could ruin his plans if he did not act quickly. Gorg cocked his arm.

Before Gorg could throw the grenade, Tricklock crashed into him like a juggernaut. Hopped up on adrenaline and sprinting at full speed, Tricklock rammed the terrorist so hard that they both launched into the air. At the moment of impact, Tricklock could feel that the terrorist wore body armor under his loose robes. The armor explained why Gorg looked thicker than the average, reed-thin Afghan. Gorg screamed in frustration as he and Tricklock sailed through the air. When they hit the ground, Tricklock was the fortunate beneficiary of the law of gravity. The terrorist landed on his back with Tricklock on top. Gravity gripped Tricklock's 250 pounds of rock hard muscle and combat gear and crushed him onto Gorg. Gorg was smashed between the rock-hard ground and Tricklock's considerable bulk. Gorg's chest crumpled, his ribs snapped and gave way, and his lungs emptied with a whoosh in one violence-packed instant. With his lungs completely empty, air hunger consumed Gorg. Paralysis gripped his diaphragm, and he was unable to draw a breath. Gorg's eyes fluttered wide. For the first time in his life, Gorg experienced the sheer panic of having the wind knocked out of him. His mouth gulped like a fish out of water. He couldn't breathe and felt that death was imminent. His struggle for air became his entire universe. Gorg lost his grip on the grenade.

Tricklock watched events unfold as if they were taking place in slow motion. The lethal grenade slipped from Gorg's hand and slowly plopped onto the ground, swirling up small plumes of dust. The grenade's spoon slowly flipped through the air, arming its explosive charge. Tricklock immediately recognized the distinctive size and shape of the M67 fragmentation grenade, because he always carried a couple of them himself. Unlike the old World War II *pineapple* grenade, the M67 is a smooth sphere that weighs just under a pound and is packed with a potent explosive mixture of RDX and TNT called Composition B. An exploding M67 will kill anyone within 15 feet and can seriously wound people standing as far away as 45 feet, but of more immediate concern to Tricklock was its short four second fuse. Tricklock swiped at the grenade but only succeeded in knocking it further away. Tricklock knew he only had seconds to live.

Adrenaline flash-flooded through Tricklock's arteries and super charged his muscles. For the first and perhaps the only time in his life, his clarity of purpose, his primal instinct for survival, and his nervous system all synchronized perfectly. Tricklock drove his head into Gorg's face so fast and violently, that the motion was a blur. His helmet pulped Gorg's face, spraying scarlet blood. Almost simultaneously, Tricklock clutched Gorg's body close and rolled, dragging the stunned and paralyzed terrorist along. He rolled Gorg's back onto the grenade and buried his face in Gorg's chest. Tricklock barely had time to feel the comforting hardness of Gorg's titanium body armor plate against his cheek before the grenade exploded.

Tricklock heard the grenade detonate and simultaneously felt as if he was being electrocuted by a paralyzing bolt of lightning. The force of the explosion lifted Gorg and Tricklock into the air. The very fabric of Tricklock's vision twisted and swirled—he saw stars. A split second later, he felt a swarm of fierce scorpion-like stings on his legs and arms. His nervous system was overwhelmed.

In the midst of all this pain Tricklock thought, "I'm still alive!"

Tricklock knew that the sharp stabs he felt were pieces of metal shrapnel drilling into his flesh. He rolled off Gorg, who was limp and bloody and tried to stand. He felt as wobbly as a gummy bear and was racked with pain. Standing upright proved to be a huge challenge. He scanned his body and saw he was slicked in red. He was teetering and about to fall when strong hands suddenly steadied him. His burly teammate Tank was at his side, his face wavering in and out of focus. Tank leveraged one of Tricklock's bloody arms around his neck, keeping him upright. All the world's colors were incredibly bright and shimmery—everything seemed dreamlike. A mystery person slung Tricklock's other tattered arm around his shoulders, and suddenly he was moving towards the helicopter at dream speed.

Tricklock only remembered bits and pieces of the chopper ride back to the base. He knew Tank was working on him, but he slid in and out of consciousness. The whine of the engines was strangely comforting. His scattered memories were like camera snapshots taken randomly with no attempt at chronological ordering. One snapshot Tricklock remembered was Dave hovering close, his face mostly concealed by his video camera, the lens a large glittering eyeball. Tricklock tried to give the glass eye a thumbs-up. His legs and arms throbbed and his head felt as if his naked brain lay exposed to blowing sand.

Tricklock yelled over the engine noise, "Lollipop, lollipop!"

Another snapshot—a smiling Tank holding a Fentanyl lollipop. Fentanyl is about 100 times stronger than morphine and very effective in lollipop form. Tank taped the stem of the pop onto Tricklock's forefinger and guided it into his mouth, admonishing Tricklock not to crunch-up the pop in his teeth but rather to suck, absorbing the analgesic gradually. People in very severe pain tended to chew the pop, trying to get immediate pain relief, which is why PJs usually give Ketamine to those patients. The lollipop filled Tricklock's mouth. It was delicious and tasted of tart citrus.

Tricklock laughed in his head, "I have a serious badass guardian angel to have survived that grenade explosion! Damn, but I feel like I'm covered in toothaches."

He giggled at the thought of rotten teeth with exposed nerves, sprouting all over his arms and legs. He greedily sucked on the deliciously flavored pop and felt soothing warmth gradually creep down his body, dampening the throb in his legs and banishing the pain.

And the Fentanyl lollipop said, "Pain, I banish thee! Leave this wounded man in peace!"

Tricklock's vision was a large square of light that shrank to smaller and smaller squares—just before the smallest square of light disappeared, Tricklock laughed inside his head, "I love lollipops."

Chapter 5

THE GREAT FACE EATER

What you don't know can't hurt you, may be the most fallacious expression in the English language. What Tricklock didn't know, could not only hurt him, it could kill him. Tricklock didn't know there was a terrorist named Khaled Ayoob. In fact, very few Americans possessed any useful information about Khaled. Those few people who did know of him worked in the US, British or Israeli intelligence communities, but even they didn't know his true name, his current whereabouts, or the extent of his involvement with al Qaeda. That's because in his communications and work on behalf of al Qaeda, Khaled always used an alias. Khaled was in fact an al Qaeda commander and a rising star in the organization. He currently lived and worked in Southern Afghanistan in the city of Kandahar. Afghanistan's second largest city, Kandahar has a population of more than half a million people. Alexander the Great founded Kandahar in the 4th century B.C., making it one of the oldest cities in the world. Kandahar is a bustling metropolis with an international airport and a thriving tourist industry.

Although Khaled now lived in Afghanistan, he had originally been raised and educated in Egypt. Khaled's formative years in Egypt were relatively un-remarkable. Although his family was Sunni Muslim, they were not fanatics or activists. His father was a mechanical engineer, and his family was upper middle class and financially comfortable. Khaled was radicalized while he studied broadcast journalism in college. At the university, he became an active member of the Muslim Brotherhood and resolved to fight against the West and particularly America. He hated the United States for raping the oil-rich Arab nations of their natural resources and for their political meddling in Muslim countries around the world. He also hated America's puppet Israel for usurping Arab lands and for their cruel and oppressive treatment of the Palestinian people. But he hated Israel most of all, because Israel had fought and so easily defeated Egypt in the Six Day War. Khaled blamed America for Egypt's ignominious defeat at the hands of the hated Israelis. The United States bolsters Israel, providing them with the weapons and means to prevail against their Arab neighbors.

Khaled was obsessed with Jihad, particularly the past and current struggles in Afghanistan. He wanted to follow in the footsteps of those freedom fighters that had traveled to Afghanistan to fight against the Soviet Union and later the United States and its allies. Khaled studied Afghan history and learned to speak fluent Pashto. He was absolutely convinced that Allah sanctioned his righteous cause. He romanticized Jihad and its heroes, such as Osama Bin Laden, in much the same way that Americans idolize famous World War II generals, such as Patton and Eisenhower, and admire their brilliant strategies that crushed the evil Nazis and the Imperial Japanese Empire. Khaled venerated Osama Bin Laden and Khalid Sheik Mohammed, but he especially admired his fellow Egyptian and new al Qaeda leader, Ayman al-Zawahiri. He viewed the pantheon of charismatic al Qaeda leaders as brilliant Islamic military commanders in the vanguard of a struggle to save the world from godless Western culture. Khaled's life goal was in lockstep with al Qaeda's plan to defeat America and her infidel allies, and to establish a worldwide Islamic caliphate.

Khaled was of medium height and slight build. He had a light complexion, wore glasses, and appeared bookish. He was rather nondescript, and at first glance he looked like an Arab computer nerd. But when Khaled first attended an al Qaeda training camp in Pakistan, he gave truth to the proverb *never judge a book by its cover*. He was much tougher than he looked, and proved to be mentally as strong as steel. Khaled proved his dedication to the cause by fighting with al Qaeda in Iraq. He participated in numerous actions against

Shiite Muslim heretics and the Americans and their mercenary puppets. He showed himself to be a fearless fighter and quickly earned the respect of his superiors. Khaled was utterly ruthless and appeared totally indifferent when al Qaeda's suicide bombs maimed and slaughtered innocent women and children. He believed that collateral damage in the service of Allah was justified.

Khaled was a fanatic and became known for his skill at making stubborn prisoners talk using only a pair of pliers, a hammer, and a sharp knife. But the beheading ritual occupied a special place in Khaled's heart. He genuinely relished the theater and drama of execution, the stark backdrop with black masked men, cruel curving swords, and grim Islamist banner. He cherished the ritual, the helplessly bound and blindfolded man placed center stage, his plaintive cries for mercy callously ignored, and then the bloody act of sawing off the victim's head while he screeched out the final moments of his life. The video images of the executions created a powerful and chilling spectacle. Khaled was a gleeful murderer and sociopath.

Immediately following the American invasion and conquering of Iraq in 2003, the Iraqi militias united in their hatred of the American occupiers and became active insurgents. Nearly a thousand militias came together to fight their number one enemy, the United States of America. Foreign jihadists such as the Jordanian born Abu Musab al-Zarqawi fought under the banner of al-Qaeda and received money from Osama Bin Laden. By 2006 the militias dominated the insurgency, and al Qaeda in Iraq was ascendant. They rapidly extended their control over vast reaches of Iraq. In the beginning, the Iraqis viewed al Qaeda as a fellow Muslim group that was helping them fight against a common enemy. The militias naively welcomed Bin Laden's Islamist group with open arms and embraced them as allies and brothers.

The relationship between al Qaeda and the Iraqi militias soon began to sour. The terrorist organization quickly sought to dominate their Iraqi partners. Al Qaeda began to impose their harsh, fundamentalist brand of Islamic rule over the Iraqi communities—their methods were brutal. They carried out ruthless campaigns against Iraqis, lopping off limbs and chopping off heads for minor infractions against their program. They harshly punished the slightest infractions. They even executed an Iraqi merchant for merely selling a magazine to an American. Al Qaeda stacked the squalid alleys with the bodies of their Iraqi allies. The life blood of murdered Iraqis flooded the cobbled streets, brimming the roadside gutters and gurgling down clotted sewers. Al Qaeda beheaded fathers in front of their families and slaughtered wide-eyed children. Their righteous arrogance and horrific atrocities eventually became unbearable. Al Qaeda ruthlessly sought to control all aspects of Iraqi neighborhood life, but they dramatically overstepped and soon displaced the Americans as the Iraqi militia's number one enemy. The Iraqis were finally fed up with al Qaeda.

As a result of al Qaeda's heavy handedness, some important Iraqi militia leaders decided to ally themselves with the Americans and turn the tables on al Qaeda. They resolved to exterminate al Qaeda and their foreign minions and restore peace to their neighborhoods. The Americans eagerly supported these militias and the tide quickly began to turn against Bin Laden's terrorist organization. This sea change became known as the *Anbar Awakening*. Luckily, the awakening coincided with the American surge and the innovative leadership of top American generals. As part of the new strategy, the Americans began to venture out from their fortified enclaves and into the neighborhoods and communities. They established small outposts scattered over wide areas which were better able to respond to, and protect, the local populace. More and more Iraqis embraced the new status quo. These anti-al Qaeda militias were known as the *Sons of Iraq* and quickly swelled their ranks to over 100,000 fighters. The Americans widely acknowledged these events as the turning point in the Iraq war.

This is not to say that al Qaeda meekly faded into the night. Initially, the terrorist group resolved to turn back the tide of anti-al Qaeda sentiment by eliminating key leaders in the Iraqi militias that were working with the United States. Khaled was infuriated by the Anbar Awakening and viewed the Iraqis as ingrates, turncoats, and defilers of Islam. Khaled helped lead a major raid on the compound of a key Iraqi militia commander as part of al Qaeda's plan to make a dramatic statement and reverse the tide of Iraqi defections to the American side—the planned attack was ambitious and bold. Al Qaeda mustered 150 men for the battle, a much larger than normal raiding force. Khaled and the other organizers of the military operation badly miscalculated. Al Qaeda did not realize the full extent of America's military assistance to the militias. The Iraqis had American advisors and upgraded weapons, but most importantly they had American combat air support.

The al Qaeda raid was ambitious. Khaled and the other al Qaeda commanders launched a coordinated night attack on a key militia compound. They assaulted with a formidable force of men supported by mortars, rocket propelled grenades, and crew-served heavy machine guns. What they lacked was local intelligence and the intimate knowledge of battlefield geography they normally obtained from Iraqi insiders. This time their grasp of the terrain and the enemy's fortifications was sparse and imperfect. When al Qaeda launched their surprise attack, the scene quickly devolved into a confused morass of thunderous explosions, blinding flashes of light, and the agonized screams of dismembered soldiers. It was quickly evident to Khaled that the compound had formidable defenses and vigilant guards. The element of surprise was not the force multiplier the terrorists had hoped for, whether it was because of Iraqi traitors or American surveillance and early warning systems, Khaled did not know. What he did know was that the compound's defenders were holding strong and even repulsing the attack.

Ghostly tendrils of acrid smoke snaked among the fighters and gathered into a putrid miasma that coalesced and hung above the battlefield. An American attack helicopter arrived and began to wreak havoc on the al Qaeda assault force. Khaled resolved to quickly get his men inside the compound's outermost defensive perimeter where the helicopter would be reluctant to fire its missiles and cannon for fear of hitting its own soldiers. Khaled rallied his fighters and led a desperate charge through withering machine gun fire. Khaled was stunned by the ferocity and tenacity of the defenders. Unknown to Khaled, the U.S. had anticipated the need to protect the leaders of the Iraqi militias from al Qaeda retribution. They had reinforced and strengthened the compound's defenses and had helped establish a defensive perimeter. They provided the compound's defenders with American explosives, weapons, and air support. Khaled refused to quail in the face of this stiff and unexpected resistance and continued to press the attack. The ink-black night strobed with dazzling bursts of light, and the air rocked with ear splitting thunderclaps of explosive concussions. The al Qaeda attackers reeled under the compound's formidable firepower. An American claymore mine detonated off to one side of Khaled, flattening him into the dust and sending hundreds of ball bearings at supersonic speed that turned half of his squad into flying body parts and red mist—Khaled did not waver. He rose from the dirt, a fierce and terrible apparition with dilated eyes and a heart filled with blood lust. He fired a rocket propelled grenade to clear a way forward and dashed the remaining few feet to the enemy's lines. His rocket breached a gap through wicked coils of razor wire. Khaled clawed his way through the carnage, over the earthen breastworks, and leaped into the midst of the enemy's defensive positions. His men followed and soon they were fighting hand-to-hand for their lives with Iraqi soldiers and militiamen. Khaled fought like a man possessed, but he seemed to be overmatched when he encountered a burly Iraqi commando. The Iraqi giant threw Khaled onto the ground and leaped on top of him, briefly stunning Khaled.

Khaled's men were powerless to help him, as they fought for their own lives against determined soldiers. Iraqi regulars fought alongside the compound's defenders and they soon began to dominate the al Qaeda fighters. Initially Khaled appeared to be losing his battle against his massive foe. Khaled lay helpless on his back. The imposing Iraqi loomed over him with intent black eyes and a bushy moustache that framed a savage sneer. The commando was trained in Brazilian jiu-jitsu and quickly threw Khaled onto his back and straddled the smaller man. In moments the larger man would begin his attack, and Khaled would be bludgeoned to death by rock-hard fists and crushing elbow drops. Khaled reached his arms around the back of his attacker's neck and pulled his head down with the adrenaline boosted strength of a man fighting for his life. When the Iraqi first started screaming, it was hard to tell what was happening. Instead of attacking, the commando was suddenly in a panic to escape. The Iraqi spasmodically abandoned his assault and flailed his arms to break the grasp of the madman beneath him. Khaled clutched the Iraqi with an iron grip and ferociously began ripping and gnashing the Iraqi's neck with his incisor teeth. Blood splashed in a hot red flood when Khaled ripped open the commando's carotid artery. The Iraqi rained panicked blows down upon Khaled, but the mad Egyptian clung to him like a nightmarish demon, methodically slashing, chewing, and tearing away the Iraqi's cheeks, lips, and facial flesh until Khaled's teeth scraped against bare bone. The commando's nose was gone, his cheeks hung in crimson tatters, and his lidless eyes flickered erratically. The Iraqi's desperate attempts to escape Khaled soon degenerated into palsied twitches and the spastic jerks of a dying man.

Khaled had used the Filipino martial art of kina mutai to defeat his Iraqi attacker. He had learned the art from a Filipino Muslim in Egypt while he was attending college. Filipino Muslims from Mindanao have been fighting against Catholic Filipinos on the big island of Luzon for centuries. Kina mutai is the devastating and brutal art of biting, gouging, and mauling. A kina mutai practitioner bites with his sharp incisors not with his weak front teeth and strives for a devastating uninterrupted bite that an opponent cannot escape.

There are twelve kina mutai positions, and each position has four variations. There are nine places on the human body where teeth can rip open an artery, causing rapid unconsciousness and death. There are many vulnerable points on the body that are jam-packed with sensitive nerves and fragile blood vessels. Some areas of the body are hypersensitive to pain, such as nipples, eyebrows, eyelids, ears, and cheeks. When a person cannot escape and is helpless to prevent his attacker from biting and gnashing through their tender facial nerves, soft flesh, and blood vessels, the panic and pain is so all-consuming that the screams sound like they come from the tortured depths of hell.

When he first learned of the *art of biting*, Khaled resolved to become an expert. He did not have years in which to master complex combat systems such as Brazilian jiu-jitsu, boxing, or karate. Many of the American and British commandos started training in the fighting arts as children. Once they joined the military they learned advanced jiu-jitsu and striking. If Khaled ever had to fight hand to hand against such a formidable adversary, he needed an edge, an unexpected way to defeat a larger, better trained opponent. His Filipino teacher taught him the secrets of kina mutai. Grip strength is an important aspect of the art. A kina mutai practitioner needs an iron grip to prevent an opponent from escaping. He needs to hold his opponent in place long enough to inflict a crippling, uninterrupted bite. Khaled was obsessed with increasing his grip strength and practiced continuously. Even when he was not training he always squeezed a special rubber ball. Although physically smallish, Khaled could grab a man's forearm and bring him to his knees simply by squeezing.

Khaled also worked to increase his bite force. He used some of the same techniques that professional eaters used, often filling his mouth with multiple packs of gum and chewing long past the time when the gob became stiff and inelastic and his jaw muscles ached and clenched. He practiced his kina mutai technique on raw beef roasts wrapped in tee shirts or old blue jeans. Initially he found it almost impossible to chew through the cloth-wrapped meat, but with practice he was eventually able to use his incisors to rip through a denim covered roast in seconds.

Khaled's biting had just helped him defeat an elite commando, but the writing was on the wall. Khaled and the other al Qaeda fighters were losing the battle. When his soldiers went to retrieve him, Khaled was crouched over his opponent like a ravening animal. The Iraqi's face was a bloody patchwork of raw flesh and white bone. His throat was torn open and pale red bubbles formed and popped from tears in the dying man's windpipe. Khaled's loyal soldiers pulled him off the limp Iraqi and supporting him between them, scrambled away from the compound. The al Qaeda fighters fled the battlefield in a rout. The attack helicopter continued to destroy targets of opportunity and killed many retreating al Qaeda soldiers. It was a miracle that Khaled and his group survived, and that was only because a small force of their fighters made a valiant suicide charge, diving among the enemy and detonating their grenades among the compound's defenders. Their selfless acts of martyrdom allowed Khaled and the surviving al Qaeda fighters to escape. Once he was removed from the immediate life and death struggle and was clear of the destruction, Khaled's eyes cleared and he quickly regained his sanity and senses. He immediately assumed leadership of the tactical retreat until they were finally out of danger.

During that battle al Qaeda lost 85 killed and almost every survivor was wounded to some extent. The tale of Khaled's personal bravery and his defeat of the huge Iraqi commando spread among the al Qaeda rank and file. For his extraordinary actions against the commando, Khaled earned the nickname, *The Great Face Eater*. In the immediate aftermath of his fight, Khaled's face and shirt were clotted with the life blood of his adversary. No one could remember seeing anything remotely akin to Khaled's savagery. He had gained new found respect from his comrades in arms. The tale of The Great Face Eater became legend.

Al Qaeda clings to various passages and interpretations of the Koran to justify their ruthless behavior. This provides a moral framework and rationale which many Muslims blindly accept. Various spiritual advisors and clerics quote parts of the Koran to warrant al Qaeda's barbarous tactics. When Muhammad conquered Mecca he proclaimed that whoever fought for Allah and slaughtered non-Muslims, enemy occupiers, or those warring against Islam, had a *get out of hell free card*. Other verses of the Koran seem to encourage Muslims to strike off the heads of non-Muslim enemy invaders. Islam has no supreme authority analogous to the Catholic Pope to rule on matters of interpretation and church doctrine. Almost any obscure cleric can issue religious edicts called *fatwas*. There isn't even an accepted standard on who can craft a fatwa. This is perfect for Islamic fringe groups who can always find *someone* to justify even the most abhorrent practices. The Islamic landscape is littered with contradicting fatwas, but this seems to bother no one. Khaled fit in perfectly with this insane philosophy and thrived.

Khaled continued to gain responsibility and authority within al Qaeda. The terrorist group's leadership allowed him to plan and initiate activities. His successful schemes gained him increased latitude and trust. He filled his enemies with fear and jam-packed his terrorist resume with accounts of sophisticated operations and victory in battle. After Khaled planned and carried out a devastating assault on an American checkpoint that killed dozens—the top tier of al Qaeda leaders finally acknowledged him as a key al Qaeda player.

At the urging of his superiors, Khaled left Iraq to become educated in other aspects of the terrorist organization. He continued to actively move in Islamist circles and gradually connected with other al Qaeda commanders. Although he was willing to serve as a frontline fighter, his education and unconventional cleverness made him more valuable as a leader than as a rifle-toting foot soldier—Khaled had paid his dues. Khaled was assigned to work closely with prime movers and decision makers. He was a quick study and demonstrated a knack for organization and logistics. Over time he garnered the terrorist leadership's full trust and admiration.

Khaled wanted to be where the action was. He eventually decided to emulate his hero Osama Bin Laden and move to Afghanistan. With his college education and broadcast and journalism background, he easily found employment within Afghanistan's burgeoning television and radio industry. In his alter ego as a journalist, Khaled fit the stereotype with his unassuming appearance, soft voice, and technical sophistication. He was a mild mannered Arab version of Clark Kent, but instead of changing into Superman to protect truth, justice, and the American way, Khaled transformed into The Great Face Eater to destroy the forces of the imperial United States of America. Khaled landed a job at Kandahar RTA, one of the largest and most popular radio and television media outlets.

Khaled worked as an investigative reporter and broadcast technician. He mostly labored behind the scenes preferring to stay in the background, providing information and insight to his superiors and TV anchors. He was in the perfect position to stay on top of political and military developments and to exploit this knowledge on behalf of al Qaeda. Khaled actively networked and used the Journalist Association and Press Club to his advantage. In Afghan society, it is a well-known and accepted practice that insurgents will phone journalists, especially in Kandahar. The Taliban hate it when the media depicts them as weak or incompetent, and they often provide information to journalists to bolster and spin their side of the story. For obvious reasons, Khaled encouraged insurgents to phone him and built reliable information conduits into the Taliban—he received a lot of inside information. He also used technology to his advantage. Khaled owned the latest smart phone and had access to computers and the internet. His position at the TV station provided him with all of the technical resources he needed to monitor the major U.S. and European media outlets. He was particularly interested in American and British reporting on the war in Afghanistan. The information helped him to exploit various situations and worked to al Qaeda's advantage.

It was in Afghanistan that Khaled had come up with his idea to expand and strengthen al Qaeda's intelligence network for the purpose of tracking and killing those who assassinated key al Qaeda members. His organization's ability to carry out major attacks was diminished, but by pursuing Khaled's new policy of grassroots retribution called *Operation Powerful Vendetta*, they would exact a steep price from America's special operators. It was important to claim responsibility when they were successful. He was extremely disappointed that his attempt on Tricklock's life at the dry well had failed. Unfortunately it had only increased the American's stature.

When Khaled heard about the foiled attack on an American rescue helicopter, also involving Tricklock, it immediately piqued his interest. The story was very dramatic and was made even more so by an American videographer who captured the action. Khaled fumed that the attack had failed, making a hero of the American pararescueman named Tricklock. Given the United States' relentless war against Islam and the one true God, Khaled was mystified and frustrated as to why America continued to enjoy military successes around the globe. American and Israeli dominance in the Middle East, the birthplace of Islam and the heart of the Muslim world, was incomprehensible and embarrassing. As an Egyptian born patriot, Khaled was mortified by Israel's rapid crushing of Egypt's military in the 1967 Arab-Israeli conflict, also known as the Six Day War. The 22 Muslim countries that completely surround Israel are 640 times Israel's size and dwarf the Jewish state. From the beginning, Israel's Arab neighbors single-mindedly pursued Israel's extinction. Khaled bristled that despite the Arab countries' advantages in size and population, the tiny Jewish state remained militarily invincible.

Khaled also hated that America had twice demolished Iraq's military with embarrassing ease and rapidity. At the time, Iraq fielded the mightiest Muslim fighting force in the world. Despite its godless ways, America was a strong, implacable enemy and had easily smashed the Taliban and ousted them from the government of Afghanistan. In the years since that initial invasion, America systematically devastated al Qaeda's leadership and practically dismantled their organization. But what really made Khaled tremble with rage, was that because of all their easy military victories, the infidels could actually lay claim to the notion that God was on their side—this was intolerable! In comparison with the West, the Arab nations seemed militarily backward and bumbling. The injustice of it all continuously fueled Khaled's hatred of America and he resolved to do as much damage to their society as he could.

In the days following the failed helicopter ambush, the fawning world-wide media coverage of the event sickened Khaled. No one had claimed responsibility for the ambush on the chopper and the identity of the attacker remained a mystery. To satisfy his personal curiosity, Khaled began to probe his Taliban sources for information. He was astonished to learn that the attack had been carried out by Gorg, the rebellious son of Mullah Abdul Nabi, a powerful Taliban commander in the Helmand Valley. Al Qaeda and the Taliban had worked closely together in the past, coordinating attacks against NATO in Afghanistan. But much of the cooperation between the two groups had been based on the personal friendship between Mullah Omar, the leader of the Taliban, and Osama Bin Laden the head of al Qaeda. Currently there were relatively few al Qaeda fighters in Afghanistan, in fact there were less than a 150. Since the Americans had killed Bin Laden, many Taliban commanders were reluctant to get involved with al Qaeda. They now thought of al Qaeda as diminished and thought that associating with the terrorist group was more of a liability than an advantage. The Taliban was more interested in securing political power once the coalition left Afghanistan. Khaled knew that without Taliban help it was almost impossible for al Qaeda to operate in Afghanistan. It was getting harder and harder for Khaled to obtain Taliban support for al Qaeda operations.

Khaled dreamed of carrying out a spectacular attack which he would unleash in the midst of America's cowardly withdrawal from Afghanistan. He would attack during a time when the coalition was most vulnerable. The unexpectedness, sheer magnitude, and unprecedented violence of the operation would cause maximum disruption and chaos. Khaled's fame in al Qaeda would soar if he could make his plan a reality. He wanted to stage the largest attack since September 11, 2001. In order to succeed, he desperately needed Taliban help. Maybe there was a way he could exploit this situation with Tricklock. It appeared that Mullah Abdul Nabi had lost his eldest son Gorg during the failed ambush on the Pave Hawk. Khaled would closely follow news coverage of the event and learn as much as he could about Tricklock. If Khaled could somehow kill Tricklock, this gesture of friendship and revenge might ingratiate him with Mullah Abdul Nabi. With Taliban help, Khaled could deal a deadly blow to their mutual enemy, the United States of America.

In the days that followed, Khaled watched the media slobber over Tricklock. He hoped to glean some nugget of information he could exploit. When it came he almost missed it. During an interview Tricklock casually let slip that when he returned to America he planned to go camping with his son in the Pecos Wilderness in the state of New Mexico. A quicksilver thrill of excitement shivered down Khaled's spine as the beginnings of a plan began to take shape in his mind. What a blow it would be to the Americans if he could somehow kill Tricklock and his son in the bosom of their own country. Gorg's father would almost certainly be grateful and might grant Khaled the Taliban assistance he urgently needed in order to carry out his grand attack on the American forces in Afghanistan. Khaled knew that al Qaeda had agents in America. He could easily form a team to hunt down Tricklock, but he would not trust this mission to faceless men a world away. He would personally lead this operation, and he needed to move fast if he was to succeed. This mission would kill two birds with one stone. He could assassinate Tricklock and also curry favor and cement an alliance with a powerful Taliban commander. Jake Tricklock was now the primary focus of Operation Powerful Vendetta.

Chapter 6

HOMECOMING

Dave Jasper was beside himself. He was more excited by his video of the attack on the Pedro than any other event he had ever filmed. The fact that if successful, the ambush would probably have killed him along with the rest of the helicopter crew, hardly even registered. The entire incident was incredible, and the footage of Master Sergeant Jake Tricklock manhandling that terrorist and throwing himself on a grenade was nothing short of spectacular. He had captured every second of Tricklock's life and death struggle with the Taliban fighter on high definition video; Tricklock had saved the helicopter and the entire crew! Tricklock had rolled himself and that insurgent on top of a live frag grenade and survived! He had heard about such heroics, but for a journalist to actually film such military heroism first hand is extremely rare. Not only had he watched the events unfold, he had documented them on video. Visions of journalistic awards and prestigious accolades danced in his head, and this story was just beginning. Tricklock's shrapnel wounds were not life threatening, and Dave slavered at the prospect of follow-up interviews with the hero of the day—Master Sergeant Jake Tricklock.

For his part, Tricklock was not amused; he was virtually imprisoned in a hospital bed. Although he was grateful for the state-of-the-art medical care he was receiving, his shrapnel wounds were more an annoyance than anything else. As the cliché goes, they were only flesh wounds. He now faced a new challenge, coping with psychologists and members of the *Traumatic*

Stress Response Team. He knew that they meant well, but he hated all that *touchy feely* stuff. As far as he was concerned, the bad guys were the ones who needed counseling. Gorg was the one who was dead or seriously fucked up. He didn't know which because the cleanup crews had not recovered Gorg's body. Tricklock thought he was probably dead, but Gorg had worn body armor so it was possible he had survived.

In the end everything had turned out perfectly for Tricklock, but the shrinks still wanted him to talk about his feelings. He had almost died, but Tricklock didn't understand why the doctors thought that *almost* was supposed to traumatize him. Tricklock had almost died on numerous occasions. Twice during training he had experienced parachute malfunctions while skydiving, and in each case he was forced to cut-away his main canopy and activate his reserve parachute. The ironic thing about high-speed parachute malfunctions is that when you have one, you have the rest of your life to fix the problem. If Tricklock had not kept his composure and performed proper reserve parachute procedures, he would have ended up a syrupy red splotch on the ground. Of course he still loved to skydive despite those two close calls. In Tricklock's mind, those near-death experiences had actually given him additional confidence—his backup parachute had worked as advertised!

Tricklock patiently tried to explain his rationale to the doctors, but his reasoning didn't seem to register with them, "Look, I know you think I must be extremely traumatized and stressed, but I'm not. I won, and the bad guy lost. I'll grant you that I'd probably feel differently if I'd lost all my arms and legs and was a drooling vegetable, or the helicopter exploded and killed all my friends, but that didn't happen. I'm alive and whole, the helicopter is undamaged, and my flight crew and friends are unhurt. So considering the outcome, I had about as much fun as a person should be allowed to have—I had a splendid adventure."

The doctors were taken aback and even seemed disappointed that Tricklock's mind didn't seem to be scarred, but the counselors finally relented and left him alone. What *did* traumatize Tricklock was all the media attention. Jasper had filmed Tricklock's action packed encounter with Gorg and the video was plastered all over the major TV and cable news shows. The tidal wave of media coverage was unstoppable, seeming to gain momentum over time. Tricklock's exploits had gone viral. His military bosses urged him to cooperate with the media as this was extremely good press at a time when the war rarely offered any good news. Air Force Public Affairs briefed him on the *dos and don'ts* of radio and TV appearances. Tricklock learned firsthand why reporters are called newshounds. Once reporters get a whiff of a sensational story they are as relentless as bloodhounds on the trail of an escaped convict. The radio interviews began while Tricklock was still in his hospital bed. He talked with national radio personalities and with local New Mexico radio stations.

Like it or not, Tricklock was a celebrity. During his hospital stay he had visits from all sorts of important people. He talked to high ranking military officers and officials in the Afghan government. And of course he had plenty of visits from his brothers in arms. He also debriefed extensively with military intelligence. He told his story over and over and asked them to research the word *shahid*. He eventually learned that the word means both witness and martyr. It's an Arabic word used to honor a Muslim who dies fighting to protect his family or country. Gorg spoke that word right to his face, knowing that Tricklock wouldn't know its meaning. Tricklock couldn't tell the difference between the Arabic and Pashto languages. Although most Afghans spoke Pashto or Dari, one could not draw any conclusions from that one Arabic word. The Afghans have been fighting alongside foreign Arab fighters for decades. To Tricklock, Gorg and Abdel had appeared to be Afghan but he could not be sure.

Gorg had called Abdel his brother. Abdel could be his real brother, or a just a brother in jihad. Military intelligence also confirmed Tricklock's suspicion that there had never been a firefight in that area. It was possible that a Taliban fighter shot that little kid just to stage the helicopter ambush. The enemy is unbelievably ruthless. Islamic fanatics routinely blow themselves up and set bombs off without a single care for innocent women and children who might be killed, even other Muslims. It's hard for a civilized person to grasp the Islamist's complete disregard for human life—they are an evil scourge on this earth. Tricklock thought that when all was said and done, the strategic effect of the suicide bombers would be zero. It amused Tricklock to image the surprise on the faces of the delusional suicide bombers when they awoke in the afterlife only to find themselves in hell.

Tricklock also suggested to the intelligence shop that they investigate Gorg. The terrorist probably only told him his name because he thought that Tricklock would soon be dead. Maybe Gorg was important. Abdel was also a person of interest. He had escaped in the confusion after Tank had rushed to Tricklock's aid.

After what seemed like an eternity of days, the doctors finally told Tricklock that they were discharging him from the hospital and flying him back to the states. Tricklock didn't want to leave his team, but apparently he had no say in the matter—orders from on high. Looking on the bright side, he could probably take some leave, visit his family, and maybe arrange a visit with Simon. It had been a long time since he had seen his son. He felt that his father/son bond was weakening and feared that his chance to rekindle his relationship with Simon was slipping away. Maybe a good long camping and fishing trip in the New Mexico wilderness would be the perfect remedy.

Tricklock's fellow PJs and CROs all gathered with the rest of the helicopter crews and support personnel to see him off. He felt guilty that he was leaving Afghanistan early and didn't want anyone to make a big production out of his departure but it was not to be. Tricklock was already a hero back in the states, and the brass was not going to waste this media opportunity. Marine Major General Mike Davis was slated to present the Purple Heart Medal to Tricklock in an official ceremony. Many other dignitaries would be present including high ranking British officers, NATO officials, the U.S. Ambassador, and top Afghan officials. Tricklock was fully aware of the honor that America was bestowing upon him and treated the situation with humility. After the officiating officer read the citation and General Davis pinned the Purple Heart on Tricklock's chest, the crowd erupted in raucous cheering and applause. Tricklock glanced over at Dave Jasper standing next to his video camera. Dave was grinning ear to ear having just filmed the whole ceremony. Tricklock knew this would add more fuel to the already substantial media firestorm.

Afterwards Tricklock received a long line of well-wishers and congratulators. When the din finally died down, he moved to the squadron area where the only people present were his teammates, the helo crews, and the maintainers. All the PJs and CROs gathered around Tricklock.

Tank was the first to give him a bear hug and clap him on the back, "Hey hero, make sure you drink a couple of beers for me when you get home."

Tricklock shot back, "Dude, don't start with that hero bullshit, but I will have some beers for you, probably more than a few. And by the way, you're also considered a hero."

"I'm only a minor hero, you're the one who jumped on a grenade and saved everyone." Tank said, "And I'm jealous of that mean looking scar on your jaw. That's badass! It's too bad that shrapnel lopped off your penis."

"Do *not* start a rumor that I lost my dick!" said Tricklock.

Tank went on, "Too late tricky man, the word's out now."

Tricklock stoically endured the long series of plane flights necessary to get back to New Mexico. When he finally arrived at the Sunport International Airport in Albuquerque, he was all traveled out. Long flights, jet lag, and erratic sleep had combined to make him tired and irritable. When he walked off the plane and out of the secure flight area he was met by a large crowd, colorful welcome home banners, and TV cameras. His unit commander was there to greet him along with several of his fellow PJ instructors. Tricklock realized he would have to say a few words for the cameras. He immediately transitioned into his public, politically correct persona.

Even though he didn't want all the attention, he understood the dynamics, "Adapt and overcome." he murmured to himself.

He could play the game when he had too, and he was genuinely appreciative of the sentiment. He didn't want to offend anyone who was showing their heartfelt support for the military or just trying to be nice. Representatives of the University of New Mexico Lobos football and basketball programs presented him with sports logo gear. The Isotopes minor league baseball team also gave him logo gear. He answered a few brief questions for local TV stations and when it was all finally over he was exhausted. He collected his car from the base and drove home only to find his house besieged by a jostling throng of eager journalists. He felt like Dr. Frankenstein seeking refuge in his stone castle. The only thing missing among the mob were flaming torches.

He pulled into his garage and once safely ensconced inside, he mixed a drink, turned his bedroom TV to a generic science fiction movie, and fell into a deep, dreamless sleep.

When news of his exploits had first hit the wire, Tricklock had phoned his parents and then Simon to assure them he was OK. Later, he talked to his ex-wife and explained his idea for a father and son camping trip. Given all that had transpired, it was hard for her to object; for the time being Tricklock was a national hero. In fact, BA and Simon were being hounded by the press as well. Tricklock sincerely apologized for the inconvenience. He understood, because he was also irritated by the media's constant intrusion into his private life. BA said she would talk to Simon about the proposed camping trip. A few days later, Tricklock talked directly to Simon and explained his plans. Simon reluctantly agreed to the visit but he didn't sound too enthused about the whole idea. They were fast growing apart, and Simon's life interests seemed to be aimed in other directions.

Now that he was back in Rio Rancho, Tricklock had hoped that all the hub-bub would die down. His hopes were dashed the previous night when he had to penetrate a journalistic cordon just to enter his house. When he woke up and looked out his window, his street was clogged with news vehicles and his front yard was crowded with TV cameras and satellite dishes. Thick bundles of cables led to a van that served as their Mobile TV command post. All the equipment on his street crystallized his resolve. He would escape from the spotlight as soon as possible. He was tired of dodging reporters who were angling for a story. When Simon arrived he would give these newshounds the slip, pick up his son from the airport and drive straight to the Pecos. He was grateful that both Simon and his mother had agreed to the visit. Tricklock was almost completely recovered from his shrapnel wounds and was looking forward to this vacation.

Tricklock had not seen his son in over a year, but his close brush with death had put things in perspective and lent urgency to his plan to reconnect with Simon—life could be short. Once he collected Simon they would visit his parents and then off they would go to begin their fishing and camping trip in the Pecos Wilderness. He hoped that tenacious reporters and paparazzi didn't try to follow him into the woods. During one of his many interviews he had let slip his camping plans. Even so, Tricklock doubted any reporters would be able to follow where he was going. He planned to drive deep into a remote area where few people visited, then hike even deeper into the rugged mountains to a little known fishing stream.

While Tricklock fretted nervously about his son's visit, Simon was working out his own issues. Like millions of other Americans, Simon and his mother had watched Tricklock's heroics on TV. His father's fight with the terrorist was essentially a battle with the Grim Reaper. The video of his dad's heroics had quickly gone viral and all the major network and cable news outlets replayed it over and over. Overnight Simon's dad had become famous. As soon as he was able, Tricklock had phoned and talked to Simon and his mother. His dad planned to travel back to the states as soon as the hospital released him. When his dad got back he wanted to take Simon to visit his grandparents and then go camping in the Pecos Wilderness. Given the circumstances it was impossible to say no, even though Simon was not thrilled with the prospect of primitive camping. He wanted to see his dad but as the years had gone by he and his father seemed to have less and less in common. After the war began, his dad had spent more and more time deployed overseas and their visits together had become few and far between. Simon's interests had slowly diverged from his father's. Simon was not a big outdoors person, preferring indoor creature comforts and pastimes, such as reading, playing computer games, and watching movies.

Simon's mother had nothing but disdain for Tricklock and the military. When Simon was conceived, his mom had insisted that his dad choose between her and a career in pararescue. Tricklock had stunned her with his decision to stay in the air force. She saw herself as a woman scorned. Simon's mother was a girly girl, meaning she was super feminine. His mom fit the stereotype of a woman of privilege and refinement. She relished all things of sophistication and good taste and abhorred all outdoor recreation, except maybe a cruise on a luxury yacht. She was high maintenance and acted like an aristocrat. It was bizarre. Simon's parents were polar opposites. They were Yin and Yang, day and night, oil and water. His mother was the embodiment of the ultra-feminine and his father was a finely tuned example of the ultra-masculine.

Simon was nine when his mom married David Peace, a personal injury lawyer. Dave was a prolific bread winner and an OK step father, but Simon never considered him a replacement dad. Compared to Simon's father, Dave was a sissy. Simon knew that his dad thought Dave was a weasel. Dave's idea of parenting was to buy Simon all the latest computer gadgets and games, and Simon had no problem with that arrangement. Dave spent a lot of time at his law firm and was gone almost as much as Simon's real father. Although Dave rarely criticized Simon's father, Simon knew that Dave did not consider Jake Tricklock his social equal—Tricklock was a mere enlisted man in the military. Politically, Dave was very liberal and like Simon's mother was no great fan of the military. In fact, Dave and his mother saw eye to eye on most issues. Simon's dad always referred to BA and Dave as the Princess and the Weasel. Simon knew that his dad worried that he had adopted some of the Princess and the Weasel's liberal philosophy, and to some extent he had.

The only time Simon ever participated in sports or outdoor activities was when he visited with his dad. Before the war, his visits with his father were more frequent and he had always had fun. The last few years his dad was often gone, stationed overseas or deployed for months at a time, and Simon had gradually drifted into a different life groove. He was fascinated with computers and technology and saw himself pursuing a technical or scientific career, something creative and challenging. The school authorities had tested Simon and classed him as a gifted student. With his high IQ Simon was encouraged to take more advanced science and math courses. Despite Dave's disparaging opinions about the intellectual quality of military men, Simon knew that his dad was exceptionally intelligent. He had proved that to Simon time and time again during their past visits. Simon knew that his dad also appreciated the finer things in life, such as art and music, probably more so than Dave. That's probably one of the things that had attracted his mother to his dad in the first place.

Shortly after his dad's *hero mission,* TV crews had besieged their home. Tricklock had warned them about the coming media blitz and apologized for the many inconveniences that he knew were coming their way. His mother tried to shelter Simon from the major brunt of the intrusion, but Simon still had to deal with a lot of extra attention at school. Because of his father, Simon was now a celebrity in his own right, and if the truth be told he kind of enjoyed the notoriety. Especially the flirting he received from some of the prettiest and most popular girls at school. Simon knew his dad would approve of his success with girls. In fact, Simon planned to thank his dad for that unintended consequence of his famous mission.

In fact, if anything could derail Simon's academic dedication and his pursuit of a scientific career, it would probably be girls. He seemed to have a real weakness when it came to the opposite sex. It didn't help matters that all the most popular girls seemed to be attracted to him. Simon's friends lived and breathed their pursuit of the opposite sex and were mostly rebuffed. They were continually amazed that Simon tried to avoid romantic entanglements but still ended up with the prettiest girls. Girls actually pursued Simon, and his friends were jealous. Simon made a real effort to keep some distance, but he was rarely successful. Girls were always inviting him over to their house, ostensibly to help them with their homework. He could already see into the future in some respects. When he was older he was going to face some serious temptations.

During the following weeks, Simon packed carefully for his trip. He planned to bring plenty of his own entertainment. If his dad was going to push his brand of fun on Simon, then Simon would introduce his dad to some of his own interesting pastimes. Simon was confident that his dad would find some of his hobbies intriguing. Simon was particularly looking forward to his father's reaction when he told him he was studying a martial art. His dad was big into mixed martial arts, but when he found out what Simon was learning it would throw his dad for a loop. Simon smiled to himself as he pictured his dad's face when he revealed his mystery martial art.

Simon knew that his dad was no stranger to technology. In fact, his dad was way more tech savvy than most ordinary people. His dad used a computer at work to do almost everything. He wrote reports, made slideshows, used spreadsheets, and used web-based programs. He often heard his dad complain that today's military member's had to master numerous databases and computer programs just to function at a basic level. The modern U.S. Air Force practically ran in cyberspace. As a PJ, his dad also had to operate various types of complicated radios, GPS receivers, night vision devices, heart defibrillators, and map software. Surprisingly, where he seemed to be lacking in knowledge was in using smart phones, tablets, and the associated skills that go with those devices—he texted like a snail. His dad was also ignorant of the many apps that were out there. And as far as computer games went, forget it.

Where technology was concerned, Simon was taking his game to the next level. He didn't just want to operate technology; he wanted to understand and build devices. He studied electronics and the science behind all the gadgets. He didn't just want to use applications; he wanted to write his own code. Simon was already quite skilled in a number of technical disciplines. He liked to operate remote control helicopters and UAVs. He even enhanced their capabilities by adding power and installing miniature cameras. As new models were released, many with upgrades Simon had already added, he modified and improved those as well. An outsider looking in would say that Simon was a budding engineer.

Simon was convinced that a lot of the problems that older folks have with new technology is tied to what science and devices were commonplace while they were young. He remembered his grandparents talking about the difficulties *their* parents had when new devices, such as simple rotary phones were introduced. The phones actually came with directions! Imagine needing directions to use a rotary phone. Many older people still can't use DVD players. Even simple remote control units throw them for a loop. When smart phones and tablets came out, adults learned to use them, but they never achieved the instinctive skill of the younger generation who grew up with these gadgets. Phone texting was a perfect example of Simon's hypothesis. Watch any teenager text and their thumbs fly across the phone. Contrast that with an older person and their slow, clumsy texting. They're like cavemen suddenly thrust into the future.

Another hobby of Simon's was high end audio and music technology. This tied in with his interest in electronics but with added dimensions. Simon liked to buy old, class A power amplifiers and stereo receivers to conduct high tech autopsies. Thanks to his step father's generosity, he also owned modern high end audiophile equipment including a media server with state of the art digital audio converters. He collected multi-channel super audio CDs and downloaded high definition music from the internet. High definition audio is to ordinary CD music quality, what crystal clear high definition TV is to old fashioned blurry TV images. Simon aggressively exploited wireless technology and system integration. His home theater, computer, laptop, tablet, media server, game systems and phone were all connected. He had created an electronic symbiotic system that was almost a life form.

Simon couldn't understand how people could casually use technology that was so amazing that it bordered on magic, without trying to understand the underlying science. Scientific knowledge seemed to progress at a mind blowing rate, increasing geometrically each year. The present day reality was science fiction only a few years ago. Simon thought that his generation would probably witness several seminal moments in human history. Simon would be in his prime when the world experienced the *Singularity*. A physics singularity is the center of a black hole. Imprisoned by mighty gravity, even light beams can't escape. At the bottom of the gravity well is a mysterious, unknowable realm. When computers equal then exceed human intelligence, maybe even attaining self-awareness, no one knows what will happen. The human race will experience a technological singularity beyond which nothing can be known. Even though present day supercomputers can crunch massive numbers like nobody's business even defeating chess grandmasters, overall they are about as smart as a rodent. Computer processor speed and memory capacity doubles every two years. Some futurists predict the technological singularity will occur in the year 2045, but others calculate the date as early as 2030. The resulting *Super Intelligences* could save mankind or destroy it. It may be that the normal progression of life in the universe starts with billions of years of organic evolution, resulting in biological beings who build smart mechanical machines. At some point the machines become more intelligent than their builders, become self-aware, and wipe out the organic beings. It is heady stuff to contemplate, and Simon was excited that he might get to witness the event. Simon wondered if his dad knew about the singularity.

When Tricklock had recovered enough to earn his discharge from the hospital, he had called Simon to coordinate times and dates for their vacation. Simon's mom reluctantly made plane reservations for Simon to fly into Albuquerque. Simon resolved to keep a positive attitude. He was looking forward to seeing his dad and his grandparents Isaac and Alice. Like a nervous hen watching over her only chick, his mom chirped unending advice which passed in Simon's one ear and out the other without even registering on his mental Richter scale. When they went to the airport, his mother was in tears as Simon left her to make his way through security. He soon forgot her as he steeled himself for security screening. Afterwards he realized that TSA employees may actually be outer space aliens; they are often responsible for missing time and anal probes.

Simon had checked two suitcases jam packed with clothes and other essential items. He had also brought along many of his little tech gems. He had his tablet and smartphone in his carry-on bag, but had the bulk of his property in his check baggage. Simon earnestly hoped that no one stole any of his gear. Many of his toys were expensive and would be tempting targets for any dishonest folks searching through his baggage. All he could hope for was that the reports of theft and stolen bags he saw on TV were exaggerated and sensationalized. He would find out when he landed and collected his things. He boarded the plane with mixed feelings. Maybe because of all the surrounding events that had led up to this visit, he had a premonition that this trip would be unusual. His eyes suddenly widened. He had just experienced a déjà vu moment. Simon interpreted déjà vu flashes as confirmation he was doing what he was supposed to be doing at that moment in his life, a short replay of events already lived. He settled back into his seat feeling better. He ignored the flight attendant's unreasonable demands that he power down all electronic devices and surreptitiously started playing a game on his tablet.

Chapter 7

THE PECOS

Tricklock packed his truck with supplies and all the camping and hiking gear he would need. He planned to carry the bulk of the weight on the hike, but he had a medium sized backpack that was a perfect fit for Simon. He knew that Simon was not exactly thrilled to be going camping. Given a choice, Simon would probably rather have badgers eat his face than go camping. Computer games held a much stronger attraction for Simon than forested mountains and gurgling brooks. Despite Simon's druthers, Tricklock thought it would do the boy good to ditch the computers for a while and spend some time outdoors. Tricklock looked forward to teaching Simon basic fieldcraft, such as how to pitch a tent, catch fish, and make a campfire. Tricklock had stayed in contact with Simon over the years spending as much time with him as his military commitments allowed. As Simon grew older, the vague beginnings of a nameless discord began to encroach on their previously idyllic sojourns. Recently Tricklock had the heart wrenching realization that he and Simon were growing farther and farther apart. He felt powerless to prevent the rift. Tricklock accepted that the situation was his fault. His military duties and overseas deployments made him an absentee father. He resolved to reconcile with Simon—guilt was a conspicuous splinter in Tricklock's mind.

This camping trip would be a good chance to reconnect with his son and have some fun. Simon's mother wasn't evil, but it was only natural that some of her anti-military, anti-Tricklock feelings would rub off on an impressionable teenager. It also didn't help that BA's husband was a slimy, ambulance chaser. Dave's idea of fathering was to buy Simon whatever the gadget-of-the-day happened to be. Without Tricklock's influence, Simon was becoming less and less physically active. All that his son seemed to be interested in was playing computer games. He no longer seemed to like outdoor activities or sports. He was becoming a cityfied couch potato and a computer nerd. As far as Tricklock knew, Simon had never even been in a fist fight. Hell, Tricklock didn't think Simon had ever been in any kind of trouble at all—given his DNA, which was half Tricklock's after all, that was just unbelievable. Tricklock was all about supporting whatever career choice Simon wanted to pursue; he never wanted or expected Simon to follow in his footsteps. But he had always thought that they would share some of the same interests, and that when Simon was older they would occasionally watch a football game or go hunting or fishing together.

Tricklock got into his truck and pushed the button on his visor that activated his garage door opener. He backed down his driveway, ignoring shouted questions from the reporters that thronged around his home. They didn't know it, but he would not be returning until his camping trip was over. Simon was due to arrive at the airport in less than an hour. After collecting Simon, he planned to go straight to his parent's ranch—Simon could unpack there. Tricklock had everything they would need for their camping expedition stuffed into the back of his truck.

At the airport, Tricklock left his vehicle in short term parking and sauntered over to baggage claim. Right on time, Simon called Tricklock's cell phone and told him that his plane had just landed. Tricklock was incredibly excited to see his son. It had been a couple of years since he had seen his boy in the flesh. Tricklock watched Simon descend the escalator and walk towards the baggage carousel. He was a good looking boy. He had black hair like his father, but instead of Tricklock's blue, gray peepers, he had inherited his mother's intense dark eyes. He was tall for 14 years old and a bit gangly. Tricklock could see that with a little weight lifting and exercise he would fill-out nicely; he had a wiry, athletic frame. Simon was dressed in shorts and a tee shirt. He looked very fashionable and GQ. He obviously paid a lot of attention to his appearance—he seemed like he was a bit of a pretty boy. Tricklock would be willing to wager that Simon had no trouble attracting girls at school. It was probably a little late for "the talk" but Tricklock still planned to broach the subject at an appropriate time and place.

Tricklock caught his son's eye and Simon changed course to meet-up. Tricklock gave him a bear hug and a pat on the back, "You're looking good son."

Simon replied, "You're looking good too—still all in one piece and obviously still crushing weights."

"Always." said Tricklock, "I've got to stay in shape with all these up and coming young PJs nipping at my heels. You should do a little cross fit yourself and put some muscle on those bones. Are you doing any sports at school?"

"No, just studying hard. I'm not into all that macho, jock stuff." replied Simon.

Tricklock laughed, "Chicks dig jocks. You have a girlfriend?"

"No one serious." said Simon.

"I should hope not." said Tricklock. "You're too young to get serious. Let's go and get your bags, we have a long day ahead of us. After we get your luggage we're driving up to visit your grandparents for the rest of the day, and then it's off into the wilderness. You ready to live off the land with just a knife and a loin cloth?"

Simon shook his head emphatically, "Nope, that's not my idea of a good time."

Tricklock shrugged, "Just kidding. You don't need a knife." He laughed at Simon's expression, "Let's get your stuff."

"By the way," Tricklock asked, "What's in the purse?"

Simon was snippy, "First off, this is not a purse. It's a shoulder bag. And secondly, it holds my tablet and computer stuff."

"Right on." said Tricklock, "I'm just curious; no need to get your panties all in a bunch."

They grabbed Simon's two large hard-shell suitcases off the carousel and headed off to Tricklock's truck. Tricklock paid the parking fee at the exit kiosk, and they drove off and were soon cruising north down I-25. The drive to

Isaac's ranch would take a couple of hours, plenty of time for Tricklock and Simon to get reacquainted.

"So how is BA?" Tricklock asked.

"Mom doesn't like you calling her BA. That drives her nuts. She prefers Barbara or Barbara Ann."

Tricklock chuckled, "Well la de da. That's nice, except BA doesn't stand for Barbara Ann. BA is short for Butt Angel—she used to love that nickname."

Simon turned beet red, "That is so wrong!" he said.

"I don't know, your mom had quite the exceptional derriere—she used to be quite the looker, probably still is."

"I think I'll change the subject." said Simon, "Looks like you're all recovered from being blown up by that grenade."

Tricklock grinned, "Yeah, I guess I was pretty lucky. I just have a few shrapnel wounds, nothing serious. Good thing the bad guy was wearing body armor. There were three titanium plates between me and the grenade blast, one on his chest, one on his back, plus the plate I wore on my chest; I did get tossed around a bit though."

"Whatever happened to the bad guy?" Simon asked.

"Nobody knows for sure. His partners probably dragged his body away. It's unlikely he survived but it's possible. I don't know much more than that. What about you, what are you into nowadays, besides computer games?"

Simon visibly perked up at the question, "Actually, I'm currently in to something right up your alley. I've been studying an ancient martial art."

Now it was Tricklock's turn to show interest, "That's awesome! Which martial art are you studying?"

"It's called Go," Simon explained, "and it's the most ancient board game in the world. The Chinese invented it more than 4,000 years ago. Go is also very popular in Japan, and Korea."

Tricklock snorted, "Are you serious? Of all the martial arts on earth, you choose a board game. Why do you even think a board game qualifies as a martial art?"

"It's not just me," said Simon, "chess has grandmasters, but Go masters hold black belts with degrees. There are tenth degree black belts in Go. In fact, the other martial arts adopted their rank system from Go."

Tricklock was visibly skeptical, "So what qualifies Go as a martial art?"

"Because Go is all about war, strategy and tactics." explained Simon, "It's very elegant and complex, and very much a martial art."

Tricklock was incredulous, "I've never even heard of Go. I thought chess was the ultimate game of strategy."

Simon explained, "For one thing, a chess board only has 64 squares, but a Go board has 361 squares. That means that in Go there are a lot more possible moves. Chess is a single battle that mostly uses the left side of the brain—the left side deals mostly with logic. Go is not just a battle, it's an entire multi-front war and uses the whole brain. The right side of the brain is creative. One of the most impressive things about Go is how difficult it is for computers to master the game. Computers can play chess at the grandmaster level, but even a supercomputer can only play Go at an intermediate level. Go is all about surrounding territory and capturing enemy pieces, or from the opponent's point of view, avoiding being trapped or encircled."

"Check out the big brain on Simon! You know, you don't talk like the average fourteen year old." marveled Tricklock, "I'm kind of impressed despite your strange choice of a so-called martial art. I still remember when you drooled and pooped your pants."

Simon turned red, "Everyone does that when they are a baby. And you're right, I'm not average. My school tested me and they say I have a high IQ. I'm almost a genius."

"That's nice." said Tricklock, "I'm almost a gynecologist. Go still won't help you kick ass in a fist fight or get you a hot date."

Simon rolled his eyes, "That's very insightful commentary from Mr. Etiquette and Father of the Year."

Tricklock laughed, "Despite your obvious sarcasm, I'll take that as a complement."

Simon wanted his dad's take on a subject he had heard his mom and step-dad talking about, "So, I hear that soon the military will allow females in combat and even have women SEALS and PJs."

Tricklock laughed, "Yeah, that's what they say. We'll see how that works out."

Sensing he had touched a nerve, Simon pressed on, "You don't sound too thrilled."

"Do you seriously want to hear my take on this, or are you just trying to have some fun with your old fashioned male chauvinist dad?"

"No, I seriously want to hear your take." said Simon.

Tricklock explained, "Well, just about all the PJs I know, myself included, have no problem with women trying out for pararescue, with one condition."

"What's that?" Simon asked.

"Women should be able to try out for pararescue as long as they don't change the PJ course standards. If they keep the current standards, none of the PJs I know would have a problem with women PJs. But if history is any judge, the first thing the generals and bureaucrats will do is lower the physical standards because of political pressure."

Simon was skeptical, "That doesn't sound fair. Why do you think that will happen?"

Tricklock went on, "Because it already has happened in the military. One way the brass gets around the *standards* issue is to keep the same physical fitness test for instance, but then they do what they call *gender norming*. The result is that, even though a woman does 50% less pushups than a man for instance, she will get the same score. In effect, women get a handicap. And this is not limited to pushups; it pertains to running and all the physical exercises. The brass will say the standard is unchanged. The standard is still pushups, running, and swimming. What they won't advertise is that women can do fewer repetitions of exercises and have slower run and swim times and still pass. If you put aside hair splitting technicalities, I think that any honest person would say that is changing the standard. There will be enormous pressures to not fail women out of training, but a man who achieves a woman's minimum passing scores will fail out."

"Are you sure about that?" Simon asked, "That doesn't sound smart or fair."

Tricklock chuckled, "It isn't smart or fair and it isn't right, especially when lives depend on the standard. Another thing the *powers that be* will say is that the standards are set too high. Amazing that the bureaucrats didn't think the standards were unrealistic during the last 70 years when pararescue washed out 85% of all male applicants. Imagine the thousands of men who failed to make the grade. They didn't have the option to claim that the standard was unrealistically high. Having high standards is how you create elite forces. And remember, PJ standards were established when women were prohibited from applying for *any* ground combat jobs. The standards were not designed to keep out women; they were crafted to keep out men who were not suited for the profession. Women PJ wannabes were not even an issue at the time."

Simon was shaking his head, "I find all this hard to believe. Don't you think there are women who can make it through training with the current standard?"

"Sure." Tricklock answered, "But probably not enough to satisfy the politicians. Let's take this down to basics. Women don't compete against men in any professional sport where money and actual performance are on the line. Women have separate competitions in the Olympics, tennis, golf, basketball, and boxing. Can you imagine if women were forced to compete against men in Olympic events? They would never win a single medal. Then everyone would be screaming, "Unfair!" and clamoring for separate competitions for women. The very best women athletes cannot compete against the best men athletes. Special operations soldiers are the very best professional male athletes in their fighting disciplines. If you lower standards to artificially introduce women onto SEAL or PJ teams, then those teams will no longer be the best that they can be."

Simon asked, "What about all those the other arguments, such as the concern that men will try to protect the women?"

Tricklock said, "You know, I could give a rat's ass about all those other rationales. Those are irrelevant and obviously nonsensical arguments meant to distract from the real issue, which is decreased capabilities. If you lower the standard to allow women onto special operations teams, you will indeed have decreased capabilities. The only thing that bothers most operators is the looming prospect of lower standards and degraded capabilities. And before you ask, I could also give a shit about gays in the military. In fact that means you can join now."

Simon sputtered, "That's crap! I'm not gay!"

Tricklock let out a belly laugh, "I'm just messing with you. You're a little sensitive aren't you? If you were gay I wouldn't care. I'd take you shopping and stuff."

"You are not a normal dad."

Tricklock nodded his head, "That seems to be a theme of yours. You should be glad I don't care if you're gay."

Simon said, "I told you I'm not gay."

"Quit being a hater. There's nothing wrong with being gay."

"You suck dad."

Tricklock's imminent visit with his parents triggered fond memories and thoughts of his childhood. During Tricklock's formative years, his father Isaac was a hard-assed Marine who thought that boys should be raised as if they would one day have to fight and survive in a post-apocalyptic world. If you hurt yourself while playing, Isaac was the type of father you wouldn't run too, unless blood was squirting or broken bones were poking through your skin, and even then you had better not be crying.

When the school sent Jake home for fighting, Isaac would only ask two questions, "Did the other kid start the fight?" and "Did you finish it?"

If the answer was yes to both questions, Isaac would clap his son on the back and tend to any injuries all the while cursing that sissy liberal school for sending his son home despite his being in the right. Isaac hated when *Harvey Milquetoast* civilians acted as if both parties were always equally in the wrong no matter who started the fight. He hated it that some people thought there was never a good reason to fight.

Isaac would rant, "I suppose those eggheads think that America was equally to blame for World War II, even though the Japanese sneak-attacked Pearl Harbor. Or that there was no reason to fight Nazi Germany, even though they tried to take over the world and wipe-out an entire race of people. Whoever said that violence never solved anything was full of shit! America kicked ass and saved the world!"

Isaac's animated tirades were usually jam-packed with military and historic references. Jake learned a lot about history by researching people and events he heard his father mention. That's how he learned about World War II, the great Winston Churchill and the colorful allied generals who saved the world from tyranny. He also learned about the great World War II Marine battles like Iwo Jima, Guadalcanal, and Okinawa where thousands died and America prevailed. Isaac also regaled young Jake with vivid accounts of Marine heroics during the battle of Chosin Reservoir in the Korean War. Best of all was Isaac's first-hand account of the battle of Koh Tang Island at the end of the controversial Vietnam War. According to Isaac, the war was only controversial because we lost, even though we won every single battle. This was because of a news media that for the first time in history influenced the outcome of a war and not in a good way. Isaac believed that if the modern media had covered World War II, we would probably be speaking German or Japanese today. Isaac was somewhat bitter, because he blamed the liberal media for turning the American public against the soldiers who were fighting for their country. He had served faithfully at a time when citizens spat on returning soldiers and called them baby killers.

Jake liked military history, but he was also intrigued by the cultural upheaval of the 1960s. He was particularly fascinated by hippies, because his mother had been a flower child. His mother Alice had actually lived at what later became known as ground zero in the sixties counterculture movement. Born and raised in Arizona, Alice ran away to California when she was only seventeen years old. It was late 1966 and the best time to be a hippie. She hitch hiked her way to San Francisco's Haight Ashbury, the epicenter of the hippy movement. She shared a huge house with a motely crowd of other hippies and sold trinkets and beads on the street. It was a mini-commune with members staying for a while then moving on, soon replaced by others joining the scene. She lived there during 1967, afterwards dubbed the summer of love. It was an amazing experience. She smoked pot and listened to obscure rock bands that are now iconic symbols of that time and place. Bands like The Jefferson Airplane, the Doors, The Grateful Dead, and Janis Joplin.

The hippies were changing the world, and young people from all over the country streamed into the city. There was a sense of community and sharing. Everyone was enjoying life and struggling to create an alternate model of society. Everything was interesting: the diverse clothing, the psychedelic art, street theater and free meals courtesy of the *Diggers*, an anarchist group. Hippies reveled in the sexual freedom and anti-war protests; *make love not war* was their mantra. Men grew their hair long and women burned their bras and demanded equality. There was a lot going on, but human nature is Jekyll and Hyde, and it wasn't long before the Mr. Hyde's started ripping apart the fabric of the hippie movement from the inside out. People from all over the country streamed into San Francisco, and the Haight rapidly became overcrowded. Soon it was terminally infected with drug dealers, junkies, and desperate homeless people. The criminals mercilessly preyed on the young, the weak, and the naïve. Violence and rape became commonplace. The police cracked down to restore order. By the fall of 1967 everything had changed—the summer of love was over. The Haight was now a dangerous place, and Alice reluctantly fled a utopia in deadly decline and moved to San Diego. That's where she met Isaac, who was on shore leave.

At first glance, a match between Isaac the Marine and Alice the hippy seems improbable, but sometimes opposites attract. Or maybe deep inside, Isaac and Alice weren't really so different. They were both young and vibrant with an unquenchable sense of adventure. After all, Alice had run away to be a hippy, and Isaac had joined the Marines and acted on his dream to see the world. They were soul-mates before anyone knew what that meant. Alice possessed Marine penetrating radar that could see through Isaac's gruff, rock-hard exterior and peer deep into his kind heart. Isaac and Alice married in 1974.

Jake was born six years later. With her loving and nurturing personality, Alice eagerly took to motherhood. She read to young Jake constantly, thrilling him with fairytale adventures. She was very animated and changed her voice for each story character. Occasionally she pointed to a brightly colored illustration and would encourage a detailed examination of the drawing, asking questions all the while. A budding artist herself, she nurtured Jake's creative talents. As a result, the refrigerator was always a colorful mosaic of Jake's crayon creations. Alice was yin, the perfect counterbalance to Isaac's yang. Alice was sincerely concerned about Jake's scrapes, bruises, and other play injuries even if they weren't squirting blood. Jake learned empathy and compassion from his mother. Alice taught him to respect people as unique and interesting residents of our mysterious planet. She taught him to marvel at the diversity that flourishes in a free society and makes for a wonderful, intriguing reality. Jake developed empathy for human frailties, even though he found it hard to understand weakness and cowardice. He absorbed the best of Isaac the hard charging Marine, and Alice the free spirited hippie. Isaac and Alice were Jake's moral compass and the foundational centerpieces of his life. Mom and dad couldn't have been more different from each other, and to Tricklock they couldn't have been more perfect.

After a long picturesque drive, Tricklock pulled into the entrance of a meandering gravel driveway framed by a metal ranch gate. Tricklock loved his mom and dad's retirement ranch. His parents had purchased the property in 2000. After his military retirement, Isaac started a gunsmithing business at his ranch. The remote location was perfect. Isaac even set up a firing range on his property to check his gunsmithing handiwork. Despite the awesome shooting range, Tricklock guessed that Simon would probably be more interested in his mother Alice's oil paintings, but he did intend to get Simon some time on trigger.

A short drive down a winding gravel road led them to the main house, a sprawling single story residence built of wood and adobe. With its rustic color scheme and aged wooden beams, the ranch house seemed like a natural part of the landscape. As they parked in front, Tricklock's parents emerged to receive them with warm hugs and effusive greetings. Simon couldn't help but respond to their genuine love and affection. Alice bundled Simon off to the kitchen to force feed him New Mexican delicacies, leaving Tricklock momentarily alone with his father.

Isaac embraced his son, "Great to see you in person Jake, although Lord knows I've seen enough of you on the news."

"Yeah I know." said Tricklock, "I'm sorry to put you and mom through all of this."

Isaac spoke seriously, "This is a military family. You did a hell of a job and we're both proud of you. You saved a lot of lives."

"Thanks dad." Tricklock went on, "Do you agree with the plans I suggested on the phone?"

"Yeah, although I don't really see the need, but Sheriff Ortega has agreed to keep an eye on the place while we're gone."

"I know you and mom don't want to leave, but the media might storm this place to try to get inside information on my camping plans. I think it's the perfect time for you and mom to take a well-deserved vacation. By the way, I'd like to put Simon through some paces on your range. I'd like to try him out with some different guns and maybe borrow a revolver for him to take on this trip."

"What kind of a gun did you have in mind?" asked Isaac.

Tricklock thought for a second, "Maybe that sweet Smith and Wesson 686-Plus, 357 Magnum, seven shot revolver. Didn't you mention that you machined the cylinder to accept full moon clips?"

"I sure did." said Isaac, "Full moon clips are twice as fast as speedloaders, and I tuned the trigger down to 2 ½ pounds. I also have a gun belt and holster that will fit Simon. Are you thinking to use 38 special rounds in that gun?"

"Yep, even with a three inch barrel the 686 is a hefty gun. The 38 special rounds will have pretty tame recoil in a gun that heavy, especially a revolver made for the more powerful 357 Magnum cartridges. I'm thinking it will be pretty comfortable for Simon to shoot, especially if you put on some small grips—he still has teenage hands. And for backup, maybe a 38 special pocket pistol would be good."

Tricklock went on, "I'm taking my Glock and my Ruger LCR 357 magnum as a pocket backup. Let's give Simon a while to chit chat, and then we can put some lead on those new falling steel targets you've been bragging about."

While they talked, Tricklock and Isaac gravitated to the house and found Alice and Simon talking in the kitchen. The floor plan of the ranch was open and spacious. The kitchen and living space merged together forming a large airy room. The walls were tastefully decorated with Alice's nature-themed oil paintings. The furniture was made of quality hardwood and supple leather. The only obviously modern items were the large, flat screen TV and sound bar. A large, functional stone fireplace and numerous houseplants completed the décor, which was decidedly Southwestern. The large living room opened onto a big patio overlooking high desert spaces with naturally growing wild grasses, sage, cactus, and mesquite trees. Off to one side were some small out-buildings that Isaac and Alice used as workshops, studios, and storage sheds. Behind the workshops Isaac had built a shooting range. The range was not just for fun, Isaac's work as a gunsmith often required him to test fire weapons to verify his handiwork.

Tricklock told Simon they were about to do some shooting, "Come on son, time to launch some lead down range."

Simon asked, "Why do we have to take guns camping anyway?"

"Well," explained Tricklock, "there are bears and mountain lions where we are going. It's always a good idea to be able to protect yourself from wild animals. There are also rattlesnakes out there. Plus, you never know when you might cross paths with a poacher or someone who might want to do you harm. The bottom line is that it's always good to carry a gun, because you never know when you might need to shoot someone."

"I can understand the bear and lion threat." said Simon, "But seriously, one of your reasons for carrying a gun is because you never know when you might need to shoot someone?"

Tricklock laughed, "That's right. I'm not being frivolous either. If you have a gun and don't need to use it, it's no big deal. But if you do need a gun, for whatever reason, and you don't have one it can be a very big deal. It's kind of like wearing a seatbelt. You will probably wear a seatbelt for years without ever needing it but when you do need it, it can save your life."

Despite himself, Simon actually understood his father's logic. Tricklock, Isaac, and Simon ambled over to the shooting range. If Simon thought he would immediately start to blast away at targets, he was sadly mistaken. Tricklock proceeded to give his son a crash course on weapon safety and marksmanship. Simon was surprised and annoyed that both Isaac and his father seemed to be obsessed with safety rules.

"Alright already, I get it!" proclaimed Simon.

"Ah the folly of youth, Ok, Let's make a deal then." offered Tricklock, "We'll start shooting, but every time you violate a safety rule you have to do ten pushups."

Simon was confident, "You have a deal."

Isaac fitted Simon with a gun belt, holster, and his revolver. They decided to start with paper targets at ten yards. The targets were colorful depictions of threatening zombies.

"I forgot to mention another reason to carry a gun." said Tricklock, "You never know when you might have to deal with a herd of rampant zombies."

Tricklock demonstrated the proper technique to load ammo into the revolver. When Simon began to load his gun, he inadvertently pointed the muzzle of his revolver at Isaac. He did ten pushups as a result. During the next hour, Simon had a surprisingly awesome time shooting zombies. He also did more than a hundred pushups. When they switched to falling steel targets at 15 yards, Simon had even more fun. He ended up becoming quite enamored of his new revolver. Firing it was like playing a first person shooter video game, but better because it was real. He loved the recoil and feel of power, the smell of gunpowder, and the clang of lead on steel. Despite his initial misgivings, Simon had fun.

The light was failing and Isaac suggested they call it a day. Isaac provided tools and supplies to clean their guns and afterwards they all went back into the house. Upon entering the ranch, steamy tendrils of savory aromas drifted off delicious foods and infiltrated their unguarded nostrils. Simon's mouth immediately began to water. Alice had warmed up a pot of green chile chicken stew. Warm tortillas and sopapillas with organic honey completed the feast. Simon had experienced a long and eventful day and was feeling the effects of jet lag. After dinner, a satiated and exhausted Simon sleepily retired to his room. The adults moved to the patio to enjoy the evening breezes. The men nursed large tumblers full of ice and Black Maple Hill Bourbon and fired up a couple of double maduro cigars. Alice sipped a glass of chardonnay and occasionally puffed on an electronic cigarette.

"Thanks mom." said Tricklock, "That was an awesome meal. I really miss your cooking. I haven't really had time to talk to you much. How have you been doing?"

Alice smiled, "Besides worrying about you, I've been doing great. My paintings are selling as fast as I can finish them."

"Your mom's being modest." added Isaac, "Alice is becoming the new Georgia O'Keeffe."

Alice laughed, "I told you a million times not to exaggerate. I can't complain though, I'm having more fun painting than I ever have."

Tricklock replied with obvious sincerity, "That's great. You both seem to be having the time of your lives. I hope I can be as happy when I retire. I'm not sure about life after pararescue."

"I felt the same way about leaving the Marine Corp." said Isaac, "Anyway; you have a long time before you have to worry about retirement. On a different note, how are things between you and Simon?"

Tricklock frowned, "OK I guess. Things could be better. It's hard to stay connected with Simon with me being gone so often. I'm also not thrilled with BA's anti-military and anti-man influence, not to mention that lawyer husband of hers. But I guess things could be worse. At least I'll have Simon to myself for a few days. I plan to make the most of our time together."

Alice smiled, "If I were you, I wouldn't worry too much. Simon's a good boy, smart too. He's not a baby anymore. He can figure things out for himself."

Tricklock nodded, "I know. I'm proud of how he's doing in school. I'm glad he's into science and art, after all he probably inherited a lot of that from you, *Mrs. famous oil painter.* Just don't cut off one of your ears! After this camping trip I have a surprise for Simon—a visit to the Smithsonian."

Both of Tricklock's parents agreed that Simon would really enjoy a trip to the museum. They chatted for a while longer before they all decided to hit the hay. Before they retired, Tricklock took out a map and quizzed Isaac on the location of his favorite fishing hole. The little known trout stream was well into the backcountry and off the beaten path. Tomorrow would be a long day. They planned to all rise and shine at the same time. Alice and Isaac would leave for their vacation immediately after Tricklock and Simon left the house.

The next morning, Tricklock decided to forgo eating breakfast at the ranch. He wanted to pay a visit to his favorite diner, which was on their way. After morning ablutions, he pulled his truck out front and loaded their bags. He and Simon said their goodbyes, promising to stop by on their way back to Albuquerque. They hopped in Tricklock's truck and waved as they drove off. Isaac and Alice stood arm-in-arm and waved back.

As the truck pulled onto the main road Simon remarked, "It continues to amaze me how awesome and normal my grandparents are. How in the heck did you turn out to be so strange?"

Tricklock chuckled, "I'm not strange—I'm eccentric."

Simon smirked, "Uh huh. Maybe weird is the right word."

Tricklock was glad to be finally heading into the forest. "Before we hit the trail, what say we get a good breakfast?" he suggested.

For once Simon agreed without a debate. A few minutes later Tricklock pulled into the parking lot of a small cafe appropriately named, the Roadrunner Roadside Diner. He parked the truck, and they both went in and settled in a booth upholstered with red, cracked vinyl. A young waitress with a name tag that read "Katie" brought water, coffee, and breakfast menus. When she returned, Simon ordered bacon, eggs, and toast. Tricklock ordered his usual hash browns, bacon and sausage, and two orders of rye toast slathered with real butter.

"No eggs?" asked Katie.

Tricklock replied, "No thanks. I don't eat eggs."

Katie asked, "Are you allergic?"

"I'm not allergic. I had a traumatic experience with eggs when I was a kid."

"Now you've made me curious. What kind of traumatic experience could you possibly have had with eggs?" she asked.

Katie had thought Tricklock was joking, but now his face turned grim.

Simon cut in, "I thought you just didn't like the taste of eggs."

Tricklock said, "No, there's more to it than that. When my younger brother Sammy and I were four or five years old, we were eating sunny-side-up eggs for breakfast at the kitchen table. Sammy couldn't finish his eggs and my dad, who was a mean bastard, got all bent out of shape. He told Sammy that he couldn't leave the table until he finished all his eggs. Sammy was stubborn and just sat there with his pudgy little arms crossed and his face all scrunched up. For a while it was a Mexican stand-off between Sammy and dad. Finally, dad snapped. He snatched up the plate of cold eggs, and smeared them right into Sammy's face. The cold yolks had the consistency of yellow glue and gummed up Sammy's eyes. Maybe cold egg yolk is harmful to eyeballs or maybe it was just the salt that burned, but Sammy clutched at his eyes as if someone had tossed acid in his face and fell onto the floor screaming. Before dad could stop him, Sammy stumbled to the door and ran outside, blind from the thick yolk caked in his eyes. The poor little guy was terrified. He was sightless and disoriented, and in a blind panic he staggered right into the busy street in front of our house. A man driving a car at forty miles an hour saw Sammy at the last second and tried to stop, but it was too late and he slammed my brother square on. To this day I can still see my little brother as if in slow motion, cartwheeling through the air like a ragdoll. When he thudded onto the street he hit so hard he cracked the pavement and bounced twice before coming to rest in a tiny crumpled heap. Somehow Sammy survived, but the car had shattered his leg bones into hundreds of jagged fragments. The doctors did what they could, but they finally had to amputate both of his legs."

Katie's face had turned chalk white and her lower lip was trembling. She was mortified and wished she'd never brought up the subject of breakfast eggs.

Tricklock locked eyes with her, "Well, he's really my half-brother."

When Tricklock started chuckling, Katie finally got the joke and laughed nervously along. She was actually relieved that the story *was* a joke.

When Katie left, Simon shook his head, "You're messed up dad."

Tricklock laughed, "Well, I think that's been universally established."

When they finished eating, Tricklock paid the 15 dollar bill and left Katie a 10 dollar tip for her solicitous service and for being a good sport. Tricklock and Simon waddled out of the diner with full bellies and climbed into their truck.

After Tricklock started the ignition he pulled out a map from the glove box, "Simon, do you know how to read a map?"

Simon said that he did.

As Tricklock tossed Simon the map he said, "That surprises me a little. Where did you learn to read a map?"

"A lot of my computer games have maps. You have to know how to read them if you want to get to the higher levels."

Tricklock handed Simon a large square of folded paper, "This is your personal map. I've even marked our campsite."

Tricklock flipped open his pocket knife and placed the point on the map, "We are here—follow along and see if you can keep track of where we go."

"OK, easy day." said Simon, "And why did you use your knife that way?"

"Never use your finger to indicate a spot on a map, because your finger is too fat to point accurately and can cause confusion."

Tricklock elaborated, "Use a small twig, blade of grass, or a knife, anything but your finger; it's a basic rule of using a map and compass. Now pay attention, we're about to drive onto some mountain roads."

Calling the obstacle course they traveled a road would be overly generous. Only the most tricked out four wheel drive vehicles could pass over the deeply rutted jeep trails—even a dirt bike would have difficulty on these trails. Simon felt like an early American pioneer. They traveled many miles deep into wilderness. Finally, Tricklock pulled his truck off the trail, drove a short distance and parked behind a grove of trees. He walked back to the main trail. From where he stood his vehicle was hidden from view—excellent!

"Jock up Simon. We're heading out."

Pecos Wilderness Day One: Tricklock and his son shouldered their packs and walked into the forest. They had a long way to travel, but initially the terrain was relatively flat and easy going. Tricklock took the lead. He used a map and Silva compass. He was an expert navigator and used terrain association to skirt around steep hills. They needed to travel 20 kilometers to reach their destination and establish their camp. They were not following a path. They were traveling overland through wilderness forest. Tricklock effortlessly carried five times the weight that Simon carried. Tricklock had brought along a lot of gear and was prepared for any eventuality. He carried an extensive medical kit, two-man tent, forest axe, fishing gear, food, and cooking implements—he also carried plenty of water.

Simon was enjoying the hike. H saw all kinds of wildlife and interesting plants. The hiking boots his dad had provided were sturdy and comfortable. His dad had also insisted he put duct tape on his heels to protect against blisters. At his dad's insistence, Simon also wore dense wool socks even though it was warm outside. Surprisingly, his feet were comfortable and not hot. During the hike his dad constantly and matter-of-factly passed on bits of wisdom and fieldcraft. It was all interesting stuff that seemed to be commonsense. Simon was getting an outdoor education without realizing it, and his dad's constant tips helped to pass the time. Simon didn't know it but if he had attempted this hike on his own, his lack of knowledge and his inexperience would have been immediately telling and possibly fatal. He would have been miserable and probably experiencing numerous medical issues. With Tricklock running things, Simon was oblivious of the potential dangers and was virtually unaffected.

Tricklock talked while they walked, "I can't understand why you were so resistant to this camping trip. I thought we always had fun visits when you were younger."

Simon replied, "You had fun because you're crazy, and I had fun because I was too young to know any better."

"What's that supposed to mean?" asked Tricklock.

"Dad, you taught me all the wrong names for stars and constellations. When I went on an overnight school field trip I bragged that my dad was a PJ and taught me the names of important stars. Then my teacher asked if I would share with the rest of the class—I was so proud. Then I pointed at Orion's belt and said, 'See those three stars in a row? They're called Larry, Curly, and Moe, and the constellation is called the Three Stooges.' My teacher was not amused, and I was embarrassed."

Tricklock let out a guffaw and literally started rolling on the ground laughing.

"That's not funny dad. Big Ladle, Little Ladle, you taught me stupid names for everything!"

In between belly laughs Tricklock managed to gasp out, "That's some hilarious shit!"

Simon was not amused, "Yeah, you think it's funny. That's messed up teaching little kids wrong stuff like that."

Tricklock had somewhat recovered from his laughing fit, "No it's not. Those names and constellations stuck with you, even after all these years. All you needed to do down the road was learn their correct names. I also taught you to call your penis a winky. It didn't take you long to figure out it's your penis though, did it? Or do you still call it your winky?"

Simon snorted, "See, that's what I mean. You are not normal. Normal dads don't talk to their kids that way."

"Well," said Tricklock, "Normal dads are pussies."

"I rest my case." said Simon.

"You need to lighten up and grow a sense of humor." countered Tricklock, "You're a teenager now, not a little baby. You know what they say; you can judge the size of a man's penis by the size of his sense of humor. I rest *my* case."

Simon was incredulous, "You just made that up."

"Don't forget, I've changed your diapers."

"I'm a lot older now." said Simon.

Tricklock just smiled and said, "Uh huh."

Simon shook his head, "You continually set new standards of inappropriateness."

Tricklock laughed, "I'm known for that."

Suddenly Simon laughed, "Dad, you actually did a ROFL."

"What's that?" asked Tricklock.

"ROFL is internet slang that means rolling on the floor laughing, but that's the first time I saw anyone actually do that. Now that I think about it, technically you did an even more advanced move known as ROFLMAO which means rolling on the floor laughing my ass off."

Tricklock arched an eyebrow, "Do I detect the beginnings of a sense of humor? Maybe there is still hope for you."

Around noon Tricklock called a halt for lunch. He also wanted to check Simon's feet to make sure he wasn't getting any blisters. They ate sandwiches, drank some water, and rested in the shade. When it was time to get moving, Tricklock asked Simon to take out his map and compass to try his hand at land navigation. Simon looked through his gear and realized he had left his map in the truck. He was upset because he had marked the map and wanted to show his dad what he could do. Tricklock just shrugged and let Simon borrow his map. During the hike Simon had such a good time that he hardly realized that he was acquiring skills. His dad had a way of teaching that made learning fun. During their next rest break, Tricklock switched from using a map to using a handheld GPS called a Garmin Rino, which also has a built in 5 watt walkie talkie. A cool feature of the Rino is that a person with one of these radios can use GPS satellites to track someone else who also has a Rino. So if Simon wandered off exploring and got lost or injured, Tricklock could get his GPS position and locate him as long as Simon had his Rino turned on. Tricklock had fitted each Rino with a memory chip that added a scalable topographic map display.

Tricklock had brought three of the Rinos, two for him and Simon and another for backup. He also brought along some extra charged batteries. Tricklock was all about redundancy, a habit he had learned as a PJ. He always had a plan A, B, and C. As a PJ he normally carried a GPS, a backup GPS, and map and compass in case both GPSs failed. Tricklock faithfully applied that principle to almost all his gear, including knives and guns. Tricklock showed Simon how to use the Rino to navigate to GPS coordinates. Of course Simon thought that the GPS was much easier to use than the compass. It was like a mini-computer with menus and different screen pages, in short it was a gadget that Simon quickly mastered.

When they finally reached their campsite near the trout stream, there were only a couple of hours of daylight left. Simon was exhausted from the day-long hike over rough ground and hilly terrain. Tricklock set up the tent and arranged the interior with sleep pads and warm fluffy sleeping bags. Tricklock constructed a fire pit ringed with rocks, gathered wood, and started a campfire. He dragged some logs over to sit on and broke out some hot dogs and buns. They speared the dogs on skewers that Tricklock had brought and roasted them over the flickering orange flames—it was a delicious feast. Simon was famished and thought the hot dogs were some of the tastiest food he had ever eaten. Afterwards they toasted marshmallows for dessert. Simon could feel energy pouring back into his spent muscles. He was tired, but it was a good tired.

The setting sun colored the mountain peaks glorious shades of purple. The sun finally sank below the high ridges and its pale reddish light gradually faded. The crackling flames warmed and mesmerized as the night sky darkened to indigo and the stars appeared in all their glory. With no city lights to wash them out, they were brilliant in the jet black sky. Simon could even see the pale haze of the Milky Way, earth's own galaxy, stretching across the heavens.

Tricklock said, "Look, there's the Three Stooges constellation and burst out laughing."

Simon also started to laugh. In his head he reluctantly acknowledged that his dad's star jokes were pretty funny once he thought about it.

"Tomorrow, if we're lucky we'll be eating fresh pan fried trout for dinner." Tricklock went on, "You done much fishing Simon?"

Simon shook his head, "No, my mom and stepdad are not much into fishing."

Tricklock said, "Well, you're in for some fun times. Fishing is a blast."

"We'll see." said Simon. "It sounds messy and primitive to me."

Tricklock chuckled, "That's BA and the weasel talking out your face. Trust me, you'll have a great time, but right now it's time to hit the sleeping bags."

As if to punctuate the moment, a meteor streaked across the sky, its silvery tail quickly fading into the night. Tricklock and Simon crawled into the tent and situated themselves. Tricklock hung a green chemical light stick from the ceiling to provide some light in case nature called during the night. They snuggled into their cozy sleeping bags and soon drifted off into pleasant dreams.

Pecos Wilderness Day Two: The next morning they awoke bright and early. Simon groaned. His joints and muscles were sore and stiff from the previous day's exertions. When Simon asked about the bathroom, Tricklock laughed. He handed Simon a small lightweight folding shovel, and showed him how to do his morning bathroom ritual well away from their camp. When Simon returned, he asked about breakfast.

Tricklock had a sly smile on his face, "While I go and perform my morning rituals, why don't you start a fire?"

Before Simon could sputter out a response, Tricklock grabbed the shovel and walked off into the bushes. When he came back, Simon was fumbling around the fire pit to no good effect. There was no fire, not even the beginning glimmerings of a spark.

Tricklock asked his son, "Are you hungry?"

Simon quickly answered, "I'm starving!"

"Well," said Tricklock, "would you like to have some dried beef jerky, or bacon, eggs and toast?"

Simon snorted, "Duh, bacon, eggs and toast of course!"

Tricklock remarked, "Well, if we want to eat like kings, then we need to build a fire."

Tricklock then taught Simon the step by step procedures for building a fire. He demonstrated each step, then had Simon do each step. Soon they had a crackling fire. Simon was obviously proud of himself. He felt even better after his dad produced a frying pan and some camping utensils. His dad quickly whipped up some bacon, eggs, and toast. Delicious food smells wafted around them and stoked their appetites. After they had eaten, Simon declared that their simple breakfast was awesomely delicious.

When they finished cleaning dishes and ordering their camp, Tricklock proclaimed that henceforth, Simon would be responsible for starting all of their campfires.

"I am Fire Marshall Simon!" he exclaimed. He was actually looking forward to his campfire duties.

While they were preparing their fishing gear, Simon started another controversial conversation, "Mom and Dave say you are racist against Muslims."

Tricklock retorted, "Those two crack me up. They're always trying to analyze me. I'm not against every Muslim, just the crazy ones who want to kill every man woman and child in America. This is a serious war, if terrorists could set off a nuclear weapon in a major city they would do it—they're nuts!"

"But not all Muslims act like that." said Simon.

Tricklock shook his head, "I didn't say they did, but there are about 1.6 billion Muslims in the world. If we discount the very ill, very young, and very old as threats to America, that leaves about 1 billion. If only a quarter of a percent of those billion Muslims are America-hating fanatics, that's still two and a half million terrorists. It's depressing to think about. BA and Dave-the-weasel think that if America is nice to the Islamists they won't want to kill everyone, but those two are not known for their penetrating political insight. They're actually dangerously naïve."

Simon frowned, "What's so naïve about their point of view?"

"At school you've probably seen bullies in action. You think a good strategy against bullies is to be nice to them? Give them your lunch money and then they'll be your friends?"

Simon laughed, "No, that won't work. If a kid tries that, the bully will try to get even more money."

Tricklock nodded, "I'm glad you can see that. You may as well try being nice to a hungry tiger or an angry cobra, but some folks just don't get it. That philosophy is called appeasement and has failed every time it's been tried throughout human history. But enough of all this serious stuff, what say we do a little fishing?"

"OK." said Simon, "I have a feeling I'm going to be a natural at this. Watch out trout! By the way, where are we going to get worms?"

Tricklock just laughed and shook his head, "Almost a genius huh?"

Chapter 8
STORM CLOUDS GATHER

While Tricklock had languished in the Bastion hospital making preparations for his return to the United States, Khaled was making his own very different arrangements. Khaled had closely followed the news coverage of Tricklock's convalescence and had learned of the American's plan to visit with his son. Khaled quickly arranged to take an extended leave of absence from the TV station and booked a flight out of the country—his destination was Albuquerque, New Mexico. He did not seek approval from his al Qaeda superiors for fear they would balk at the audacity of his plan. Rather, he planned to provide them with a fait accompli. He had contacted two men living undercover in the United States, a college student and a college professor. The men were actually al Qaeda soldiers, albeit low level operatives. America was full of untrained al Qaeda wannabes, but Khaled needed trained fighters he could trust. The two men he selected were both fellow Egyptians, which Khaled saw as a plus. Both men had been vetted and trained in an al Qaeda camp before moving to the United States. Youssef was known to Khaled by reputation and was attending college in Texas on a student visa, while Waleed was teaching Egyptology in Denver.

Although Youssef and Waleed both dreamed of serving al Qaeda while in America, they realized that the chances were slim that they would ever be called upon to act. The past years were not exactly full of successful al Qaeda attacks carried out on American soil. The odd attacks usually involved

American-born Muslims who decided to fight for al Qaeda and who inevitably and unwittingly enlisted the help of the FBI to construct their bombs. But nonetheless, both Waleed and Youssef dutifully checked a certain website daily, hoping to see a coded phrase which would set in motion certain actions and procedures. And then suddenly the phrase had appeared on the website. Without any previous knowledge of each other or of mission specifics, their protocols guided them to other Jihadi websites where they obtained contact procedures.

Eventually, the two undercover terrorists each found themselves talking on Tracfones to a mysterious man. They strictly followed orders and made arrangements to take leaves of absence. Khaled gave preliminary instructions to Youssef and Waleed and arranged to meet the two men in Albuquerque, New Mexico. Both men possessed useful assets and skills that fit with Khaled's planning. Youssef looked much younger than his 30 years but had killed men in battle. He was a foreign student, and although he didn't realize it, he was now an assassin supporting Operation Powerful Vendetta.

Waleed had been born in America while his parents had been visiting his uncle who owned an import and export business. His parents still lived in Egypt, but Waleed had later taken advantage of his U.S. citizenship and moved to America. Long before moving to the states, Waleed had joined al Qaeda and trained at one of their many camps. When al Qaeda found out that Waleed could claim American citizenship, they arranged for him to move to the U.S to serve their cause. As an American citizen, Waleed had been able to stockpile guns and ammunition and owned a Ford Explorer that could easily tow a camper trailer big enough to sleep three men. Khaled decided that during this operation his team would only use concealable handguns and knives. If they had to track Tricklock into the forest, he wanted his team to be able to pass as hikers and nature enthusiasts. Openly carrying assault rifles, especially in an area open to hunting, would most certainly attract unwanted attention from nosey fish and game officers. Their cover story if questioned was that they were friends who shared an interest in high desert geography and wildlife. They would even carry cameras and a book on New Mexico animals and birds to complete the deception.

The three Egyptians met at a small coffee shop in the Nob Hill district of Albuquerque to make plans. When Youssef and Waleed realized their commander was the famous Great Face Eater, they were in awe. Their hearts swelled with pride and importance. Their commander's identity underscored the importance of this mission. Khaled assigned each of his soldiers various tasks to accomplish. Although he didn't expect to spend much time in the actual forest, they needed basic camping and hiking gear to remain inconspicuous and to carry out their plan. They also needed to rent a camper trailer to use for shelter and as a command post, and of course they needed to stock the camper with food and other essentials. Khaled also wanted maps and compasses, walkie talkies, and some hand-held GPS receivers. He handed Youssef a thick wad of money and directed him to purchase a small used dirt bike. Khaled had easy access to substantial cash reserves. Khaled had researched Tricklock and discovered that his parents lived in Pecos. Khaled had also learned, by following local media reports and interviews, that Tricklock had not yet left his home in nearby Rio Rancho, in fact he had only just returned to New Mexico. Attacking him at his home was out of the question; a media circus had sprung up around his residence. Tricklock was surrounded by a force field of journalists angling for interviews, and paparazzi hoping to take a candid photo. Khaled would have to follow Tricklock to Pecos and attack him when he was isolated.

Once in Pecos, they would use the camper trailer as their mobile base of operations. As soon as possible Khaled would put Tricklock's parent's house under surveillance. Youssef would use his motorcycle to scout the residence. The bike was less noticeable and could travel where the SUV and camper could not. Khaled had learned that Tricklock would take his son Simon to visit his grandparents before beginning his camping trip. When Tricklock left for the forest, Youssef would unobtrusively follow him on the bike, keeping Khaled updated. Meanwhile Khaled and Waleed would visit Isaac and Alice. Khaled considered himself an expert at coaxing information from unwilling prisoners, and Tricklock's parents should have detailed information about their son's plans. He trembled with anticipation when he thought of how he would make the old couple suffer, using their love for each other against them. He genuinely relished the prospect of torturing and killing Tricklock's parents. After their coffee house meeting, the three Egyptians went off to accomplish their tasks, agreeing to link up the next day.

Khaled and his men met again at a small cafe in the afternoon of the following day. The eatery was filled with oblivious young students from the University of New Mexico taking their lunch, hunching over I Pads, and talking on smart phones. In their midst the three killers sipped tea and plotted Tricklock's destruction. Youssef had purchased a small dirt bike, and Waleed had rented a camper trailer. Khaled handed them each a list of supplies and equipment to purchase. They hunched over a road map and discussed various details of their plan. Khaled knew that compared to past operations that involved many months of detailed planning and analysis, this operation had been hastily cobbled together, but Khaled felt divinely inspired. Only he had recognized this small window of opportunity and had boldly seized the moment. With Allah's blessing this successful mission would set in motion events that could result in the deaths of thousands of enemy unbelievers.

Khaled glanced around the cafe and scrutinized the motley group of patrons with disgust. The longer Khaled stayed in America, the angrier he became. The difference between America and Afghanistan, and even Egypt, was stark. The prosperity that surrounded him rankled, and it had only been obtained by raping the poor countries of the world of their natural resources. This was Khaled's second visit to the United States, and his firsthand experiences further steeled his resolve to successfully complete his mission. Compared to the Middle East with its poverty, political instability, and ubiquitous fighting, America was practically a utopia, but one built on a foundation of imperial exploitation and evil. The social injustice was staggering. Hatred radiated from Khaled like heat from the sun.

Waleed was concerned, "Khaled, you look as if you are ready to explode. You should calm yourself before you attract attention."

Khaled took a deep breath and slowly let it out, "Yes, you are right. There will be plenty of time to indulge myself later. We must finish our preparations today so we can leave tomorrow as planned."

The next day, they placed the motorbike into the camper and headed onto I-25 North. An hour and a half later they neared their destination. The terrain had changed dramatically. They were surrounded by mountains covered with juniper, piñon, and bristlecone pines. The geography was very different than the flat desert spaces they had driven across on their way to the Pecos. They were surrounded by greenery and the temperature was much cooler.

Khaled had researched the area during his planning. The Santa Fe National Forest and the Pecos Wilderness cover an area of about 230,000 acres. The Pecos Wilderness is a part of America's National Wilderness Preservation System. In much of the preserve, vehicles of any kind are prohibited and the only way to travel is on foot or on horseback. In large tracts of the wilderness there are no roads, homes, or even campsites. The forest is filled with wild animals and there are 20 lakes and more than a hundred miles of fishing streams. The Pecos Wilderness is enormous. In the foothills the elevation is 6,000 feet and rises to 13,000 feet at the top of Truchas Peak. In September the days are usually mild, but the nights can be frosty.

As they had studied the map, Khaled was forced to acknowledge his team's inexperience with American maps. They had picked up a few different types of maps, but they were hard to understand. Even though they all spoke conversational English, they were unfamiliar with technical and scientific map terminology. Khaled only knew the basics of using a map and compass; he was not an expert. The GPS was also hard to figure out—it was a miniature computer. In order to use a GPS, one had to be familiar with its features and be able to enter coordinates. His team was smart, but they were hampered by language and cultural differences. Where they came from the average person did not own a GPS, and they were not accustomed to keeping pace with rapid technological advances. The result was that it took much longer than Khaled planned to familiarize themselves with their electronic devices and equipment. During operations in Iraq, Khaled had mostly used city street maps for their attacks on checkpoints, police stations or specific buildings. When he had operated in rural areas in Iraq and especially in Afghanistan, they always had local guides and soldiers who had grown up in the area and were intimately familiar with all the mountain passes and secret hiding places.

Their unfamiliarity with their maps and GPS receivers made it even more critical that they be able to clandestinely follow Tricklock into the forest, or if that was not possible, torture his exact camp location from his parents. Khaled planned to place the ranch of Tricklock's parents under immediate surveillance. When they arrived in the Pecos region, Khaled parked their trailer at a small roadside camping space only a few miles from the Tricklock ranch. Khaled insisted that Youssef immediately place the ranch under discreet observation, and moments later Youssef hopped on his motorbike and drove off towards the ranch. He carried a paper roadmap with the ranch location circled in pen. Youssef concealed his bike off the side of the road a few hundred meters from the ranch entrance and picked his way through scrub trees and sagebrush to a vantage point on a small forested knoll where he could scrutinize the residence.

While Youssef began his surveillance, Khaled and Waleed went about the business of setting up their command post. They left the camper hooked up to Waleed's truck in case they needed to move quickly in pursuit of their quarry. Besides, the rental place had attached the camper to the truck and it appeared complicated. None of the three Egyptians were familiar with campers, or with camping in general. The man who rented them the camper had explained the various external and internal workings, but Khaled and Waleed had already forgotten many of the details. They were frustrated with the difficulties they were having. At first the tap water didn't work. They wasted half an hour before they found the switch that turned on the water pump. The trailer also had a bewildering number of outside compartments that contained essential equipment, such as the trailer's batteries and generator.

There were separate controls for the generator, water pump, heater, air conditioner and lighting. There was a toilet and shower that worked differently than their household counterparts. There was a propane stove and a refrigerator. The beds were suspended platforms that had electric controls to raise and lower them, and there were couches and tables that came apart and stowed away in clever places. The furniture was designed to fold away to conserve space. The camper was like a giant jigsaw puzzle. Some of the contraptions were ingenious, but confusing to anyone who was unfamiliar with camper trailers. They wasted a lot of time dealing with camper issues—Khaled fumed and fidgeted. Since his partners had been living in the U.S. for some time, he had assumed they would be familiar with everything American. He now realized that was an unrealistic expectation.

An excited Youssef returned before sunset, "I saw the American and his son. They are at the ranch. I watched them unload some baggage from a green truck. I think they just arrived. Later I heard gunfire. I think they were shooting at targets. When it started getting dark I left."

Khaled beamed. He was pleased that at least one thing had gone right this day.

"Why didn't you immediately phone us or use the radio to inform me?" asked Khaled.

Youssef answered nervously, "I tried Khaled, but the phone had no signal and there was no response on the radio. Maybe there is something wrong with the device."

Khaled focused an accusing gaze upon Waleed who had a stricken look on his face.

Waleed explained nervously, "I forgot to turn the radios on. It will not happen again."

Khaled let it pass, "Having just arrived at his parent's house, the American will not leave today. Youssef, you will pick up your surveillance at daybreak."

The Egyptians convened a war council inside the camper to go over the next day's activities. Afterwards, they attempted to settle in for a good night's sleep. They struggled with the camper controls but eventually resolved their issues. Khaled eventually fell into an uneasy, dream-filled sleep. Youssef left before first light the next morning and made his way to his observation post of the previous day. The ranch was still dark as he settled in to watch. When the sky began to lighten, the high desert creatures began to stir. Youssef heard the rustle of small animals stirring in the underbrush. He was a city person and wild animals and dangerous looking insects made him nervous. As the sky slowly brightened and the desert began to shake off the night, he also began to detect movement within the Tricklock residence. Slowly the house seemed to rouse itself and come alive. One by one the ranch's dark windows brightened into glowing squares of warm yellow light. As the Tricklock family began to move about, their shadows flickered on the amber hued window shades. Soon it was light enough for Youssef to see color and details in his surroundings. After a time, Tricklock left the house and moved his truck close to the front door and began loading luggage.

Youssef used his walkie talkie to contact Khaled and tell him that Tricklock was preparing to leave. Khaled told him to continue to observe, and when Tricklock left the ranch Youssef was to discreetly follow the American and periodically update Khaled. Once Tricklock left the ranch, Khaled would visit the American's parents and painfully extract some helpful information. Youssef made his way back to his motorcycle and positioned himself to observe the ranch gate. When Tricklock's large green pickup truck pulled onto the main road, Youssef followed at a discreet distance. When the truck parked at a roadside diner, Youssef called Khaled and then settled in to wait for the Americans to finish breakfast and leave the diner.

Khaled and Waleed left the campground and drove to the Tricklock ranch. Khaled was tingling with anticipation. He pulled into the driveway and brazenly parked in front of the residence. He knocked numerous times, but there was no response. With growing frustration Khaled searched the grounds. The elder Tricklock's were not there. Khaled wanted to torch the ranch, but that would draw too much attention. Also, if their attempt to follow Tricklock failed, they might need to return here to find out where Tricklock planned to set up his camp.

At the urging of their son, Isaac and Alice had agreed to leave town for a week. Tricklock had been worried about the press intruding on his parent's privacy, but his insistence that they leave had inadvertently saved them from Khaled. As soon as Tricklock and Simon had driven off, Isaac and Alice had left for Denver where they would spend some time with one of Isaac's old Marine buddies. They planned to return home after five days to host Jake and Simon when they returned from their camping adventure.

Meanwhile, Youssef had been watching the diner where he assumed Tricklock and his son were eating their morning meal. He had been waiting for 30 minutes when he received a phone call from Khaled informing him that Tricklock's parents were not at the ranch. It was now crucial that Youssef keep close tabs on his quarry. The success of the three terrorist's entire mission depended on Youssef's ability to track the American. Tricklock and his son finally left the diner, got into their truck, and pulled out of the parking lot. Youssef followed at a safe distance. When possible he kept one or two vehicles between his bike and Tricklock's truck. When Tricklock pulled off the main road onto a dirt jeep trail, Youssef waited at the turn-off for a spell and then slowly followed.

Youssef drove gingerly, following the truck's dust like a trail of bread crumbs. The billowing brown cloud also helped conceal Youssef from Tricklock's view. They traveled the rutted dirt road for quite a few bewildering and jarring miles before Tricklock parked his truck off the jeep trail in an area concealed by a thicket of trees. Youssef watched from a distance as the father and son put on backpacks and ambled into the forest. He tried to contact Khaled but could not get phone reception or a radio signal. Youssef warily approached Tricklock's truck and peered inside. He thought for a moment and then smashed a window and entered the vehicle. He spent 20 minutes at the truck and then returned to his bike. Before Youssef left the area, he made a cairn of rocks to mark the spot where Tricklock's truck had left the jeep trail. Youssef impatiently drove the considerable distance back to his prearranged rendezvous point at the campground. Khaled was pleased that Youssef had successfully followed Tricklock to the trailhead, but now they would have to track the American to his campsite. Man tracking is very difficult, and Khaled had serious misgivings about their chances for success. Then Youssef smiled broadly and pulled out a map. The map had Tricklock's destination campsite labeled and circled in pencil.

Khaled's face lit up as he realized what he held in his hands, "How did you get this?"

Youssef beamed, "After Tricklock parked his truck and left, I broke in and searched the interior—I found this map. I do not know if the strange doodles in the margins have special meaning."

Khaled bowed his head, "You have done well Youssef, and it is clear that Allah has truly blessed this undertaking. Tricklock has a substantial head start, but this no longer matters. We now know their final destination."

Khaled paused and smiled, "We also know their final resting place."

Pecos Wilderness Day One: Youssef led the way on his motorcycle, and Khaled and Waleed followed in their SUV towing the camper. The trail was extremely rugged and the going painfully slow. When the trail became almost impossible to negotiate, Khaled decided to park the trailer in a clearing even though they were still a couple of miles from Tricklock's truck. It was evident that many other campers had previously used the small glade. There were tire tracks where camper trailers had parked, and there was even an abandoned fire pit. Khaled ordered his men to organized their gear and supplies. Their heavy backpacks contained mostly pistols and ammunition. They packed very little actual camping gear. Khaled decided they would pack light and not burden themselves with too much useless camping gear and water. Water was very heavy, and he figured they could refill their water bottles from one of the many mountain streams. The terrain was steep and the altitude made the air thin. It was late afternoon, and Khaled did not want to travel at night. He had a map marked with Tricklock's campsite, and even though he was anxious to begin, he decided to sleep in the camper and go after Tricklock the next day.

Denver, Colorado Two Days Earlier: Tanya Brown was supremely confident and ambitious. In her humble opinion, she was the complete package. She was smart, attractive, and independent. She had grown up in rural Colorado and loved to camp, hike, and fish. Raised a tomboy, she was athletic and comfortable in the outdoors. Her parents owned a ranch and she grew up riding horses and had even competed in some amateur rodeos. In school she easily achieved straight A's and IQ tests confirmed that her intelligence was well above average. She was also blessed with stunning good looks. Tanya was tall with lustrous black hair. Her emerald eyes were arresting, and if one looked closely, her irises were flecked with copper colored artifacts. There was something slightly asymmetrical and mysterious about her face that was hard to define. Maybe her mouth was a bit too wide, or her nose was not perfectly straight. Whatever the reason, the small imperfections only added to her beauty—her striking good looks were intriguing. Although she had an amazing figure, the gazes of most men were inexorably drawn to her face. Men tended to stare at her, subconsciously trying to solve the riddle of her appeal. She was a force of nature that radiated energy and personality. Most men found it almost impossible to concentrate when she was around. Tanya was aware of the effect she had on men, but she refused to rely solely on her good looks to advance her career—she worked hard and smart. This was not to say she did not take advantage of her *feminine charms* when it helped her to achieve her goals. Tanya did not hesitate to exploit all of her assets to get what she wanted; to Tanya this was only common sense.

As a matter of principle, Tanya had no reservations about using her God-given beauty to further her career. In fact, she had strong opinions about the feminists who looked down upon attractive women. She thought that type of feminist was misguided, arrogant, and condescending. These same so called feminists liked to protest restaurants and magazines that they thought exploited women as sexual objects, which in their opinion was shallow and degrading. Tanya thought that there was some hypocrisy and fishy goings-on with that brand of feminism. First of all, could it really be a coincidence that most of the feminists, who complain that men exploit attractive women, are themselves often unattractive or even lesbians. It also didn't seem to matter to them if the poor downtrodden victims loved what they were doing and were making excellent money.

It amazed Tanya that some feminists looked down on women who took advantage of their God-given good looks and sexy figures to make successful careers as models, actresses, or dancers. In Tanya's mind, the key phrase in all of this was, God-given. God-given beauty, athletic ability, artistic talent, or even brains—it was all an accident of birth. Tanya imagined two scenarios: a woman is born a genius and capitalizes on her superior intelligence to become a highly paid rocket scientist. Another woman is born with exceptional beauty and a sexy figure and goes on to become wealthy and famous. In Tanya's opinion both career paths had equal value, because in each case the women were born with their respective talents and then with hard work parlayed their genetic gifts into lucrative careers. Both smarts and appearance are genetic.

Both are accidents of birth and therefore, Tanya reasoned, physical beauty and intelligence are equal. Tanya was blessed with intelligence *and* good looks and unabashedly used both of God's gifts to her advantage.

After college Tanya pursued a career in journalism and landed a job with a local TV station in Denver. Over the next few years she paid her dues and single mindedly worked her way up the corporate ladder, finally landing an on-camera slot as an investigative reporter. She was especially impressive in front of the camera. She was exceptionally photogenic and her live broadcasts sounded natural and unforced. She had a talent for speaking live in front of a camera. But her greatest strength was her skill at behind the scenes detective work, sniffing out clues and navigating unerringly to the heart of convoluted stories. She had a knack for steering her way through the labyrinths of misinformation that white collared criminals built to disguise their schemes. Her good looks and non-threatening demeanor often got her in the door where others would have been barred admittance, and once inside she usually landed interviews with people at the heart of the controversy. Her friendly and somewhat timid approach was disarming. Her initial queries were deceptively innocuous but soon gave way to hard hitting and penetrating questions that often caught the subjects of her interviews off guard. Her subjects often revealed much more information than they intended. Before they realized their mistakes, they had often let slip nuggets of information that eventually led Tanya to the unvarnished truth. Public figures soon realized that Tanya Brown was no puff pastry, but her growing reputation was making it harder and harder to obtain interviews. Her career path was not without its obstacles, but she overcame them with grace and intelligence.

Like the rest of the nation, Tanya had watched the video of Tricklock's heroics with fascination and admiration. On a purely personal level, she thought he was the most humble, brave, and handsome man she had ever seen. He had been relatively reticent and guarded during the interviews she had watched. She had the feeling that his military bosses had pressured him to make himself available to the press. Sergeant Tricklock lived close by in neighboring New Mexico. Tanya would love to get an interview with him one on one. She thought she could get him to open up and provide the public with a truly fascinating expose of a real national hero. During one of Tricklock's interviews, Tanya picked up on a casual comment he made. Tricklock was not a practiced public personality and thus was not very media savvy—she was sure his comment was a blunder. Tricklock had let slip that he planned a father and son camping trip in the Pecos Forest in New Mexico. That night visions of sugar plums, sporting Tricklock's rugged features and maroon PJ beret, danced in her head.

By the next morning she had formed the outline of an audacious plan. With her skills, Tanya had confidence she could find Tricklock in the Pecos and land an on-location interview. An exclusive and penetrating discussion with the reluctant hero would garner huge ratings and bolster her career. The Pecos Wilderness was easy driving distance from Denver, but first she had to convince her boss. That morning, she marched into Oscar's office and launched into a well-reasoned and impassioned pitch supporting her plan to interview Tricklock in the Pecos. She completely overwhelmed her poor boss; he was only partway through his first cup of coffee. She argued convincingly that the potentially huge payoff of an exclusive interview, far out-weighed the minor effort and expense.

Oscar finally threw up his hands in a mock defensive gesture and said, "Ok! Just try and keep your expenses down and be sure to stay in touch and keep me posted on your progress."

Anticipating her boss's acceptance of her plan, Tanya had already loaded her Jeep with camping gear before driving to work. After leaving Oscar's office, she hopped in her vehicle and headed straight for New Mexico. She was loaded for bear, but she was hunting a Tricklock. If she was lucky, she would arrive in Pecos before the enigmatic PJ hero.

Tanya had hastily conceived a rough plan and would first try and get some information in Pecos town. She had learned some basic facts about Tricklock and his parents and had a few notions on how to use that knowledge. If her plan to acquire information in town didn't pan out, she would watch Isaac's house until he showed up. When Tricklock left for the wilderness, she would follow him and later pretend to stumble upon him and his son. Initially, she concocted an elaborate scheme that involved playing the unprepared female hiker, possibly feigning some dilemma or injury. Tricklock's chivalry and natural male instincts to rescue a damsel in distress should attract him to her, especially such a sexy damsel as herself. But in the end her conscience got the better of her, and she decided that given the chance she would approach Tricklock boldly. She would be upfront and honest. If she didn't get any good tips in town and struck out while spying-out the ranch, she could hike to some popular fishing and camping sites. If she was lucky, she might stumble across the hero and his son. Maybe Tricklock would consent to an interview if she could convince him that she was sincere in her motives.

Tanya had researched Tricklock and his family. She walked confidently into Sam's Sporting Goods Shop, the largest outdoor recreation store in Pecos town. She was hoping that as a gunsmith in a small community, Isaac would be known to most of the gun shops in town. She casually strolled over to the glass cases that held various models and types of firearms. The clerk was an older gentleman who wore a plastic name tag that read *Karl*.

Tanya smiled, "Hi Karl. I was wondering if you could help me."

Karl smiled back, "Why sure. What can I do for you?"

Tanya asked, "Do you know Isaac Tricklock, the gunsmith?"

"Sure I know Isaac; we've been friends for years."

Tanya gave Karl her biggest smile, "You ever go fishing with him?"

Now it was time for Karl to smile, "Why, Isaac is one of my closest fishing buddies. Why do you ask?"

Tanya knew how to turn on the charm, "Oh. I'm sorry! Here I am asking all these questions and I haven't even introduced myself. My name is Tanya Brown."

When she offered her hand to shake, Tanya's heart was pounding. It seemed like she'd struck pay dirt on her first attempt.

Karl warmly shook her hand and Tanya continued to explain, "Isaac knows of an out-of-the way fishing hole, and I was hoping to try it out. I finally made it out here from Denver, but Isaac is out of town. I was hoping you could steer me in the right direction."

Karl had instantly taken a shine to the young lady. She seemed like good people, easy going and friendly. She was properly dressed for hiking and fishing, and he liked women who knew their way around the outdoors. His wife Martha hated camping, fishing, hunting, and any activities that lacked air-conditioning and a spotless bathroom. Although Tanya had not claimed actual friendship with Isaac, her familiar use of Isaac's name led Karl to assume that Tanya was close friends with the gunsmith. Tanya pulled out a topographic map of the area and spread it on the counter.

Karl said, "I think I know the exact stream you are referring too. You know the jeep trails are pretty rough and will only take you so far. It's quite a hike in, but the big fish are worth the effort."

Tanya put his mind at ease, "I have a four wheel drive Jeep and am also prepared for a long hike."

Karl and Tanya hunched over the map and Karl traced out the jeep trail and the hiking route that he and Isaac usually used to reach the trout stream.

Tanya pointed to a different jeep trail, "What about this road here?" she asked. "This looks like it gets a lot closer to the stream."

Karl chuckled, "Yep, but the map is real deceptive. The terrain has changed a lot since this map was made. A big forest fire and then flooding and erosion really re-landscaped that whole area. The hike from there is shorter but it's a bear, well-nigh impossible for a man of my advanced years. But on second thought, maybe not so hard for a fit young lady."

Tanya asked Karl a few more pertinent questions, thanked him with a big hug and said her goodbyes.

Armed with her new found knowledge, Tanya was feeling more hopeful than ever. Next up was a covert trip to Isaac's house to see what was cooking at the elder Tricklock residence. So far, Tanya seemed to be blessed with good fortune on this assignment. During her research she had easily located Isaac and Alice's ranch. Given their age, they were understandably somewhat old fashioned and were actually in the Pecos phone book. She had found their location online before leaving Denver. She punched in their address into her GPS and headed out.

Tanya parked a good distance away from the ranch gate and approached the residence on foot. She moved slowly, being careful to stay concealed among the scrub trees. She felt like a TV private eye as she crouched among the mesquite and scurried from tree to tree. After traveling a couple of hundred yards she reached a good vantage point amidst concealing vegetation where she could secretly observe the ranch. She took out her binoculars and dialed in the focus. Her good fortune continued as she recognized Tricklock's green pickup truck parked in front of the residence. As she scanned the area she saw Tricklock, accompanied by an older man and a teenager, walk to some outlying buildings and sheds. Tanya guessed that Tricklock's companions must be his father Isaac and his son Simon. A short time later Isaac seemed to be setting up targets—it appeared that he had his own shooting range.

As she watched Simon, apparently getting a lesson in gun safety, she saw a flicker of movement off to her right. She swung her binoculars to where she had seen the brief flash of color. She zoomed in on a slightly built, dark complected man dressed in blue jeans and a brown leather jacket. He also had a pair of binoculars trained on the shooting range.

Her heart started pounding, "Now isn't this an interesting development?"

She had discovered a fellow spy and closely scrutinized the mysterious stranger. A herd of thoughts stampeded through her head. One disturbing possibility was that she was being scooped by a reporter from a rival news outlet. This competitor could spoil her plans for an exclusive. The man was so focused on watching Tricklock, that he was oblivious to her hidden presence. When he began to pull out, Tanya followed at a good distance.

She stayed out of sight but was still able to observe the secretive man's progress. He walked a fair distance from his spy hole and retrieved a dirt bike from where he had concealed it behind some bushes. He donned a helmet and drove off, looking like a typical recreational motorcyclist out for a joyride. It appeared that Tricklock wasn't going anywhere for a while, so Tanya resolved to follow the biker spy. The motorcyclist stopped only a few miles down the road where a Ford Explorer hooked to a trailer had set up at a roadside camping spot. As she drove past she noticed two other men. She also noted the SUV's tag number. When she had gone a safe distance past, she jotted down the number on a scrap of paper. This was very depressing. It appeared as though another TV station had sent an entire film crew. She only had a small portable video camera, nothing to compare with the production equipment a three man film crew could carry in a camper.

She immediately dialed her DMV contact in Denver, "John, this is Tanya; I was wondering if you could do me a favor. I have a plate number I'd like you to run. I'm on a story and it looks like another crew is trying to scoop me. Get me a name and whatever information you can, and maybe I can figure out who my competition is. I'll call you tomorrow to see what you come up with."

She paused to listen to John's response, "OK, thanks, I owe you one."

Afterwards Tanya checked into a small motel and began to inventory the contents of her backpack. Although her focus was on obtaining an interview with Tricklock, she could not afford to ignore the obvious; she was about to hike for a day and a half through wilderness. This was a serious endeavor and she needed to thrive and survive.

Tanya needed to pack smart in order to camp comfortably. Individual items had to weigh as little as possible. She had a long way to hike, much of it uphill, and she wanted to travel light. She was 5 feet 8 inches tall and weighed an athletic 135 pounds. The backpacking rule of thumb is that a person should carry no more than 30% of their body weight. Tanya was shooting for a pack weight of no more than 40 pounds.

There was little chance for serious thunderstorms, so she decided to go minimalist and pack a Sil Tarp. The high-tech tarp only weighed a few ounces, but it made a sturdy waterproof shelter. For her sleeping comfort she would carry a closed cell sleeping pad, a lightweight fiberfill sleeping bag rated to 20 degrees, and a compressible pillow. She had a four day supply of dehydrated meals, but most of the weight she would carry would be drinking water—she would not skimp on water. Anyway, as she drank her water, her pack would lighten. This was also good motivation to drink a lot of water and stay hydrated. Once she reached the trout stream she would have plenty of water, but she would have to purify it before drinking. Nearly all the streams in the U.S. contain Giardia, a protozoan parasite that will make a person as sick as a dog.

The next morning Tanya checked out of the hotel while it was still dark and drove to Tricklock's ranch. She quietly picked her way back to the same spot she had used the previous day. She was curious to see if the other reporter would be in his spot. She would find out when the sun rose. She didn't have long to wait. The impenetrable black of night slowly morphed into progressively lighter shades of grey. With dawn's arrival the night noises faded, replaced by the delicate sounds of furtive creatures beginning their day with a breakfast hunt. Small birds chirped and fluttered among the shrubs and cacti.

Tanya focused her binoculars where she had previously seen the mystery man. Just as she suspected, the enigmatic spy skulked among the bushes scoping-out the ranch. Tanya divided her time between watching the ranch and watching the man watching the ranch. Soon she saw shadow people moving behind shaded windows as they turned on room lights and began their morning rituals. An hour or so later, she saw Tricklock move his truck near the front door and begin to load bags into the back seat—it looked like he was preparing to leave. Tanya watched as the family gathered near Tricklock's truck, hugging, kissing, and obviously saying their goodbyes. Tanya planned to follow Tricklock, so it was time to head back to her Jeep. When she glassed the other observer's location, he was already gone. She walked back to her Jeep, picking her way through the cacti and thorny vegetation. When she positioned her Jeep to follow Tricklock's truck, she almost drove up on the mysterious motorcyclist. She saw him just in time and stopped before he could see her. It appeared that she would be following a man who was following a man. This was a novel experience but exciting. Things were getting curiouser and curiouser.

Tanya followed at a good distance, unseen by the motorcyclist who was laser focused on the vehicle he was tailing. When Tricklock pulled into a diner, the biker stayed well back. It appeared as though he planned to wait for Tricklock and Simon to come out of the restaurant. Tanya drove right past the bike and parked her Jeep. She strode into the diner and sat where she could keep an eye on Tricklock and his son. She ordered a light breakfast and tried not to stare. Tricklock and the waitress seemed to be engaged in an animated conversation. When the waitress left, Simon was shaking his head. He seemed to be annoyed with his father. Tanya finished her food and paid her bill. She sipped on black coffee, and when Tricklock and Simon left the diner, she walked out after them and got into her Jeep. When the green pickup left the parking lot, she waited for the motorcyclist to follow and then pulled onto the main road, following at a discreet distance.

Tanya noticed that her GPS showed they were heading towards the jeep trail she had learned about at the store in Pecos. When the biker following Tricklock turned onto the trail she had marked on her map, it was good confirmation of her information. They continued down the road for some miles. The dirt road was heavily rutted and she was glad she was driving her trusty Jeep. When she neared the point that Karl had marked as the starting point for the hike, the motorcyclist slowed and Tanya pulled off the trail and parked. She crept through the foliage staying out of sight. By the time she reached a vantage where she could see Tricklock's parked his truck, he and his son were just disappearing into the trees. Seconds later she spotted the motorcyclist, now dismounted and approaching the pickup which was parked off the dirt road behind a copse of trees. She was shocked to see the dark skinned man casually smash the truck's driver side window and ransack the vehicle. He eventually rose with what looked like a folded map in his hand. Next he opened the hood of the truck and bent over the engine compartment. When he emerged he grasped a tangle of wires and cables.

She remained hidden while the man mounted his bike and drove past her concealed position back the way he had come. Tanya glanced at her phone—she had no service. She decided to drive back to the main road. She needed to make a phone call. She decided she would use the other route to the fishing stream and shave some miles off the hike. Despite Karl's warning, she was young and in shape and was not worried about the rough terrain. When she had a couple of bars on her phone, she called John to see if he had run the license plate of the Explorer. John answered on the third ring.

"John, it's Tanya. Have you had a chance to run that plate?"

"Hello Tanya. Well I did check that license plate. The vehicle belongs to Waleed Ali. After a little digging, I found out that he's an American citizen of Egyptian descent. He teaches Egyptian studies at a university in Denver."

Tanya was confused, "I thought he might be working for a TV station."

John continued, "I'm no detective, but as far as I can tell he's just a professor."

Tanya was more confused than ever, "Ok, thanks John."

"I hope that helps. You owe me one Tanya. I'll talk to you later."

Tanya was baffled. Why would a college professor be part of a team spying on the parents of Jake Tricklock and following Jake's vehicle? And why would he break into Tricklock's truck and disable the engine? There were a lot of unanswered questions. She headed her Jeep towards her hotel. She would get a good night's sleep and head out first thing in the morning. She would hike the shorter trail that would take her by an alternate route to Tricklock's fishing hole. Tomorrow she had a rough drive and an arduous hike ahead of her. She would have plenty of time to mull over the implications of today's mysterious goings-on.

Chapter 9

OPENING MOVES

Pecos Wilderness Afternoon Day Two: Tricklock had given Simon a crash course in fly fishing, and now they were trying their luck from the edge of the stream bank. Simon was learning that having an intellectual grasp of a concept, such as fly casting, does not immediately translate into physical mastery of the skill. Simon was frustrated. His movements were bumbling while his father's motions were smooth and graceful. They were using artificial trout flies for bait, not worms. No wonder his dad had fallen down laughing when Simon asked about using worms for bait. Simon had started off clumsy but was slowly getting the hang of fly casting. Suddenly, the tip of his rod bent down violently as a large fish gulped his fly. A fleeting glimpse of a glittering trout immediately dispelled his gloom and instantly transformed his sullen mood into joy. Simon's heart pounded as adrenaline and excitement commandeered his nervous system. The trout fought desperately to escape, leaping into the air and shaking off silvery spangles of water before splashing back into the rippled brook. Simon's mind raced and his hands trembled as he fought against the fish.

As if from a great distance, Simon heard his father call out encouragement and advice. Simon experienced a moment of overwhelming fear that he would lose the fish. The trout was strong and somehow pulled Simon, little by little, off the bank and into the rifling creek. Every time the fish leaped, Simon almost swallowed his heart for fear the trout would throw off the hook. As he reeled the fish closer and closer, he experienced a moment of sudden panic when he realized he didn't know what to do next. And then his dad was at his side with a landing net. Simon kept the tip of his fly rod up, following his father's urgent entreaties, and suddenly in one swift motion his dad scooped up the struggling fish.

Back on the dry creek bank, Simon was frenetic. He hopped from one foot to the other so excited he couldn't stand still. Tricklock weighed the fish and pronounced it an awesome three pound rainbow trout. Simon was stunned by the fish's beauty. Its coruscating scales were decorated with an amazing pattern of dark speckles set on a backdrop of gleaming silver. A slash of ruby ran down each side of the fish, a master stroke of God's paintbrush. The trout's vivid colors were a living mural animated by the electricity of life. As the trout died, its colors lost their vibrancy and gradually faded to dull shades of their former luster. Tricklock snapped some photos of Simon the triumphant angler, his face split ear to ear with an irrepressible grin. They put the fish on a stringer secured to the bank and slid the fish back into the icy cold water to keep him fresh.

Tricklock was elated that Simon was having an adventure, "Great job Simon! That's a beautiful fish. That's what I call pure fun. You were really living in the moment!"

Simon was exuberant, "That was awesome! I want to catch another one."

Tricklock laughed, "Alright, let's do it. I need to catch up. Looks like I'm up against some serious beginner's luck here."

Tricklock caught movement out of the corner of his eye and snapped his head around to get a better look. He was surprised to see a young woman walking towards them. She was still about a hundred yards away, but he could see she wore a good sized backpack and grasped a trekking pole in each hand. The hiker had spotted them and seemed to be making a beeline for their place on the stream bank. Tricklock was surprised to see another person out this far in the woods, especially a young woman on her own. He and Simon stopped fishing while they waited for the stranger to arrive. As she got closer, Tricklock could see that she had dark hair gathered into a ponytail and pushed through the back of a Broncos ball cap. She looked to be athletic and in her late twenties, and he couldn't help but notice that she was very good looking.

The pretty stranger boldly approached the two fishermen, extended her right hand and said, "Sergeant Tricklock I presume?"

Momentarily taken aback, Tricklock recovered quickly. He shook her hand and introduced Simon, whom she already seemed to recognize.

"And you are?" he asked.

"My name is Tanya Brown. I'm a TV reporter for a local station in Denver. My original plan was to find you and get an exclusive interview."

Puzzled, Tricklock cocked his head, "Your original plan? What's your new plan?"

"Can I talk to you for a minute?" she asked. "As strange as this may sound, I have a lot of things to tell you."

Tricklock acquiesced, "What say we all take a break in the shade, and you can tell us what's on your mind?"

They walked to a small grove of broad leafed trees a short distance away and sat down shielded from the sun. Tricklock studied Tanya intently, intrigued by the sudden turn of events.

"Does the name Waleed Ali mean anything to you?" she asked.

"I can't say that it does." Tricklock answered, "Why do you ask?"

Tanya frowned, appearing to struggle with what to say next, "This is awkward, but I'm just going to lay it out."

She went on to explain her movements of the last couple of days. She told of her surveillance of his parent's ranch where she had stumbled onto the mysterious stranger who had also been spying. She talked of her subsequent discovery of the strange man's partners and their camper and her conversation with her friend John who had researched the license plate of the SUV. She related the events of the previous day, her breakfast at the diner and how she had trailed the man to Tricklock's parked truck. After she described the shocking break-in of his truck and how the man apparently disabled the engine, Tricklock stopped her.

His face was serious, "You say he took a map from my truck?"

"That's what it looked like." said Tanya.

Tricklock and Simon locked eyes, "Simon, you said you accidently left your map behind?"

Simon had been closely following Tanya's story, "Yeah and I had our campsite circled."

Simon was confused about the meaning of all these strange happenings, and felt uneasy because his father seemed very concerned.

Tanya continued her account, "I decided to take a shorter route here, and when I re-acquired phone reception, I called my friend about the plates. He told me the truck was registered to Waleed Ali, an Egyptian American who teaches in Denver.

Tricklock mulled things over before responding, "And you said there were three men together, all dark complected?"

"That's right." she answered, "If I was profiling, I'd say they all looked Middle Eastern. I know that Waleed is from Egypt and the other two look as if they could be his brothers."

"I'd say breaking into my truck rules out your initial guess that they are reporters. Would you ever do anything like that to chase a story?" asked Tricklock.

Tanya was emphatic, "Never in a million years! And I don't know any reputable journalists who *would* do such a thing. And why would a reporter rip out wires from the engine?"

Tricklock took a deep breath, "Why indeed. Maybe that man wasn't a reporter, but someone with sinister motives who wanted to disable my ride. I think we may have a real problem."

Simon was worried, "What's going on dad?"

"I hope I'm wrong, but this may be connected to my mission in Afghanistan."

Tanya spoke up, "I came as fast as I could, and in hindsight I probably should have notified the police. I don't know what is going on, but I have a bad feeling about those men."

Tricklock asked Tanya to repeat her story, taking care to recall even the smallest detail, and this time he halted her narrative frequently to ask questions. He picked her brain for every nuance she could remember. Tanya was an investigative reporter and a trained observer—she had an excellent memory.

Afterwards Tricklock pulled out his map and pointed to a feature with the tip of his knife, "Simon, I want you to take your backpack, GPS, and these binoculars and go to the top of this hill with Tanya."

Tricklock programed the coordinates of Simon's destination into a GPS and gave instructions, "Just follow the arrow like you did on the way to our camp. If you have any trouble, just call me on channel 5. Once you get to the top of the hill, find a vantage point where you can watch this camp with the binoculars. These glasses are designed to work well even in low light. They have a large objective lens and a huge exit pupil—they're the next best thing to actual night vision goggles."

Everyone huddled round the map while Tricklock explained his general plan. He also detailed their emergency actions in case something happened to him.

"You two will have to rough it for a bit. Stay quiet, and of course there can be no camp fire or lights. From now on we're in stealth mode."

Simon was visibly nervous, "What are you going to do exactly?"

"Well, I want to verify that these guys have bad intentions, so I figure I'll arrange a meeting to find out. We have about four or five hours till sundown. That should give us plenty of time. I'm going to break down our former camp and set up a decoy camp. Sadly, you will have to leave your fish. We won't get to eat it, so you will have to let it drift downstream. Some lucky animal is going to have a great meal. Don't forget to radio me when you get to the top of the knoll, it's only a couple of kilometers away. Look for a flat space on top and I'll setup the camp when I get back. Tanya says she's an experienced outdoorsman so you two should be fine. Are you both confident you can do this?"

Tanya put her arm around Simon's shoulders and they both nodded yes. Tanya was impressed. When Tricklock took charge it seemed totally natural and unforced. She was very independent and strong willed. Normally, she would have bristled at someone issuing orders and taking for granted her co-operation. But somehow none of that bothered her. She realized that Tricklock wasn't bullying. He was a confident, natural leader who obviously knew what he was doing.

While Simon went to set his trout adrift, Tricklock talked privately with Tanya. When Simon returned they all huddled for final instructions and encouragement, then Simon and Tanya marched off towards the distant peak. Satisfied that they would be safe, Tricklock walked to the stream, filled a water bottle and then jogged the 300 meters back to camp. When he neared the campsite he stealthily circled around looking for evidence of intruders. When he was sure the coast was clear he entered the camp. He packed up his tent and replaced it with a small lean-to shelter he constructed from an old tarp. He collected all his essential gear, but he wanted to leave the impression that the camp was still occupied. He left the water bottle he had filled and one of his three GPS radios and started a small fire in the pit. There was an obvious path leaving the camp and leading towards the trout stream. Where the path narrowed, bordered on each side with thick stands of pine, Tricklock used his small folding shovel to dig three trenches across the path, each about two feet deep. He spaced the trenches about a foot and a half apart and sharpened sticks and embedded them in the sides of the holes angling the spikes both downwards and upwards at 45 degrees. Then he concealed the tops of the trenches with a thin screen of twigs and leaves. When he stepped back to examine his handiwork, the trail looked natural and undisturbed.

A little farther down the trail he strung para cord across the path just below knee height. One strand of the olive green cord can dangle 550 pounds without snapping and is used to suspend parachutists below their canopies. PJs always carry a supply of para-cord. Much like a pocket knife, para-cord has a million uses in the outdoors. Tricklock measured out a length of cord, doubled it for extra strength, and secured both ends of the line to strong trees on either side of the path. He tensioned the cord as tight as a bow string. In low light conditions the dull green cord would be invisible. Tricklock was protecting his escape route with simple, but what he hoped were effective booby traps.

Tricklock concealed himself off the path, but within sight of the camp. When Simon called on the radio, Tricklock reiterated that both he and Tanya were to keep quiet and not use flashlights or start a fire. Daylight was rapidly fading, and Tricklock settled in to wait and see if unwelcome visitors would invade his camp. After half an hour had passed, he heard branches crack in the distance, He stilled his movements and breathing—his senses were on high alert. The sounds got louder and closer and then abruptly stopped. Tricklock could almost feel the men searching the camp with their eyes to see if it was occupied. Eventually, three men fitting Tanya's description, cautiously slogged into the open, looking exhausted.

The men talked softly among themselves as they methodically searched the camp. Tricklock was too far away to hear them clearly, but it sounded as if they were conversing in a foreign language. Tricklock quickly figured out who was in charge by observing the group dynamics. Two of the men obviously deferred to a third man who appeared to be their leader. Although he acted less tired and more animated than the others, to Tricklock, he looked like the stereotype of a meek librarian. He seemed frustrated with his two exhausted companions. One of the men soon found the Garmin GPS that Tricklock had planted. Tricklock had set it to a different radio channel than his other two radios. When one of the men started gulping water from the bottle that Tricklock had filled, he smiled to himself.

These men were definitely not your average hikers and campers. For one thing, ordinary folks do not just walk into another person's camp and make themselves at home. And they do not conceal themselves and wait to ambush the returning occupants of the camp. But Tricklock had to be 100% sure of their intentions. Now came the most dangerous part of the plan he had hastily cobbled together. The sun had completely set and the camp was only illuminated by pale moonlight filtering through the trees and the dull orange embers of the dying fire. In the gathering gloom, color had fled the forest and everything appeared in shades of grey. Tricklock owned the element of surprise and planned to deliver the equivalent of a psychological sucker punch. Hopefully he could knock them off balance and jolt them into revealing their cards.

Tricklock stepped from behind the thick bole of a tree and onto the moonlit path. His thunderous voice shattered the silence, "WHAT ARE YOU DOING IN MY CAMP?"

The intruders involuntarily jerked, startled by Tricklock's sudden appearance and stentorian voice. They froze in their hiding places.

Tricklock boomed, "WALEED ALI, WHAT ARE YOU DOING HIDING IN MY CAMP?"

Tricklock's shocking question galvanized Khaled who smoothly drew a pistol and emptied a magazine at Tricklock. But Tricklock was no longer standing in the path; he had ducked behind a tree where he was protected from the lethal fusillade of bullets. The attacker had seemed to fire in furious anger rather than deliberate aim. The other two men were only instants behind their leader drawing their handguns and blazing in Tricklock's direction. There was sudden silence as their pistols ran out of ammo. The intruders watched impotently as the shadowy blur of a man ran away down a dimly lit path. Tricklock disappeared round a bend in the trail before Khaled and his men could reload. Khaled screamed out commands and his two men sprinted after Tricklock.

A mile away from Tricklock's confrontation with the assassins, Tanya and Simon had navigated to the top of their hill without incident. Simon was trying to spot his old camp with the binoculars but was having trouble. Even though they were on high ground, there were too many trees in the way. Tanya thought she might be able to see the camp if she climbed up a tall tree that jutted above the smaller saplings. Simon intertwined his fingers, making a stirrup with his hands, and boosted Tanya up to the first branch. Lying on her stomach, she wormed her way out on a thick limb until she had a bird's eye view of Tricklock's old camp. She balanced precariously while she brought the glasses up to her eyes.

Simon was anxious, "Can you see anything?"

Tanya was excited, "It's a little dark, but I think I see movement in the camp. I can't see your dad though. Wait! Something's happening."

Suddenly, long strings of gunshots cracked and echoed off the peaks. Simon was terrified for his father and bombarded Tanya with questions. She was startled by the abrupt turn of events. Tanya gazed transfixed at the strange tableau, all the while balancing on the narrow tree limb. The sound of the gunshots unnerved Tanya, and she experienced a momentary loss of equilibrium. Overwhelmed, she lost her balance and slipped from her precarious perch.

The binoculars flew from her hands and she flailed her arms trying to grab onto something to stop her fall. Her efforts were in vain, and she crashed to the ground with a sickening thud. Before Simon could react, Tanya lay at his feet. Gravity had buckled Tanya's ankle, and Simon heard a loud crack like a thick dry stick snapping. Tanya clawed the forest floor, ripping up handfuls of leafy loam and pounding her fists onto the damp earth. She thrashed about in an uncontrolled fit of agony. Simon rushed to her side, but he didn't know what to do. She calmed slightly when he touched her, but when he looked at her right ankle it was bent sideways at an odd angle. Tanya was in so much pain that sweat poured down her face and mingled with her tears. Simon was afraid to touch her foot. Like Simon, Tanya was also at a loss. She didn't know any medicine beyond basic first aid. Simon held Tanya's hand and tried to console her. He fervently hoped his father would return soon, but the sound of gunshots still echoed in his mind.

Waleed raced in the lead with Youssef right behind as they chased Tricklock down the dim path. Waleed's heart pounded as he ran down the shadowy trail. He momentarily slowed as he rounded a bend in the trail, scanning ahead for the fleeing American. Suddenly he pitched forward as his right leg plunged into Tricklock's spiked trench. He screamed as sharpened spikes skewered his calf and rasped his shin to the bone. He screamed again when he instinctively tried to pull his leg out of the trap. When he wrenched his leg upwards, the stakes that Tricklock had angled downwards, impaled his calf and tore his flesh. Tricklock's sharpened sticks had stabbed Waleed's lower leg as it went into the hole and as he yanked it out. Waleed was fortunate that he had slowed rounding the bend, or he would have also snapped his shin bone. As it was, he still suffered deep puncture wounds and had hyperextended his knee. Khaled soon arrived and urged Youssef to continue to chase Tricklock while he attended to Waleed.

Youssef reluctantly took up the chase and had barely reached full sprinting speed, when his shins hit the para-cord that Tricklock had strung between trees. He pitched forward and instinctively thrust out his arms to break his fall. He hit the ground hard, badly spraining his wrist. His arms collapsed under the force of his fall and his face slammed onto the unyielding ground.

He lay there stunned with blood pouring from his broken and rapidly swelling nose. Tears welled in Youssef's eyes as he slowly staggered to his feet severely dazed and shaken. Moments later Khaled arrived accompanied by a badly limping Waleed. Khaled decided to abandon the pursuit. It was dark and the American had obviously prepared for this encounter. They would return to Tricklock's old camp and regroup. His men were injured and shaken, though none of the wounds appeared life threatening. Khaled needed time to think and to re-motivate his men. They needed food, rest, reassurance, and above all a new plan.

Chapter 10
LIBERTIES

Tricklock now knew that he was being hunted by three assassins. The hail of bullets had confirmed that. He also knew that his booby traps had injured two of the men, but it didn't appear that they had incurred serious wounds. Before the three strangers retreated to his old campsite, he watched the interaction between them with curiosity. Once Tricklock had skirted around the traps he had set and disappeared round the bend, he had abruptly stopped and melted into the trees that lined the path. He watched the effect his traps had on his pursuers with interest. He was invisible, hidden in the undergrowth, and the killers were oblivious to his presence, assuming that he had continued to flee down the trail.

Tricklock momentarily toyed with the possibility of following the assassins back to his old camp and ending this right now. He had his Glock with him, but he decided it would be better to hike to civilization and contact the police. They were many miles into the wilderness and he would have to push Simon and Tanya to their limits, but he decided that escape was the best plan. He reluctantly backed off and headed towards Simon and Tanya's location. When he was well on his way and a good distance from the bad guys, he called Simon on the radio. When Simon answered, Tricklock immediately knew something was wrong.

Simon started talking too fast to understand. Tricklock interrupted, "Simon, slow down. What's wrong?"

Tricklock could almost hear Simon take a deep breath and gather his wits, "Dad, you need to get back here as fast as you can. Tanya broke her ankle. She's in a lot of pain, but I was afraid to call you. We heard gunshots and didn't know what was going on."

Tricklock tried to calm Simon, "It's OK, everything is fine and you're doing great. Take care of Tanya as best you can. I'm not that far away. I'll be back in a few minutes. Can you do that?"

Simon sounded shaky, "I can handle things for a while—just hurry back!"

Tricklock took a bearing and began to run. As the half-moon climbed higher in the clear night sky and the illumination increased, so did his pace. There was ample light for Tricklock to avoid obstacles as he ran through the night. Simon was due north of his position. The Big Dipper and Polaris were clearly visible in the heavens. Tricklock didn't waste time using a compass or GPS. He increased his speed, running towards the North Star and bounding across the ground like a two legged deer.

Back at Tricklock's old camp, Khaled and his men gathered their gear and moved desultorily into the forest. A few hundred meters away they found a suitable spot to stay the night. Khaled decided not to use Tricklock's campsite, although he did snatch the tarp to use as shelter. After the night's recent events he wouldn't put it past Tricklock to attack their camp. Khaled was mystified as to how the American had known about his team. He was even more frustrated that they had lost the element of surprise. Tricklock had even known Waleed by name; how was that possible? None of them could imagine how Tricklock came to know about Waleed. The encounter with the American was disturbing on many levels. Tricklock had even set traps for them. Tomorrow they would start early and track him down. Khaled did not know exactly where Tricklock was, but the American was encumbered by a teenager and would not be able to travel quickly.

"Waleed, bring me that map."

Khaled examined the map carefully. His finger gravitated to the very same high ground that Tricklock had picked for his new camp. Khaled gathered his men about him. They were worse for wear but still functional. Their first encounter with the infidel Tricklock had not gone well, but he was determined that their next meeting would be different.

Khaled rallied his men, "Do not be so glum. I think the American is hiding on this ridge. While he confronted us, he would have sent his son to high ground not too far away. Tomorrow he probably plans to move to this main road and contact the authorities, but he will be slowed by his teenage son. He is still many miles away from the road with rough ground in between. Tomorrow we will split up and funnel him into a trap."

Khaled traced his finger on the map, "Waleed, you and I will travel to this pond to cut off Tricklock's escape. This will put us between him and the main road. Youssef you stay here. After we leave, you will approach this ridge where I think Tricklock has his new camp. I will take the radio he left, it looks better than the ones we have. I will switch it onto our radio channel. I can also use it as a GPS if I need too. I will check to see if there are any coordinates loaded that may be useful. We will speak our language on the radio. If the American is listening he won't understand a word. I will make a schedule for regular radio check-ins."

Khaled assigned sentry duties and the three men attended to their injuries as best they could. No one had thought to bring medical supplies. They arranged their sleeping areas and discussed the next day's plan.

Tricklock was getting close to Simon and Tanya's refuge. He contacted Simon on the radio and warned him he was only a few minutes from camp. When he arrived he clapped Simon on the back and went straight over to Tanya. He asked her questions while he examined her injury. Although she was doing her best to keep it together, when asked, she stammered that her pain was about 9 on a scale of 1 to 10, with 10 being equivalent to the pain she would experience if Tricklock roasted her feet over a crackling campfire. She was pale and writhed in agony. The pain acted like a strong stimulant and she couldn't lay still. Tricklock brandished a pair of bandage scissors, cut her laces, and carefully removed her boot while Simon cradled her foot and leg. There were no bones sticking through her skin, but the foot was bent almost at a right angle. Tricklock checked the blood circulation in her foot and tested for nerve sensation.

When he was finished with his exam he frowned, "Tanya, you don't have blood flow to your foot. We are miles from any well-trafficked road and days away from a hospital. You will lose your foot if we don't act. That means I'm going to have to set your foot to restore nerve and blood supply. The good news is that afterwards, your pain level will be a lot lower on the scale. To deal with the pain, you can bite into Simon's arm while I set your fracture."

Simon blurted, "What!"

"Just kidding." said Tricklock. Despite her pain this exchange elicited an involuntary giggle from Tanya and momentarily distracted her. Tricklock took Simon off to the side and explained what he wanted to do. Simon was shaking like a leaf. Tricklock gave Tanya a small towel and told her to hold it over her mouth to muffle any noise. Tricklock wanted to act quickly before his companions had a chance to become even more nervous and afraid.

Well above her broken ankle, Tricklock wrapped his wide web belt around Tanya's upper thigh and snugged it up into her groin. He connected the ends of the belt and wadded extra clothes into thick padding and placed it between her inner thigh and the belt. Simon gripped the belt loop and braced his feet against a tree. At Tricklock's signal, Simon's job would be to lean back pulling on the loop of belt. This would anchor and stabilize Tanya's pelvis while Tricklock pulled her foot in the opposite direction. He needed to apply strong and steady traction to Tanya's foot in order to swing it back into line with the rest of her lower leg. Tanya gritted her teeth and pressed the towel over her mouth.

Tricklock gently positioned his hands around Tanya's petite foot and locked eyes with Simon, "Now." he said.

Following his father's directions, Simon slowly leaned back, hauling hard against the belt, while his dad simultaneously pulled Tanya's foot in the opposite direction. Tricklock fervently hoped that Simon was strong enough to hold Tanya's pelvis in position. Tricklock slowly put his strength into the pull. Tanya muffled her screams with both hands, shaking her head violently from side-to-side. Her long black hair swirled around her head, obscuring her grimacing face. Simon strained as hard as he could to counter his father's relentless pull. His thigh muscles bunched and his arms quivered with the strain.

Simon was just about to scream that he was about to let go, when suddenly Tanya's right foot slid smoothly into line.

Tanya was completely astonished. A second after Tricklock aligned her foot, her pain decreased from unbearable agony to a dull throb. The split second transition from hellish anguish to heavenly relief seemed nothing short of a medical miracle. While Simon slumped against a tree trunk to rest and recover, Tricklock checked Tanya's foot and cheerfully announced that blood flow and nerve sensation were restored. He took his medical kit from his backpack and securely splinted Tanya's ankle using SAM splints, padding, and ace wrap.

Tricklock didn't pull any punches, "Tanya, I hate to tell you this, but I think that ankle is going to require surgery and a good bit of hardware."

"What do you mean hardware?" she asked.

"I mean they're going to have to use screws and plates to fix your ankle." Tricklock explained, "That ankle is going to hurt you pretty bad, but nothing like it did before me and Simon sorted it out. By the way, you did an awesome job Simon. You really rose to the occasion and kept your head. I'm very proud of you."

He turned back to Tanya, "Normally I would have given you valium to relax your muscles before I would have attempted to set such a bad fracture."

Tanya thanked them profusely and insisted on giving both Tricklock and Simon a big hug. Tricklock continued his PJ magic by producing a 5mg oxycodone.

"This should help with the pain." he said. "The docs gave me this bottle of pain killers for my shrapnel injuries, but I hardly used any. It looks like they will be put to good use after all. Tricklock pitched his state-of-the-art, two-person-tent in only a couple of minutes. It was very roomy, weather proof, and most importantly it only weighed five pounds. The temperature was dropping precipitously and a light rain began to fall. Tricklock settled Simon and Tanya into the tent and donned some lightweight rain gear. He sat near the tent entrance where Simon and Tanya could hear him.

Tricklock began to talk in a soft serious voice, "I think it's about time I explained our situation to you both."

Afterwards, Simon was pensive. For the time being he would keep his thoughts to himself, but he was already beginning to analyze their predicament in terms of Go strategy. Concepts were germinating in his fertile young mind, but he was not sure how his father would react to his ideas. Simon thought that in these first stages of their predicament, it was important for them to maintain *liberties*. In Go terminology, that meant they needed to have many different avenues of escape from the men who hunted them. Right now his father's actions were in harmony with his own, in fact his dad was awesome. Once he better organized his thoughts, he would talk to his father. Maybe he could offer some suggestions that could help.

Khaled and his men were cold, wet, and miserable. They had not prepared for this rain or these low temperatures. The weather conditions were not life threatening, but the cold and damp chilled them to the bone and made for miserable sleeping conditions. The three men huddled together shivering beneath their makeshift lean-to and tried to get some rest. Khaled had made his men recite the next day's plan until he was sure they understood it completely. Once again Khaled lamented that they were ill prepared for these conditions. He had envisioned using the camper as their base, locating it close to Tricklock's location and then raiding the American. It hadn't turned out that way. When they caught up with him, Tricklock would pay for his actions. Khaled would slowly kill Simon in front of his father's eyes, maybe saw off his head with a knife or rip out his throat with his teeth.

Back at Tricklock's temporary camp, Tricklock described his confrontation with the three men to Simon and Tanya. He was a bit disappointed his traps hadn't caused the would-be assassins more serious injuries, but he smiled when he related how one of the men drank from the water bottle he had planted That water was straight from the stream. Without boiling or purification the liquid was sure to be swarming with Giardia protozoa. Whoever drank that water was going to be sick as a dog and gushing at both ends.

After listening to Tricklock's account, Simon was dumbfounded, "I cannot believe you did all that. You're crazy! You were outnumbered three to one and then you yelled at them?"

Tanya echoed Simon, "That whole scene does seem pretty extreme and risky."

"Well it seems crazy to both of you, because you're not used to this kind of thing. You have to be aggressive when your life is in danger. In fact, if I would have known that Tanya had broken her ankle, I would have followed those guys back into their camp and killed them all and ended this whole thing right then. But I thought we would easily be able to elude them and get back to civilization. I wanted to sic the cops on their asses."

Tanya and Simon just looked at Tricklock. They could not fault his logic, but they were both amazed at his nonchalance.

"Why did you leave the GPS?" asked Tanya.

Tricklock shrugged, "That may or may not work out. That was our third GPS, just a backup. But if they do use it, I can find their coordinates. As I explained to Simon earlier, we use these Garmin Rino devices at the PJ school because they are both a 5 watt radio and a GPS. If a student gets lost, I can pinpoint his location with my Rino. I brought Rinos with me on this trip so I could find *city boy* here when he got lost going to the bathroom at night."

Tanya rolled her eyes. Simon shot back, "I'm a pretty good navigator now."

Tricklock laughed, "Whatever, mountain man. Anyway, I seriously doubt that the bad guys know that I can locate their position with one of my radios. Even if they look through the menu on the GPS, the function is called "Polling" which is a pretty obscure word. I've already polled their position, but I haven't registered their location yet. They probably haven't turned the Rino. They may not even use it, but if they do we'll know exactly where they are."

Tanya asked, "What about me? After tonight they're going to be after you with a vengeance. You and Simon are going to have to move fast. I can't even walk."

Tricklock seemed serious, "I've given this some thought. We'll leave you a compass and some food. You're just going to have to crawl to the main road. I know it's many miles away over jagged rocks and through spiked cactus, but I think you can do it."

Tricklock laughed at the expression on her face, "Just kidding." he said. "Actually I'm going to carry you. Along with a comprehensive medical kit, as part of my standard hiking gear I carry an IPC. That stands for *injured personnel carrier*. It's a harness that the Israeli Special Forces use to carry an injured soldier piggyback style. It's really made for a combat emergency so you can carry a wounded man and still have your hands free to use a rifle, but I brought one in case Simon pussed out on this hike and I had to carry him. The IPC weighs less than a pound."

Simon was not amused, "Very funny dad."

Tricklock went on, "We're going to have to reach civilization as quick as we can while avoiding those three men. This is serious stuff, they are out for blood and they are not stupid. I caught them by surprise thanks to Tanya, but they have the same map we do and probably figure we'll make a beeline to the nearest road, or they might try to find our camp. He used a stick to point at the map. I think we'll go here. It's a peak about four kilometers away."

"Simon said, "But that's going away from the road and way out of this forest."

Tricklock said, "I don't want to move towards the road until I know more information. Once on that peak we should be able to see this camp with the binoculars. There are also some hot spots in this wilderness, although few and far between. If we can get phone reception on that peak, it will change everything. And if all else fails, we will have the high ground and can set up a pretty formidable defense. We have four handguns and plenty of ammo."

"Make that five guns. I brought my 38 special revolver." added Tanya.

Simon grinned, "Right on."

Tricklock shook his head, "Simon, now you're starting to sound like me and that's scary. Back to business: Simon, you and Tanya consolidate all the essential gear into my large pack, which Simon will be carrying. Just pack the necessities such as food, clothing, shelter, medical supplies, and especially water. Stuff all the extra gear in Tanya's backpack and your small pack. I'll hide them and, who knows, maybe we'll be able to collect them later. After you finish packing, we'll all get some sleep. We're leaving at two in the morning. The moon will still be up and I want to get a jump on the competition."

A moment later, Tricklock glanced over to see Simon holding a small quadcopter, "You brought a toy gadget with you on a camping trip?"

"It's not a toy, it's a remote controlled quadcopter, and yes, I'm an expert pilot. And yes I'm planning on taking it. It weighs almost nothing." Tricklock just shook his head and walked off.

Pecos Wilderness Early Morning Day Three: Tricklock dozed lightly with his mind on autopilot. He suddenly snapped awake and looked at the luminous dials on his PJ dive watch. It was 1:55 a.m. He gently rousted Tanya and Simon and packed the tent and sleeping bags. They ate a cold breakfast of granola bars washed down with water that was flavored with powdered Gatorade. Tricklock examined Tanya's splint and checked her circulation. He felt her forehead for signs of fever and closely questioned her. He had improvised a crude bathroom screened by bushes. He helped her to the makeshift restroom, and using her trekking poles as canes, she was able to use the bathroom with some difficulty. Afterwards, Tricklock gave her a pill for her pain and insisted that she let him know when she needed more. He adjusted the IPC harness to fit Tanya's petite frame and had Simon help with getting her securely strapped to his back. Tanya would be a bit uncomfortable, but the pain killers should help. His greatest fear was that he would stumble and fall with Tanya on his back. He commandeered Tanya's two lightweight aluminum trekking poles for extra stability while he walked.

Simon hoisted his father's pack onto his shoulders and groaned, "Holy crap. This mother's heavy!"

Tricklock laughed and said, "That's awful spicy language for a fourteen year old."

Simon shot back, "I'm known for that."

Tricklock chuckled, "You're a guttersnipe."

"What the heck is a guttersnipe?"

"His dad smiled and said, "A guttersnipe is a bit like a rapscallion—Google it."

Tanya interrupted, "OK boys, it's two in the morning and we have hit men stalking us. We might want to dispense with the amusing banter. It's time to blow this pop stand."

Tricklock couldn't resist a smart assed reply, "Good drugs huh?"

Tanya cuffed the side of Tricklock's head. He laughed and led the way using his GPS. The rain had paused, the low clouds had dissipated, and silvery moonlight frosted the forest. Sparkly globules of rainwater occasionally slid from the leaves overhead and coldly plopped onto the backs of their necks. Initially they walked towards the main road, but shortly after they left the muddy ground and stepped onto a grassy meadow, Tricklock changed course for their real destination, a moderately high peak a few kilometers away.

"We've been setting a false trail." he explained.

They took a short rest break every 200 meters. Tricklock seemed to carry Tanya's 135 pounds as if she were a lightly stuffed daypack. Simon grimly soldiered on, but he eagerly anticipated each rest stop. Tanya also relished the breaks. At each stop she was all painful pins and needles until she was freed from the harness and blood surged back into her limbs. While Tricklock carried Tanya, her circulation was slightly restricted by the harness pressing into her flesh, but there was nothing to be done about it and she didn't gripe. It was a few hours past sunrise when they finally reached their objective, a hill slightly higher than most others in the area. With Tanya on his back, even Tricklock's vast stamina was tested as they struggled upwards. Everyone was relieved to finally reach the top. Rivulets of sweat streamed down Simon's face as he collapsed against the bole of a tree. He was not used to hiking, especially with such a heavy pack.

Tricklock moved Tanya to an area where she could be most comfortable. He then took Simon aside and asked him to poll the position of *Spare Radio* using one of their GPS receivers. In a rare burst of creativity, that's what Tricklock had named the extra radio that Khaled now carried. While Simon worked on his task, Tricklock took out his binoculars and scanned last night's camp on the knoll, then looked over the terrain between their knoll and the main gravel road leading to civilization. Neither he nor Simon had any luck, but it was still very early in the morning. Tricklock also turned on his phone; still no reception.

Tricklock moved over to where Tanya lay with her injured leg elevated. "I need to examine your foot, plus we really haven't had much time to talk. Are you doing OK?"

"I can't thank you enough for setting my ankle and then splinting it, not to mention giving me those painkillers. And you carried me all that way on your back, up and down mountains."

"You're welcome, although *mountains* may be an exaggeration. Actually I owe you my thanks. No matter how this started, if you hadn't warned me, those men may well have killed Simon and me before we even knew they had bad intentions. You cost them the element of surprise."

Tanya said, "Well I had visions of getting an exclusive interview with you when I heard you mention your camping plans during one of your interviews. This whole thing reminds me of that saying about being careful what you wish for, because your wish might come true."

"Well don't worry too much." said Tricklock, "Now that I know what's going on I'm going to take these guys out. I have more at stake than they do."

While Tricklock checked the pulse and sensation in her foot and refurbished the splint, Tanya took out a notebook and began to ask questions. Tricklock just smiled, shook his head, and resigned himself to the situation.

"With all the exciting things your PJ job entails, what's the least favorite thing you do?"

Tricklock pondered for a second before answering, "I'd have to say scuba diving is my least favorite, but with a few alibis."

"Please elaborate." said Tanya.

Tricklock sighed, "Well, for the most part sightseeing underwater is boring unless you luck into something extraordinary, such as a curious whale, a shipwreck, or a gorgeous mermaid. Generally speaking, I only like diving if I'm spearfishing or going after lobsters, then it's an incredibly exciting experience."

Tanya followed up, "Aren't you ever scared of giant man-eating sharks?"

Tricklock asked, "Do you know what a bang stick is?"

Tanya shook her head.

"Well it's a long metal tube with a *power head* at one end that contains a waterproofed 357 magnum cartridge. In theory, if a big shark attacks you jab him with the bang stick and the cartridge fires, sending a chunk of high velocity lead blasting into the shark and hopefully killing the man-eating fish."

Tanya was wide eyed and fascinated, "Did you ever kill a shark with a bang stick?"

"Well, I used my bang stick once when I was standing chest deep in the ocean only 50 feet from shore. A shark was coming right at me and I jabbed it with the bang stick; you could see blood color the water red. At first I thought I killed a huge shark, but it was just a couple of kids snorkeling just below the surface and holding up a fake shark fin."

"You...what... No you didn't, did you?"

Tricklock dropped to the ground holding his sides and laughing uncontrollably. Tanya looked on in amazement as Tricklock flailed the ground.

He could hardly speak, "Simon." he choked out, "Tell her that thing that I'm doing."

Simon was also laughing, "He is ROFLMAO."

Tanya knew the internet slang and soon she was also laughing out loud.

When everyone finally regained their composure she said, "That was good; you sucked me right into that, I feel so gullible. You are both unbelievable with your constant joking around."

Tricklock said, "What do you mean both? I hardly think that Simon and I are marching in lockstep."

Now it was time for Tanya to laugh, "You two are more alike than you realize."

Tricklock reluctantly brought them back to reality, "Alright, interview time is over for now. It's time to get our war faces back on. This time, Simon you glass last night's camp and I'll check the GPS."

When Tricklock polled the spare radio, he registered a position. Their pursuers must have turned on Tricklock's planted GPS. He quickly laid out the map and plotted the coordinates. The location was near a pond directly between their position and the road they wanted to reach. Almost at the same time, Simon excitedly said he saw someone at last night's camp. When

Tricklock looked over at Simon, he was momentarily flashed by the bright morning sun reflecting off the binocular lenses.

"Simon, quick, put down the binoculars!"

Simon lowered the glasses and looked inquiringly at his dad, "What's wrong?"

Tricklock shook his head, disappointed with himself. For the last few minutes Simon had been inadvertently broadcasting their position with bright flashes.

"This is all on me, Simon. I wasn't paying attention to the sun. At the right angle those binocular lenses will reflect sunbeams and shine like signal mirrors. We have to hope that the bad guys didn't see us. On the bright side, I picked up the other GPS. Simon, how many men did you see?"

Simon replied, "I only saw one man."

Tricklock considered, "That makes sense. They must have split up and have their largest force cutting us off from the road."

When Tricklock checked the knoll, being careful to avoid sun reflections, he saw a man just leaving the site, moving in their direction. When he polled the spare GPS, he discovered it was also moving towards them. They were going to have to leave soon, but to where?

Chapter II

A DIVINE MOVE

Pecos Wilderness Dawn Day Three: The night had seemed endless, and sentry duty was mind numbing. Sleep was elusive and when it finally came, they tossed fitful. They started breaking camp while it was still dark. Khaled was dismayed by his poor fortune. He knew he was not living up to his men's expectations, and they were certainly not living up to his standards. They seemed soft and too used to American comforts. When the sky was barely starting to lighten, he left camp with Waleed. Youssef's broken nose had blackened both his eyes and his sprained left wrist was badly swollen. Youssef was not feeling well, and looked pale and shaky. He had bowel issues and suffered from nausea, weakness, and a pounding headache. Waleed had his own miseries. He limped badly. His calf throbbed with puncture wounds and his knee was stiff and swollen. He dreaded the coming hike.

After Khaled and Waleed left, Youssef set off towards what he hoped was Tricklock's new camp. The ground was soft and muddy. It was hard traveling, especially for one in his condition. For the hundredth time he silently cursed the American. The going was slow—mud caked his shoes and weighted his every step. He felt weak and drained, as if he had a fatal case of exotic flu. He had to make frequent stops to empty his bowels, and he had quickly used up his supply of toilet paper. Such a small thing, but it caused a disproportionate amount of suffering and inconvenience. He was forced to cut up his underwear to use as wipes, and when he had used all those scraps he had to use leaves off the ground. He was filthy, miserable, and he stank. When it was time to talk with Khaled on the radio, Youssef did not complain of his difficulties. Youssef used his map and compass, but was often confused. His biggest difficulty was determining how far he had traveled. He was unfamiliar with the concept of keeping a pace count, the technique that Tricklock and most navigators used to estimate distance traveled. Youssef's distance estimates were unreliable because of the rough terrain, his faltering steps, and his mud caked boots. Youssef primarily used terrain association to figure his position, but he was not good with a map. He was also developing painful blisters on both his heels. His hiking shoes were new and stiff, not at all suitable for serious walking.

When he eventually arrived at the high ground where Tricklock may have spent the past night, he was unsure if it was the right place. He tried to be stealthy, but he blundered through the underbrush like a spastic rhino. He had his pistol in his hand as he stumbled the final few yards to the top. In addition to his physical injuries, his lungs heaved and his thighs felt like lead. In Texas he lived at sea level, and the 7,000 foot altitude here was killing him. He couldn't seem to get enough oxygen. He possessed the resiliency of youth, but even at the best of times he was not an athlete. In fact, he was about as far from being a gym rat as one could get. When he finally topped the ridge it was barren. If this had been Tricklock's camp, it was now deserted. Youssef slumped down with his back against a tree and lit a cigarette. As he looked about him, he began to notice signs that someone had been here very recently. In fact there were fresh footprints that led in the direction of Khaled and Waleed's location. Maybe their plan would succeed after all.

Pecos Wilderness Day Three: After leaving Youssef, Khaled and Waleed had experienced their own difficulties. There were numerous gullies and drainages between them and the small pond which was their destination. On a dry sunny day their route would have been difficult, but now the steep sides of the arroyos were slicked with mud that weighed them down and made every inch a struggle. When they finally reached the pond the sun was high and they were exhausted. They hid within a small grove of trees in sight of the pond. They were almost out of water, and Khaled decreed that they would ration their supply. The pond was not what Khaled had expected. It was small and the water was fouled and dirty, they would wait to refill their bottles at a stream. When Khaled tried to talk to Youssef he received no response, and switched to Tricklock's radio. The American's radio must have been more powerful than theirs, because this time Youssef answered. Khaled learned that his guess about Tricklock's camp was correct. Youssef had confirmed that the Americans had been on the ridge. He had also spotted two sets of footprints leading in Khaled's direction. He had followed them a short way before they disappeared at the edge of a small grassy meadow.

Khaled told Youssef to remain where he was until he received further instructions. Youssef was relieved he didn't have to move any further. He crumpled next to a tree feeling totally spent. His bowels were watery and he felt weak as a newborn—he was a mess. He was grateful for the brief respite, but he couldn't keep solid food down and he was running low on water. He would need to conserve his fluids. Youssef closed his eyes and tried to rest, but soon his cramps returned and he scrambled to lower his trousers.

Khaled was the first to see the light flashes in the distance. He located the peak on his map and marked it with a pen. There was no guarantee that the flashes came from Tricklock, but that location made sense and the bright reflections certainly did not come from nature. He and Waleed began to move to a new location where they would be in a better position to intercept Tricklock. If the American was indeed the cause of the flashes, then he hadn't traveled very far from his previous camp. It seemed that the boy was slowing Tricklock down just as Khaled had predicted. Khaled and his men were slowly closing in on the elusive American. The next time he raised Youssef on the radio, Khaled gave him a new plan of action.

After he talked to Khaled, Youssef vomited into some nearby bushes. His physical condition was worsening. All he wanted to do was to lie down and sleep, but instead he had to trudge over more cursed hills in pursuit of the Americans. Both of his heels were raw and painful. His stiff new hiking shoes had mangled his feet. Youssef had developed huge blisters on each of his heels, and then the blisters had ripped off leaving large patches of skinless red meat.

His boots continued to scrape the wounds—his feet were a bloody mess. He also continued to feel sick as a dog, but he refused to let Khaled down. With his head bowed, he slogged off the ridge and picked his way towards the peak where Khaled had seen what appeared to be reflected flashes of light. In his current mental and physical state it was all Youssef could do to soldier on. He was beyond trying to hide his approach or conceal himself from possible observation.

Tricklock watched Youssef leave the far-off ridge and start walking towards Tricklock's present location. He was also tracking the other two men who carried his planted GPS. He briefly outlined the situation to Tanya and Simon. When Simon asked his dad where they were headed next, Tricklock said he was still thinking about it. When Simon asked to see the map, Tricklock spread it on the ground. Simon gathered a few pebbles and held them in his fist. Tricklock watched with interest as Simon studied the map.

"What kind of map is this again?" Simon asked.

"It's a one to fifty thousand (1:50,000) topographic map built on the Military Grid Reference System, commonly known as MGRS."

Simon wanted more detail, "What is MGRS exactly?"

Tricklock thought for a few seconds before he replied, "It's a grid coordinate system, the military version of latitude and longitude. Each grid block is one square kilometer. The whole map is divided into squares like a chess board."

Simon smiled, "It looks more like a Go board to me. In Go the two opposing sides are represented by black and white pieces called *stones* placed on the intersections of the squares, not inside the squares like in chess."

Tricklock said, "Simon, this is interesting, but where are you going with this?"

Tanya scowled at Tricklock somehow managing to call him a dick with just her facial expression.

Simon was patient, "Go has a 4,000 year history, and the whole object of the game is to avoid being encircled by your opponent. And what's our exact situation here? Oh yeah, bad guys are trying to surround us and kill us. Over thousands of years, Go masters have developed ingenious strategies to avoid being trapped. Those tactics might be extremely helpful in our present situation, wouldn't you agree?"

Tanya interjected, "Simon I think that's brilliant!"

Tricklock nodded, "OK. I'm tracking. This is so strange that now I'm curious. Please continue Sensei Simon. Where do you think we should go from here?"

Simon peered at the map which now functioned as an improvised Go board. He had Tricklock show him their location on the map and placed a pale stone where two gridlines intersected near their position. Next he placed two dark pebbles on gridline intersections to mark the locations of the assassins. Simon studied the resulting configuration of stones on the map.

He smiled at his father as he picked up a twig to use as a pointer, "If we were playing a game of Go against these hit men, their positions would indicate that they were forming a net to catch us. In Go there *is* a proven tactic to avoid being caught in your opponent's net."

Simon placed another stone on a neighboring grid intersection, "We should move in this direction."

Tricklock said, "That's exactly where I was going to suggest we move."

Simon and Tanya both made scoffing sounds and gave Tricklock the stink eye.

Tricklock laughed, "Just kidding. That actually may be a good move on our part, but what if your Go move had taken us over a cliff?"

Simon didn't hesitate, "Well then, we would just have to throw ourselves off the cliff, wouldn't we? We wouldn't have a choice. It's called the lemming effect."

Tanya had been following the discussion and burst into laughter.

Tricklock snickered, "You're turning into quite the young smart ass. I don't know where you get that from."

"I wonder." said Simon, "Anyway, Go can suggest a direction to move, but unlike the board game we can move as far as we want."

A few miles away from Tricklock's group, Khaled setup his observation post in a dense thicket. He had picked a location that was between Tricklock's hill and the main gravel road. The new spot offered a good vantage, and Khaled was betting that Tricklock and his son would ultimately make for the road in an attempt to escape the forest. Khaled had sent Youssef to flush out their American quarry. When the Americans fled from Youssef, Khaled should be able to see them as they moved towards the road. He and Waleed would then ambush and destroy the Americans. Khaled was thankful that so far, he and Waleed had only needed to travel a few kilometers over relatively easy ground. Waleed was limping badly. Khaled examined his partner's leg and scowled. Waleed's wounds oozed pus and corruption. Livid tendrils of crimson infection snaked their way out from the jagged punctures, forming a sinister matrix on Waleed's lower leg. Khaled lied to Waleed and told him that his leg seemed to be healing and would soon feel better. The two assassins settled down to observe the shallow valley that funneled down from the high ground that sheltered Tricklock. They searched for signs of the Americans. They also needed to find a stream. They were running very low on water. Soon their thirst would become a pressing issue.

Pecos Wilderness Afternoon of Day Three: Tricklock walked in the lead, hauling Tanya on his back. Simon lagged behind huffing and puffing his misery. As they walked, Tricklock thought about their situation. He knew that they could not keep this up indefinitely. Tanya desperately needed to get to a hospital. He was deeply worried about her ankle. Her pain was likely to increase and riding piggyback in a harness was not the most comfortable or healing way to travel. He was also pushing his teenage son to his limits. He had to be careful not to physically or mentally over burden the young man. His mind raced over different courses of action, but no grand strategy immediately emerged. Although Simon didn't complain, Tricklock knew that physically Simon was struggling with his heavy backpack.

Psychologically, Simon was internally processing all the ramifications of their perilous situation. It was a lot of pressure for any person to deal with, and Simon was barely a teenager. Tricklock was thankful that so far, both Tanya and Simon were keeping it together—they seemed to have bonded and were drawing strength from each other. When they stopped to rest he checked on the position of the spare GPS. It had stopped moving and remained near the wide mouth of a valley that descended from their hill towards the gravel road.

It was obvious to Tricklock that the two men in the valley had experience using terrain and battle tactics.

Tricklock and his crew fought their way up the side of a steep ridge. Sweat trickled maddeningly down Tricklock's back and his overworked heart threatened to jump out of his chest. He stopped for a moment and studied Simon. His son was nearing physical failure.

"Hey Simon, I can hear your heart thumping and your lungs wheezing from twenty five feet away. You're probably not doing it on purpose, but you're making the sounds of a female elk in heat. A big bull elk could be stalking you as we speak. If one tries to have sex with you, don't resist or he'll get angry, or maybe you could hold your breath while we walk."

Simon spat out, "That's impossible! And that elk thing is ridiculous!" He realized his dad was goading him when he saw Tanya smack the back of his dad's head with her cap.

"Be serious dad. I'm hurting here." Simon pleaded.

"OK. Hang on for a short while longer, and when we reach the top of this ridge we're done for the day. Think you can handle that?"

Simon chuckled, "As long as no elk jumps on me."

Tanya interrupted, "What's that over there?"

They walked over to investigate. When they got closer, they realized that what Tanya had seen was a berm of yellowish rock chips and tailings from an abandoned mine. As they neared the entrance, the underbrush gradually thinned and then abruptly gave way to a barren zone that encircled the dark chasm of a defunct mine shaft. The ominous black hole triggered instinctive wariness. The funnel-like entrance to the mine looked like the lair of a giant spider. When he saw the black hole, Simon experienced a quick mental image of himself lying broken and helpless at the bottom of the pit while hungry cave creatures crawled closer and closer. He shook off the morbid fantasy and thought to himself that someone should put a fence around this pit. Simon carefully inched closer to the rock-rimmed hole and peered warily into the inscrutable depths. Simon succumbed to the age old irresistible urge—he tossed in a pebble and listened for it to hit bottom.

Tricklock explained the origins of the dangerous looking hole in the side of the ridge, "The forests of New Mexico are dotted with abandoned mine shafts. Prospectors in days-gone-by, dug numerous exploratory tunnels probing for turquoise and silver. Some old mines show up on topographic maps marked with tiny crossed pickaxes, but some shafts are not marked on any map. Some mines are little more than holes in the ground, failed quests for elusive riches. This is one of the unmarked, dangerous ones. If you blundered into this pit at night you'd be history."

Tricklock ended their sightseeing and rallied his troops for the final push to the top. Despite his outward bravado, Tricklock was himself mentally and physically stressed. One of the advantages of having survived PJ training was that the instructors had pushed him to his limits on countless occasions. He could compare how he felt now, to how he had felt during those past experiences when he was at the edge of his endurance. He realized that for the time being he was nowhere close to his physical limits. Although Simon and Tanya's life depended on his skills and decision making during these life and death circumstances, he had accepted that same burden of responsibility during many past rescue missions. He was practiced at keeping his cool during crisis situations. He remained confident that they would prevail against the assassins, but more importantly he unconsciously conveyed his confidence to Tanya and Simon. His leadership was unforced and charismatic. Tricklock was Simon and Tanya's psychological rock.

Somewhat refreshed and in better spirits after their short rest, they quickly climbed the remaining distance to the top of the hill. Finally they were at journey's end, at least for the time being. Tricklock freed Tanya from her harness and went about the task of situating her. He laid her down on a smooth patch of ground and propped her up against a tree. He elevated her injured leg to help control swelling and tried to make her comfortable. Tricklock examined her splinted ankle, dispensed pain medication, and checked phone reception—still no bars on his phone.

Tricklock sat down next to Tanya, "You know these interviews go both ways, it's only fair."

The two chatted and laughed for a good 30 minutes.

Afterwards, Tricklock sat down with Simon, "I think that once it gets dark we should start a fire and have a good meal. What do you think?"

Tricklock had to laugh at the look of astonishment on Simon's face.

"Aren't you worried that the bad guys will see the fire?"

"Not only am I not worried; I'm actually *counting* on one of those guys seeing our fire." Tricklock explained."

Simon grinned, "What's on your devious little mind?"

Tricklock winked at Simon conspiratorially, "I think it's time you and I had another look at that abandoned mine."

A few miles away from Tricklock and the mine shaft, Khaled and Waleed walked down a jeep trail to check for water. There was a faint blue line on the map that was supposed to represent a stream. When they arrived at the *so called* stream their spirits deflated. It looked like at some time in the prehistoric past there might have been a creek there. Almost all the map representations of water had proved inaccurate. This was common knowledge to any native New Mexican. New Mexico has been in a severe drought for more than a decade. Most of the rivers and streams only hold water during the rare flash floods. The pristine trout streams are the exception, if you know their locations. While the two terrorists bemoaned their water situation, an approaching vehicle caught them by surprise. They were in the open, and it was too late to flee—that would definitely arouse suspicion. As the truck approached they could see it was a forest ranger. Khaled swore under his breath.

Waleed said, "Khaled, let me do the talking. I can handle this."

The truck stopped a few yards away and a ranger slid out of the driver's seat and approached them, "How are you two gentlemen doing today?"

Waleed answered smoothly, "Good afternoon officer. We're doing fine, but we're running short of water. Our map doesn't seem to be very accurate when it comes to streams."

The ranger chuckled, "Well I think I can point you boys in the right direction. Just remember to purify or boil the water before drinking. Giardia parasites infest all the streams—make you feel like you have the flu from hell.

You get giardia and you'll be leaking from both ends. Here, let me see that map of yours."

The ranger spread the map on the hood of his truck and bent over to examine it. Waleed watched intently, eager to learn of a good water supply. Khaled moved close to the ranger and leaned forward as if straining to get a clear view of the map, but instead of reading the map he pressed his 9mm pistol against the back of the ranger's head and pulled the trigger. The hollow point bullet traveled from the rear of the ranger's skull and scrambled his brains as it passed through his head. The bullet burst from the ranger's face followed by a geyser of blood and jellied brain matter. One of the ranger's eyes plopped wetly onto the hood of the vehicle. The ranger slumped forward and then crumpled to the ground as if in slow motion.

Waleed was taken completely by surprise. One moment he was chatting pleasantly with the friendly forest ranger who was about to reveal the location of the nearest water supply, and then Khaled's gun roared like a clap of thunder only inches from his right ear. Waleed fell to the ground with his head numb and ringing, and his face spattered with gore. When he grasped what had happened he was furious, but when he tried to get up he staggered and fell like a drunk. The gunshot so close to his ear, had temporarily destroyed his equilibrium. When he finally recovered his balance his eardrum throbbed and his head rung like a bell. He pressed the palm of his hand against his damaged ear.

"Are you insane?" he yelled, "Why did you kill him? He was no threat!"

Khaled glared at Waleed with black angry eyes, "You are a fool! It was no accident the ranger showed up. Tricklock must have alerted the authorities somehow."

Waleed was badly shaken, "I don't think so. There is no phone reception here. The ranger was alone and was acting friendly. Now what do we do?"

Khaled examined the ranger's body and inspected the interior of his vehicle. The hood of the truck was sprayed with blood and clumps of pinkish brain that had already begun to congeal in the sun.

Khaled reassured Waleed, "Even if you were right, we could not take the chance. If later on our presence and purpose became known, the authorities would have our description and this location to begin tracking us. We will take his water and anything else useful. Put his body in the backseat, and we will conceal the vehicle."

They searched the Ranger's truck and in addition to a good supply of water, they discovered a well-stocked first aid kit. Although Waleed was badly shaken, Khaled remained firmly in control. He directed the disposal of the dead ranger and his vehicle. He drove the truck well off the trail into a stand of trees where it was invisible from the road. While Khaled worked, Waleed slowly recovered his composure. The killing of the ranger seemed dangerous and compulsive, despite Khaled's explanation. He knew that it wouldn't be long before the authorities would mount a search for the missing ranger. Maybe they should give up on Tricklock, cut their losses and leave this evil forest. When Waleed suggested as much to Khaled, the terrorist leader flew into a rage.

"Have you forgotten that we tried to kill the American and that he has seen our faces? Have you forgotten that Tricklock knew your name? Not to mention that Youssef's fingerprints will be all over Tricklock's vehicle. No! Our only chance to escape this situation is to kill the American and his son and burn their bodies."

Waleed cringed under Khaled's angry tirade, but he had to admit that his commander made sense. Too much had already happened. No matter what transpired from here on out, they were committed to see the mission through. Their only way out of this situation was to kill Tricklock and his son. Once they had cleared the scene of all evidence of their confrontation with the ranger, they returned to their observation post overlooking the valley. They had learned one piece of important information from the ranger. They had not known that the stream water was dangerous. They were fortunate not to have taken drinking water from a stream as they had planned. The ranger's giardia revelation stirred new anxiety in Khaled and Waleed. During the next planned radio contact with Youssef, they needed to tell him about the contaminated stream water.

On top of their ridge, Tricklock explained his plan to Tanya. Afterwards he and Simon settled Tanya in a comfortable concealed position. Her refuge commanded a good view of the natural approaches into their camp and a clear field of fire. Tricklock established challenge and response passwords and procedures for entering the camp. Because of her lack of mobility, Tanya would be their camp guard.

When she heard someone approaching, she would challenge them from her concealed position by asking, "Who goes there?"

If Tricklock was entering he would respond with Stud. If it was Simon entering camp, he would respond with Muffin. Simon was initially upset that he had to be Muffin, but when his father suggested that they have a bicep contest to determine who would be Stud and who would be Muffin, he saw the writing on the wall and reluctantly agreed to be Muffin. Tanya laughed during the entire Stud-Muffin debate. Tricklock also insisted on a duress word. If either Tricklock or Simon was a captive being forced to enter camp, then when challenged they would answer with their actual names, not Stud or Muffin. This would alert Tanya to the situation and maybe allow for an opportunity for her to shoot the terrorist.

It was nearing evening and both Simon and Tanya were eagerly anticipating the first part of the plan. But first Tricklock and Simon needed to scout the abandoned mine in greater detail. This time they wiggled on their bellies right to the edge of the pit and peered in. About five feet down Tricklock spotted a small flat ledge that jutted from the side of the shaft.

"What do you think Simon, will that small flat area work for you? It's pretty narrow."

Simon smirked, "This will be a piece of cake."

While Simon set up and practiced his part of the operation, Tricklock had some preparations of his own to complete. Their plan involved luring the lone man who had been following them from camp to camp, to this exact spot on the ridge. The success of their endeavor hinged on bringing him to the mine shaft. If they did not accomplish this, they would have to resort to *Plan B*. Hopefully they would not have to use their alternate plan. Their backup plan had the potential to turn into something much more complicated, dangerous, and uncertain. One factor in their favor was the lay of the land. The topography naturally funneled a hiker to follow the path of least resistance. Their pursuer should follow the most logical and accessible approach to the top of the ridge. In fact, when Tricklock and his group had moved from their previous camp, they had also followed the easiest path to the top which had led them to the mine.

Tricklock prepared his area and watched Simon for a few moments, "That's pretty awesome son."

Simon grinned, "Thank you father unit. How are you coming along?"

Tricklock nodded his head, "It's all about faith in your gear. I will be wearing my one extra change of clothes for this event, that being my Crye uniform."

Simon shook his head, "You're ate-up with the military. Why would you bring a uniform on a camping trip?"

"A Crye MultiCam uniform is awesome for camping. It's designed for this environment and super comfortable and durable. Plus the state-of-art camouflage will make me a ninja. This MultiCam uniform is far superior to all those camo field clothes you see in the sports stores. Trust me. After I cover my skin with this camouflage face paint I'll be invisible."

"Face paint huh? You're a strange man father."

Tricklock stacked wood and set up a small pit where he thought a fire would be visible to their stalker, but he would wait for complete darkness before he lit the wood. The fire would be hidden from the other two terrorists who were on the other side of the ridge. Preparations complete, Tricklock and his son returned to their base camp. Tanya challenged them. Tricklock tried but failed to stifle a chuckle when Simon responded with Muffin.

"You suck dad."

Tricklock laughed, "You are just full of compliments today."

Pecos Wilderness Evening of Day Three: Youssef felt as if he was struggling to climb from the depths of hell. It had taken him all day to reach the place where Khaled had spotted the bright flashes. He was tormented by blazing sun, chills, and debilitating weakness. The brutal terrain had only compounded his woes. As he examined the ground he found evidence that Tricklock and his son had probably used this area as a camp. When he had last talked to Khaled on the radio his heart had sunk when he learned about the water parasites. He had a horrible feeling that the water bottle that he had taken from

Tricklock's camp was more treachery from the American. His symptoms since drinking the water certainly matched those that Khaled described. It would soon be too dark to travel, and Youssef dreaded the coming darkness. The temperature was already dropping, with his one light blanket he would surely spend a wretched night. His illness would magnify the misery caused by freezing temperatures and the damp hard ground.

Pecos Wilderness Evening of Day Three: Khaled and Waleed were also suffering. It was not raining, but the temperature must have been in the high thirties. None of the assassins were properly prepared to camp in the mountains. They only had lightweight wool blankets and no insulated ground pads. Their bones sucked-up the cold where their bodies touched the bare ground. They were forced to sit on top of their empty backpacks and huddle beneath their thin blankets, sharing their meager body heat. Khaled decided that he would no longer wait for Tricklock. Tomorrow they would find the American and end this.

Pecos Wilderness Evening of Day Three: A couple of miles away, Tricklock and his group rested in relative comfort. Tricklock was an amateur chef, and that night he planned to pull out all the stops. He lit the campfire near the mine shaft and carried Tanya down to the fire.

Tricklock proclaimed, "Ok fellow targets of Islamic assassins, it's time to relax and have some good food."

He fired up his camp stove and fixed a delicious pasta feast from a family sized dehydrated meal packet. Afterwards, Tanya, Simon, and Tricklock basked in front of the campfire which radiated heat, comfort, and safety. Tanya had received a fresh dose of pain medications and was enjoying the festivities. Tricklock surprised his camp mates by brandishing a small flask of Grand Marnier Brandy.

"Tanya, this brandy will increase the effectiveness of the pain medication. In other words, drinking this is just what doctors tell you not to do. None for you Simon, you're too young. You're still growing and won't be fully human for many years."

Simon said, "I'm human now."

Tricklock said, "Afraid not. You can't make babies yet."

Simon turned red, "That's bull crap!"

Tanya chimed in, "Stop it you two. Just enjoy the fire for a while."

The small band of refugees feasted and warmed around the campfire.

"So what's the point of all this?" asked Tanya.

Tricklock explained, "We know where both groups of our pursuers are. The fire will only be visible to the single man who has been hunting us from camp to camp. I want him to see the fire, and hopefully tonight he'll catch us."

Simon chimed in, "Don't worry Tanya this will work. Our plan is inspired and with my amazing skills we will dazzle and amaze. In Japanese Go this would be called Kami No Itte, more commonly referred to as a *Divine Move*.

"You are two peas in a pod with all you're macho bravado. I'm stuck in the middle of nowhere with a broken leg. If anything happens to you two I would probably die out here."

Tricklock held Tanya's hands, "Trust me. It only seems like we're being flippant. It's just that we might as well enjoy the moment. We're safe for now. Tomorrow will be all life and death and grim consequences. But let me assure you, those terrorist assassin goat herders, or whatever they are, have made a serious mistake going up against a trained operator, that being me. I'm certainly not going to let them harm you or Simon."

Tanya's eyes glistened, "Well, give me some more of that orange brandy. You're right, it goes great with painkillers."

Simon said, "Dad you need to teach me the finer points of macho bravado. That little speech even gave me the tingles!"

After dinner Tricklock carried Tanya to their camp up top, and he and Simon took their positions near the mine.

At the next radio contact time it was Youssef who called Khaled, "Khaled I think I see a fire. It's on a hill a few kilometers away. It fits with the direction the American was traveling."

Khaled was excited, "Tricklock has made a mistake. Leave your camp immediately. It is clear tonight and traveling should be easy if you're careful. Try to arrive before daybreak. You have a weapon and should also have the element of surprise."

160

Youssef tried to describe the location of the hilltop as best he could, but it was dark and not clear on the map. Khaled deciphered enough from Youssef's ramblings that he thought he had a general idea of the area where Tricklock was holed up. Early tomorrow, he and Waleed would move to a position where they could cut off the American's retreat if he survived Youssef's attack.

Waleed's wound was beginning to worry Khaled. His partner's leg was obviously infected and getting worse. Waleed badly needed antibiotics. When Khaled examined the injured leg, Waleed's skin was hot to the touch, another bad sign. Khaled used supplies from the dead ranger's first aid kit to clean and dress the wounds as best he could. Khaled also cut down a sapling and trimmed it for Waleed to use as a walking stick to take some of the strain off of his lame leg. Waleed was just going to have to tough it out until they completed their mission. After Tricklock and his son were dead they could attend to Waleed's medical needs.

Pecos Wilderness Early Morning Day Four: Youssef picked his way carefully through the trees trying to be as silent as possible. It was a good thing that he had left his old camp immediately. He felt very weak and drained, and he had moved over the steep geography very slowly. His hands shook and occasionally his vision jittered. His mind was playing tricks. Every shadow seemed menacing, and every sound was evidence of a concealed enemy about to pounce on him. Along the way he had stopped on several occasions because he thought he saw people crouched near thickets of trees waiting to jump out at him. In each case it had only been his imagination. The walking had kept him somewhat warmed, especially when he climbed steep slopes. His thighs burned and his heart thumped in his chest. It took all his willpower to continue. The sky was beginning to brighten as the moon climbed high in the sky. Youssef had plenty of time. It was 4:00 a.m. and the first glimmerings of dawn were still a few hours away.

Youssef had walked all night in a haze of pain—his senses were numb. Suddenly, he smelled the faint odor of a wood campfire and his senses came alive. He slowly drew his pistol from his holster. He heard the faint pop of a dying ember and scanned the area where the sound had originated. As he peered through the trees, his pistol automatically followed his gaze. Youssef saw faint wisps of smoke off to his right. He stood immobile and studied the area. He spotted the back side of what looked like a crude lean to, fashioned from branches and vegetation. Near the charred remains of the fire, there was a barren area of gravel. Youssef practically held his breath as he slowly inched towards the fire pit and the sleeping Americans. Youssef froze when he heard a strange whirring noise.

He watched in astonishment as a small aircraft rose into the air from behind the gravel berm. The rectangular craft had four rotors, one at each corner, and hovered effortlessly. The small quadcopter slowly turned and seemed to stare straight at Youssef. The appearance of the machine was so unexpected and so fantastic as to be other-worldly. Youssef was transfixed, could this be an American drone? As he brought his pistol up, the craft abruptly lowered out of sight. Youssef glanced quickly around and saw nothing. He cautiously approached the spot where the quadcopter had disappeared. As he got closer he realized there was a deep, dark hole in the ground. As he approached the edge the quadcopter zoomed back into sight and hovered at head height just out of reach.

A voice thundered behind Youssef, "Toss your weapon into the hole and lay on the ground!"

Youssef was so startled that he stumbled instinctively away from the voice and found himself teetering on the edge of the pit. His pistol flew out of his hand as he frantically wind-milled his arms to regain his balance. His eyes popped wide with terror as he realized he was going to fall. He grasped at the quadcopter in desperation as if it could prevent his fall. His flailing arm smashed the small chopper and it went skittering into the depths, careening off the rock walls. As he fell, Youssef spun to catch the gravelly lip of the shaft. His hands clawed the crumbly rim but failed to stop his fall. He screamed as he disappeared from view.

A man-shaped piece of the forest detached from a thicket and flowed towards the edge of the pit. Tricklock's camouflage was so effective, that he had been only yards from Youssef but was completely invisible to the terrorist. Simon ran down from his hiding place from where he had flown his remote controlled quadcopter. True to his boast, he had proven to be a master pilot. Father and son converged at the mine. When they peered into the depths they were shocked to see the terrorist hanging from the small ledge that had acted as the helicopter's launch pad.

Youssef dangled above the black pit. Both of his hands gripped the lip of the rock ledge. He was desperate, unable to pull himself up because of his weakened state and his sprained wrist. He glared at Tricklock and Simon. With his broken nose and blackened eyes he looked like a demon. The assassin's expression abruptly changed as realized his predicament.

He hung precariously above the rocky chasm, "Help me!" he pleaded.

Tricklock yelled down to the terrorist, "I'll lower you a rope, but first you must answer some questions and you better answer fast—it looks like your grip is slipping. Who is your leader?"

Youssef answered quickly, "He is Khaled, The Great Face Eater."

"What's your name?" asked Tricklock.

"I am Youssef. Now quickly, throw me the rope!"

"Why are you trying to kill us?"

"You must pay for killing Gorg in Afghanistan! Now throw me the rope—I'm slipping!"

"I'm sorry Youssef," said Tricklock, "I don't actually have a rope. But thanks for the information."

Youssef screamed and tried desperately to claw his way onto the ledge. For a second Tricklock thought he might even make it, but then Youssef's strength failed and he toppled backwards into the pit screeching his hate. They heard Youssef bouncing and crushing off the sides of the mine shaft until there was silence. Tricklock looked over at Simon, who was white as a sheet and put a comforting hand on his son's shoulder.

Simon shook his head, "Now there's something you don't see every day."

Tricklock nodded in agreement, "That was intense. Good work son. One down, two to go."

Chapter 12

A CLEVER MANEUVER

Pecos Wilderness Morning of Day Four: Khaled was furious, then only angry, and then worried. Youssef had missed the crucial morning radio call. Then he had missed the next radio contact time. Khaled's mind raced through possible reasons for the missed calls. The radios worked line-of-sight, which meant if there was high ground between Youssef and Khaled's location the terrain could block the radio waves. Youssef could conceivably have turned his radio off temporarily, because he was in a sensitive part of his mission. He would not want to use his radio if he was closing in on Tricklock or was at a critical moment. Youssef's radio could also be dead or malfunctioning. The worst case scenario was that something bad had happened to Youssef. Khaled would allow two more hours to pass. If Youssef still did not respond he would have to assume the worst.

Khaled had much to ponder. Waleed was feverish and practically lame from his infected leg wounds. Youssef was possibly captured or even dead, and the authorities were probably searching for the missing ranger. Khaled smiled to himself. It was at times like these that he felt closest to Allah. He had absolute trust in his God and in himself. When he had faced overwhelming odds in the past, he had kept his calm and steeled himself to persevere. He always kept faith and prided himself on maintaining his composure even during the direst moments. His ability to stay calm and collected during crises had earned him the admiration of his soldiers and formed the foundation for much of his reputation. Far from despairing, Khaled's agile mind began to calculate various courses of action in the event that Youssef was lost.

Even though Khaled was mystified, there were three people that morning who knew exactly what had happened to Youssef. Tricklock and his son approached their camp being sure to make plenty of noise. When Tanya challenged them they replied with their proper code names. Tanya was beside herself with concern and curiosity. She also looked as if her health was in decline. Her serious injury and the stress of being hunted by killers were taking a heavy toll. She was pale and sweating. When Tricklock placed his palm on her forehead, he was startled. Her skin was hot to the touch. Simon approached, oblivious to Tricklock's concern.

He smiled and held out a 9mm pistol, "Look Tanya, we found another gun."

Implicit in Simon's casual statement was the unspoken understanding that he and his father had successfully eliminated one of their pursuers. However, this was no time to celebrate. Tricklock was dismayed at Tanya's appearance and decided to give her a complete checkup and makeover. While Simon regaled Tanya with a detailed and sometimes embellished account of their encounter with Youssef, Tricklock completely removed her splint. He gently cleaned her foot and leg with a damp cloth and carefully checked her circulation and nerve sensation. Her foot and lower leg had turned various shades of purple. The bruising was to be expected, but Tricklock knew she should have been in a hospital days ago. He disinfected the splints and replaced soiled bandages with clean ones. With Simon's help, he encased her fracture site in a bulky cocoon of soft, protective padding that he formed from extra clothes and a microfiber blanket. As Tricklock finished the makeshift casting and afterwards admired his handiwork, the image of an overstuffed chair popped into his head.

While Tricklock finished his ministrations, Simon continued to command Tanya's undivided attention with his animated account of their confrontation with the terrorist Youssef. When Tricklock finished, Tanya swallowed a fresh dose of medication with a sip of water. Most of the weight in Simon's backpack had been drinking water, and as they had gulped it down, his pack had grown considerably lighter. Like his backpack, Simon's spirits were also lighter after their victory over Youssef. Now Tanya and Simon looked to Tricklock for their way forward.

Tricklock convened a war council. He and Simon sat and made themselves comfortable close to Tanya.

Tricklock first went over what they had just learned and examined the implications, "Youssef is dead which leaves us two men to deal with. The leader is named Khaled, The Great Face Eater. I don't know what the face eater thing is all about, but I think we can assume he's a mean bastard. Waleed we know is a college professor and the owner of the SUV. Their motive for all this is revenge, but I don't know any of the details. I wish I could have gotten more information from Youssef, but he had to leave suddenly."

Tricklock placed the map out on the ground and began to discuss strategy, "Well, let's talk about our next move. Right now Khaled and Waleed, whose names we now know courtesy of the late Youssef, are still in their blocking position between us and the main road. If they don't know that Youssef has been taken off the game board, they soon will. My general thinking is that we can't continue to run away. Tanya needs medical attention and I think the odds have shifted in our favor."

Tricklock showed Simon and Tanya their location on the map in relation to their pursuers. He also pointed out some nearby hilltops and where they were on the map.

Simon moved to the map and placed simulated Go stones to mark the position of their adversaries, "Now that the bad guys are down from three to two, I agree with dad. I think we need Tesuji, and before you ask, Tesuji is a Go term which means a clever maneuver. Given our advantage, we should be able to turn the tables on our opponent."

Simon commanded everyone's attention, "I think we should move to this position. He placed a stone on the intersection of grid squares close to Khaled's location. This hill overlooks their camp, if we can see them move into the interior, then we can make a dash for the unguarded road and press on to the town."

Tricklock nodded in understanding, "We'll have to move fast to get into position. They will probably stay put for a while, still hoping to hear from Youssef. At some point they may go to Youssef's last known location which is our present position or they might move somewhere in between, hoping to catch us on the move. And you're right, if we could see them move away from us, we could make a dash for the road. One more thing; once they realize that Youssef is dead they'll have no need to turn on their Rino. We will no longer know their location."

Tanya spoke up, "You two sound like generals. Everything you say makes sense, but a lot of things can happen. We're basically moving directly towards our enemy. If they see us, we won't be able to run away, they'll be too close and we can't move very fast. It's risky, but the plan feels right. After all, this is strategy from a special ops ninja and a Go master."

Tricklock chuckled, but what she said brought something to his attention. He had just been discussing life and death tactics with his fourteen year old son as if he were talking to one of his PJ teammates. Their conversation had seemed completely natural. He was beginning to realize that his son was both talented and complex. He also marveled at Tanya's toughness and resilience. Both his partners in this bizarre situation were amazing in many ways. Once again he mentally resolved to get Simon and Tanya through this ordeal no matter the cost to himself.

Now that they had a plan and a purpose, they quickly broke camp. Tricklock led the way with Tanya riding on his back. They made a slight detour to intercept a small gurgling brook. They were low on water and needed to replenish their supply. Soon Simon's pack would once again burden him. Normally a big fan of physics, Simon was learning first hand that sometimes gravity sucks. At the stream Tricklock filtered water through a special ceramic device and filled all their water containers. Just to be on the safe side, he also added two drops of chlorine bleach to each liter container. After a 30 minute wait, the filtered and treated water would be safe to drink. He also flavored the water with different colors of powdered Gatorade, but he only put a quarter of the recommended amount of powder into each water bottle. Weakly flavored water is easier to drink than a cloyingly sweet beverage or bland unadulterated water, and the powder would also provide energy and electrolytes.

Only a mile away from Tricklock, Khaled was having a very good day indeed. Khaled tracked Tricklock's progress and location on his Rino GPS with great satisfaction and delight. When Youssef failed to check in, Khaled wanted to be sure that the radio they had captured from Tricklock was operating properly. While going through the radio's screens and setup menu, he stumbled across the operating tutorial. What he learned was astonishing. Blood drained from Khaled's face and his ears rang. In stunned disbelief he read about the GPS radio's polling feature. All this time Tricklock had known Khaled's exact location! At first Khaled was embarrassed and furious that the American had tricked him. The devil Tricklock had cleverly left the radio in his camp knowing that Khaled would probably take it and use it. He must have known that it was customary and praiseworthy for Muslim fighters to exploit the weapons and equipment they captured from their enemies. Compared to the Americans their soldiers were always dreadfully ill-equipped. Islamic fighters considered it poetic justice to use their adversaries own war-fighting accoutrements against them. A treasure trove of infidel weapons was considered a bounty from Allah.

Khaled's righteous anger and indignation swiftly gave way to smug satisfaction and glee as he realized the implications of his belated discovery. He could now locate the Americans and observe their movements. In fact, at this very moment Tricklock appeared to be on the move and heading towards a knoll less than one kilometer from Khaled and Waleed's current camp. When Khaled triumphantly revealed his discovery to Waleed, he was disappointed in his fellow Egyptian's response. Khaled's discovery about the GPS tracking function was momentous and game-changing and should have elicited an excited response from Waleed.

Waleed's lethargic behavior prompted Khaled to take a closer look at his soldier. Waleed was listless and disinterested. Khaled closely examined Waleed's leg. His knee was badly swollen and tender to the touch. Khaled was no medic, but he had seen many wounds and injuries on the battlefield. Waleed had a very limited range of motion in his leg and when Khaled pressed the knee from different angles he could feel that the joint was loose and unstable. Waleed had probably torn cartilage in his knee. Waleed hobbled like a cripple and even using the makeshift walking stick it was amazing that he had been able to travel at all—Waleed existed in a haze of constant pain.

When he examined Waleed's wounded shin and calf, Khaled gasped involuntarily. The puncture wounds inflicted by Tricklock's booby trap were horribly infected. When Khaled pressed around the discolored wounds he felt a crackly sensation beneath the skin. The wounds were ghastly. They stank of decay and oozed brownish red ichor. When Khaled felt Waleed's skin it was hot with fever. Khaled feared that Waleed's wounds were gangrenous. Given their isolation it was almost certain that Waleed would die in this godless foreign land. When Khaled looked into Waleed's eyes he saw realization and resignation. They embraced quickly. Waleed was a warrior and a courageous martyr. Khaled had a final mission for Waleed. His soldier would cover himself in glory.

Tricklock approached their destination keeping a ridge between his group and Khaled's camp. He had considered leading his small group straight to the road, but there were two people remaining in Khaled's group. He knew where the spare GPS radio was located, but he didn't know where the second man was. It was possible that the two men were not together. In fact it was more likely that one of the assassins was positioned at a point where he could observe the length of the jeep trail. If the sniper had a rifle with a scope, Tricklock's slow moving party would be sitting ducks as soon as they left the cover of the forest.

Try as he might, Tricklock could not spot his enemies. His binoculars revealed only close ups of brambles and dense thickets of trees. When he next checked his GPS, he was excited to see that Khaled's GPS was on the move. It looked like whoever had the radio was making their way towards their friend Youssef's last known location. Tricklock had some serious thinking to do. Although one of his enemies seemed to be taking himself out of the picture, there was still a danger that one of the terrorists had remained behind to cover the road as a sniper. The sniper was the key, and Tricklock had to counter that threat.

Khaled sent Waleed to search for Youssef. He gave him Tricklock's radio and told him to leave it on at all times. He talked earnestly to Waleed, stressing the importance of his task and making Waleed feel he was on a hero's mission. In fact, Khaled was using him as a decoy. Tricklock would track the radio and logically assume that Khaled was moving away to search for Youssef; Tricklock would think that he was safe. Before sending Waleed on his way, Khaled marked Tricklock's position on his map. The American was nearby, just over the next ridgeline. The last thing Tricklock would expect would be an attack from Khaled. The American had no idea that Khaled had figured out his trick with the GPS. Soon Tricklock and his son would pay dearly for their arrogance and deceit.

Tricklock made a decision. He huddled with his companions and explained his plan. At first Simon and Tanya were skeptical. Eventually Tricklock convinced them that his plan was logical. It was possible that both Khaled and Waleed were heading towards where they had fought with Youssef, but Tricklock thought it more likely that one of them had stayed behind to cover the road with a sniper rifle. Tricklock had a plan to smoke out the sniper. Simon and Tanya would literally hold down the fort until he got back. When Tricklock returned, they would use their tried and true challenge and response code names. Tricklock realized that Tanya and Simon would feel very insecure while he was gone. He was purposely vague about how he would locate the sniper, if there was a sniper. His companions would freak out if they knew his exact plans.

"Simon, you're going to have to be the sentry while I'm away. Tanya has a serious injury and as capable as she is, she's injured badly and you have to take care of her. I'm being dead serious. Do you understand?"

Simon nodded his head; he knew that he was assuming a huge responsibility, "I understand." he said.

Tricklock walked over to Tanya to have a private word, "Tanya, I just had a talk with Simon and told him I expected him to look after you. I just wanted to stress the gravity of the situation. Even though you're injured you are still the adult here. Reassure Simon when he needs it. Also the spot I chose for him to occupy as a sentry was no accident. I'm going to set you up so you are concealed but can cover Simon. You both will be fine. I'll be back before you know it, plus we have the radios. I've already briefed Simon, but make sure you use the challenge and response code words, even on the radio."

Tanya was genuinely concerned, "I'm not sure what you're going to do exactly, but please be careful!"

Tricklock smiled and nodded. He set up Simon's guard position, and Tanya's concealed cubby hole. And then with a casual wave he faded into the forest and disappeared. Tricklock needed to carry out his plan while it was still daylight. He moved through the forest like a wraith. After a few kilometers he eventually reached the edge of the tree line. Twenty meters of barren ground lay between Tricklock and the gravel road. Tricklock brazenly strode across the bare shoulder and onto the road. He was counting in his head, imagining himself as the sniper would see him through his rifle scope.

Tricklock silently talked to himself, "The sniper is momentarily taken aback by the sight of his quarry suddenly in the open. He recovers, takes careful aim, taking into account the wind and distance, and then he slowly pulls the trigger."

Just before the anticipated trigger pull, Tricklock dropped to the ground and rolled to his right. Then he was up and running while mentally reciting, *I'm up, he sees me, I'm down!* Tricklock once again dove to the ground, rolled to his left, and sprang to his feet running, *I'm up, he sees me, I'm down.* Nothing happened. There were no shots at all.

Tricklock rose from behind his cover and repeated the ritual several times. No sniper shot at him. Tricklock was almost convinced that there was no shooter. He casually strolled down the road, counting in his head and giving a possible sniper plenty of time to aim. Then he dropped to the ground and rolled; still no shots rang out. He walked the road a hundred yards in each direction—there was no sniper. If there had been a sniper, he would have taken a shot at Tricklock.

Tricklock's plan had been risky. If there had been a sniper, then when the shooter had shot and missed, Tricklock would have been able to figure out where the shot had originated from. Then he planned to hunt the sniper down and kill him. Tricklock was done with being defensive. It was time to be the aggressor, but there was no sniper. Both Khaled and Waleed must have left to search for Youssef. It was getting dark. Tricklock walked back into the tree line. The fact that there was no sniper guarding the road made it safe for them to make their escape. He didn't want to waste any time. Once he returned to Simon and Tanya, they would leave immediately.

Tricklock took out his radio and called Tanya, "Stud calling PJ base camp. Come in."

Tricklock recognized Tanya's voice, "This is PJ base camp. Go ahead Tricklock."

Tricklock paused. Tanya should have responded with, "Go ahead *Stud.*" not with "Go ahead *Tricklock.*" He was not sure if Tanya had made an un-thinking mistake, or if she had used his name purposely and was being held captive.

Tricklock's mind raced to come up with a way to be sure of Tanya's mean-ing, "PJ base camp, I checked out the hilltop as planned and it's suitable for our purpose. I'm heading back and should return around ten o'clock. I'll call when I'm 15 minutes out."

Tanya responded, "That's good news about the hill Tricklock. Everything's good at this end, over and out."

Tricklock felt like he had just been tasered. Tanya knew full well that the purpose of his foray had been to reconnoiter the road and check for a sniper, not to explore a hill top. She had also used his name again. This meant that one of the terrorists, probably Khaled, had captured Tanya and Simon and was preparing an unpleasant reception for his return. For the time being, Tanya and his son were probably unhurt. Tanya had let him know that, when she had said that everything was good at their end. Tricklock had given Tanya his estimated time of arrival as 10:00 p.m., although he planned to arrive at least an hour before that. Somehow, Khaled had captured Simon and Tanya. As if to accentuate the disastrous turn of events a light rain began to fall. Tricklock began to run back to his camp. Hopefully Tanya's performance on the radio had been convincing. There was no reason for Khaled to suspect they were us-ing code words on the radio. That meant that Tricklock might still have a slim advantage, the element of surprise.

While he ran through cold drizzle, Tricklock's mind raced to come up with a plan. He had so many questions and so many fears. If Khaled managed to kill him, then afterwards he would certainly kill Tanya and Simon. Tricklock's companions were only alive, because Khaled was using them to draw him into the open. Khaled must be wary of him, especially given all that had happened. Otherwise Khaled would have announced over the radio that he had captured his son and Tanya and ordered him to surrender. Khaled wanted the advantage of surprise, but thanks to Tanya, it was Tricklock who now had the upper hand. All that he had to do was figure out a way to capitalize on his slim edge.

Chapter 13

FIGHTING SPIRIT

After Tricklock left to scout the road there was a sense of emptiness in the camp, and in the back of Simon and Tanya's mind was the depressing thought, "What if something happened to Tricklock? What if their great protector did not return?"

Even though they were well armed, without Tricklock's reassuring presence they felt vulnerable. As daylight began to fade, a chilling rain softly pattered the trees. Simon set about erecting a makeshift lean-to shelter for Tanya. He used her Sil tarp to keep off the light cascade of cold droplets. As he worked he realized that he was becoming comfortable in the outdoors. They had a tent, but Simon didn't want to set up camp. They would wait to see what Tricklock wanted to do once he returned. If he decided it was safe, they might be hiking to the road this very night.

Tanya lay huddled in her cubby hole sheltered from the rain and cold. Her ankle throbbed but the oxycodone took off the harsh edge of the nagging pain. Thank God for the painkillers. She could only imagine what this ordeal would have been like without them. She still felt guilty for breaking her leg in the first place. If she were healthy, they would have been out of this forest long ago. She largely blamed herself for getting Tricklock and Simon caught up in this life and death cat and mouse game, but there was no sense dwelling on the negative. She could barely make out Simon standing guard at his post. She had to smile—Simon was so much like his dad but didn't realize it. She promised herself that when they were out of this mess, she would hang out with Tricklock and Simon under better circumstances; it would be fun.

Simon put on a light Gortex rain jacket to protect against the drizzle. There was not much to see in the gloom. Although he had put his quadcopter to good use, he was disappointed that it was destroyed. On the bright side, he would get to buy a better one. The prospect of getting the latest and greatest remote controlled flying machine was exciting. This time he would modify it with a programmable GPS and an onboard video camera. He had aspirations of creating his own drone. His mind wandered, rain fell softly, and darkness descended like a black velvet curtain.

Waleed trudged painfully through the forest, faithfully playing his role as a decoy. He existed in a feverish delirium of weakness and pain. He staggered on hardly aware of his surroundings. He was in a trance like state, a kind of mental autopilot. Khaled's mental state was the polar opposite of poor Waleed's. Khaled's mind was razor sharp. His nerves jangled with anticipation and the effects of adrenaline. When the soft rain had begun to fall he knew that Allah had heard his prayers. The sound of the falling rain would help to mask the noise of his approach. The rain would soak the crackly leaves and twigs that carpeted the forest floor, turning them pliable and soundless. The Great Face Eater approached Tricklock's camp as silent as a panther.

Khaled slowed his approach a few hundred meters from Tricklock's camp and stashed his bulky backpack and spare weapons next to an unmistakable landmark, a rusty tin windmill emblazoned with the word Aermotor in faded paint. He traveled light and unencumbered, carrying only a knife, pistol, and spare ammunition. He picked his way silently, keeping to the shadows and being careful to use all available concealment. He moved from bush to bush and thicket to thicket stealthily closing in on his prey. It was movement that caught his eye and alerted him that he had arrived at his destination. Khaled watched as a teenage boy paced restlessly in the gloom. The boy had to be Tricklock's son Simon. Khaled moved closer, scanning the area for Tricklock.

Khaled was shocked when he heard a woman's soft voice, "Simon, stop pacing. Your father will be fine. He'll radio when he's on his way back."

Simon replied, "I know. I just feel better when I'm moving. I guess I'm just nervous."

Khaled could not see the woman, but he could tell her general location from her voice. Youssef had only observed Tricklock and his son leave the truck and hike into the woods. Who could this woman be? It was one more mystery among many. Khaled had never been involved in an operation that was fraught with so many unexpected difficulties. Given all the setbacks and unforeseen pitfalls, it seemed a miracle that he was finally on the verge of fulfilling his mission. Apparently Tricklock, his most serious threat, was away on a scouting mission. Tricklock had left his young son and a woman alone in his camp. Khaled smiled to himself. Maybe Tricklock had thought the camp safe because he had seen his planted GPS moving away from this location.

Khaled carefully circled behind where he had heard the woman's voice. He moved soundlessly. When the woman spoke again he was able to zero in on her location. He inched forward on his hands and knees using shrubs and underbrush for concealment. When Tanya shifted, Khaled saw her movement and pinpointed her position. He was within 20 feet of the woman. Khaled remained motionless, observing the lay of their camp. When Simon spoke, Khaled was able to spot the boy's hiding place as well. Khaled assumed that the woman and the boy were both armed. He did not know the connection between the boy and the woman, but he reasoned they must have some relationship. Khaled analyzed the situation from different perspectives and decided on a bold course of action.

Khaled crept closer to the woman. He approached from her rear moving excruciatingly slow. When he gauged he was close enough, he stood and moved quickly. He grabbed a fist full of the woman's hair and twisted violently. She let out an involuntary yelp then froze when Khaled jammed the barrel of his pistol into the side of her neck.

Khaled whispered in Tanya's ear, "Call the boy over or I will kill him."

Simon was alarmed by Tanya's brief scream, "Tanya, is everything OK?"

Tanya's voice wavered, "Simon, can you come over here for a minute?"

Simon thought that something was wrong with Tanya's leg and quickly went to her aid. He stopped cold when he saw a strange man twisting Tanya's head back and brandishing a gun.

Khaled smiled coldly and forced the muzzle of his pistol into Tanya's mouth, "Move very slowly and toss your weapon over here. If you try anything I'll blow her brains out."

Simon could hear Tanya's teeth click on the metal gun barrel. The sound made him cringe. He tossed his revolver next to Khaled. Khaled removed the barrel of his gun from Tanya's mouth and pointed it at Simon. He made Simon lay on his stomach. Khaled searched the area with his eyes. He spotted Tanya's revolver and tucked it into his waist band.

Khaled noticed Tanya's splint, "What's wrong with your leg?" he asked.

Tanya's voice trembled, "I broke my ankle."

Khaled searched Tanya for other weapons and confiscated her knife. He smiled and kicked her splinted leg. Tanya screamed, and when Simon instinctively rose from his prone position, Khaled backhanded him in hard in the face, knocking him down. Simon slowly got to his knees. He was no longer afraid—anger had replaced his fear. He glared at Khaled.

Simon smirked, "You hit like a girl."

Khaled laughed, "Face away from me and lock your fingers together behind your head while I search you."

After the pat-down Khaled kicked Simon in the back of the knee, collapsing his leg and knocking him to the ground. He ordered Simon to crawl over next to Tanya.

"The woman cannot move very fast," said Khaled, "If you try to escape or attack me, I will shoot the woman. Do you understand?"

Simon nodded his head.

Khaled barked, "Say it!"

"I understand." said Simon.

Khaled methodically searched Simon's large backpack. When he found Youssef's gun, he hissed angrily.

"I assume that Youssef is dead?"

Simon replied smugly, "He is in hell where he belongs."

Khaled almost hit Simon again but stopped short, "Don't push me boy! You are nothing to me, but continue to annoy me and I will give you a slow painful death!"

Khaled interrogated Simon and Tanya. They gave him as little information as possible. When he thought they were being evasive, he would casually kick Tanya's injured leg. Tanya was pale as a ghost and her hands trembled.

After he was satisfied, Khaled gave instructions to Tanya, "When Sergeant Tricklock calls, assure him that all is well and find out when he will return. Remember, both your lives depend on your cooperation."

Khaled had greatly enjoyed questioning the two Americans. If he had more time he could have had even more fun. He smiled to himself because he knew that eventually he *would* have more time. One of his favorite methods of interrogation was to wordlessly approach a helpless prisoner bound to a chair. He would order the captive's right hand to be placed palm down on a wooden table, and then he would drive a nail through the man's thumbnail and deep into the wood. Then he would place a hammer and a pair of pliers next to the captive's nailed hand. Still silent, Khaled would leave and return an hour later. During Khaled's absence, the prisoner's mind would inevitably conceive and anticipate horrible tortures. Next Khaled would order the man's mouth taped shut. It amused him to deny his prisoner the release of screaming. Right when the victim most needed oxygen to fuel his panicked and pounding heart and to feed his pain shocked nervous system, he would be forced to suck his air through his two small nostrils. He could not get enough oxygen and the instinctual terror of suffocation would layer upon the prisoner's physical pain and agony.

Khaled would pick up the hammer and pliers in turn and make a show of carefully inspecting them. Then he would nonchalantly choose the hammer and shatter the man's thumb joints. After a time, Khaled would remove the tape from the captive's mouth, allowing him to gulp in air and stave off unconsciousness. Khaled would studiously ignore the man's gibbering while he examined the pliers. He would methodically re-tape the man's mouth, and then he would use the pliers to snap the man's other finger bones. Khaled was careful to inflict many different types of breaks and fractures. He liked to leave the prisoner's fingers twisted and pointing in all directions as if he was an artist sculpting an abstract and corrupted hand. Afterwards, he would rip off the mouth tape and leave the prisoner to marinate in terror and misery. Khaled would return the next day, when the captive's fingers had swollen and stiffened into maximum tenderness. Then he would begin to torture the man in earnest. First he would tape his mouth, then by simply grabbing a broken finger and wrenching it around, he could inflict terrible agony on his victim. Khaled liked to play at this for hours, occasionally removing the tape so his victim could breathe and blubber out information.

Tanya's radio crackled, interrupting Khaled's pleasant reverie.

Tricklock's voice came over the radio, "Stud calling PJ Base Camp, come in."

While the woman talked, Khaled pointed his gun at Simon and watched her closely. He listened to detect any attempts by Tanya to alert Tricklock, but he was satisfied with the woman's performance. She was obviously too frightened and cowed to try any brash heroics.

Tricklock ran silently through the rain. He ran with urgency, backtracking the way he had come. His mood was as dark as the night and his mind raced, imagining the horrible things that could have occurred during his absence. He thought that Simon and Tanya were probably unharmed, because Khaled would need them as leverage. It was unlikely that Khaled had fortuitously stumbled upon his camp. For one thing, he would not be traveling at night unless he knew where he was going. The only explanation was that Khaled must have discovered the polling function of the GPS that Tricklock had planted. Tricklock did not have enough information to develop a detailed plan. His tentative plan was to arrive earlier than expected and sneak close enough to the camp to see what was going on. Once he understood the situation in the camp he would have to come up with a course of action on the spot.

Tricklock had a sudden epiphany. He stopped running and took a few minutes to prepare the gear he needed to set his plan in motion. He tested his scheme, running through a few rehearsals. When he was satisfied, he took off running again. It was important that he arrive at his camp well before ten o'clock when he was expected. Thanks to Tanya's clever use of his name instead of *Stud*, at least Tricklock knew there was trouble at the camp. When she went along with his story about checking out a hilltop, he knew for certain that she was in trouble. Tanya knew very well that Tricklock had gone to check the road for a sniper. He was worried sick about Simon, but his best chance to save him and Tanya was to keep his head.

Tricklock arrived in the vicinity of his camp at 8:30 p.m. He was an hour and a half early, but he needed the time to reconnoiter and set the stage. Tricklock was almost certain that Khaled, if it *was* Khaled, did not think that Tricklock was on to him. If he had suspected Tanya of deception, he would have immediately grabbed the radio and made threats and demands. Although an obvious stereotype, it was possible that culturally, Khaled had a low opinion of a woman's intelligence and capabilities. If that was true, he would tend to underestimate Tanya.

Tricklock slowly approached his hidden camp. He was well camouflaged and the wet forest allowed him to move silently. He peered through brush and scrub trees to spy out the lay of the camp. Through the trees he could see Khaled crouched close by Tanya and Simon. He was using his captives to shield himself from a possible attack from Tricklock. Even though Khaled was not expecting Tricklock to arrive early, he was taking no chances. Tricklock shook his head and frowned. It was too risky to use his pistol, especially at night. Khaled was nestled closely between his son and the Tanya, and it was impossible to predict how everyone would move and react. Tricklock could not use his gun to take out Khaled.

Now that Tricklock knew the disposition of Khaled and his captives, he moved off to setup for the coming showdown. He carefully calculated distances and angles and planted his cell phone in some thick bushes only a few yards from Khaled. When Tricklock moved off, he knew he only had 15 minutes to get set. He circled around behind Khaled and inched forward in the dim light as carefully as a lion staking game in the high grasses of the African veldt. He used trees and bushes to conceal his movements. His progress was so slow as to be almost imperceptible. He wore state of the art camouflage and was invisible in the gloom. He calmed his mind and controlled his breath. He stopped when he deemed himself at the optimum distance from Khaled and his hostages. He felt the weight of each smooth rock that he held loosely in his clenched fists. Their solid weight gave him strength and comfort as he waited.

Khaled was filled with anticipation. Soon Tricklock would be returning to this camp. The foolish American was even going to be so kind as to let him know when he was only 15 minutes away. He probably planned to move his group to the hilltop he had mentioned on the radio. The boy and the woman sat silent and immobile in the dim light, like pale store manikins. Khaled had carefully bound their wrists together behind their backs. He had tied the cords extra tight so as to cut off their circulation and cause maximum discomfort and pain. He had laughed when they complained and struck both of them with the back of his hand. His captives were only permitted to speak if he asked a question. Any unsolicited talk immediately earned both of them a sharp blow to the face. The sight of the two Americans huddled helpless and in misery gave him great satisfaction. Their faces were streaked with their own blood and tears.

Khaled was curious, "How did your group move so fast given that your leg is broken?"

Tanya reluctantly answered, "Tricklock carried me on his back."

Khaled was incredulous, "That does not seem possible given the distances and terrain you crossed."

Simon interrupted, "It seems impossible to you because you are weak, but my dad is strong."

Khaled punched Simon hard in the face. There was the crack of a bone breaking and Simon's nose spouted bright red blood. He slumped stunned against Tanya with his eyes full of water and his breath coming in ragged gasps.

Khaled had his arm raised ready to strike Tanya, when he was startled by a commanding voice from a nearby thicket, "Throw down your gun and raise your arms!"

Before arriving at the camp, Tricklock had recorded that voice command on his phone. He had an alarm clock app that allowed him to record custom wakeup calls.

Tricklock found it amusing to have his phone alarm blast his own voice saying, "Tricklock! Get your lazy ass up!"

He liked his latest message even better. After spying out the situation at the camp, he had turned the phone's volume to maximum and strategically placed it in a copse of small trees. He set the alarm for 15 minutes later and snuck into position. Then he had waited. When Khaled struck Simon it was almost more than he could bear, but he gritted his teeth and maintained his composure. When his voice boomed from the night, Tricklock threw one of his stones into the thicket where he had placed his phone. He had calculated that the sound of his voice combined with the sound of the stone cracking on branches would convince Khaled that Tricklock was actually in the trees and create an almost subconscious response from the terrorist.

Just as Tricklock hoped, Khaled reacted instinctively. He immediately rose to a kneeling position while simultaneously drawing his pistol and shooting into the trees where he had heard Tricklock's voice and movement. Behind Khaled, Tricklock rose from the ground and raced forward in a blur. He was close enough to cover the intervening distance in only a couple of seconds. Even so, Tricklock had anticipated that, despite the distraction of his phone ploy, Khaled would quickly sense an attack and turn to engage him. That's why Tricklock carried the second stone. When Khaled started to turn to meet his attack, Tricklock's second stone was already speeding through the air. The rock missile thudded into Khaled while he was still in the process of turning around. The impact disrupted Khaled, and a split second later Tricklock slammed into the assassin at full tilt. Simon and Tanya were knocked sprawling, but that was unavoidable.

Tricklock hit the much smaller Khaled like a blitzing linebacker while simultaneously chopping down on Khaled's gun wrist. Khaled's pistol went flying, and both Khaled and Tricklock crashed to the ground. Usually Tricklock felt the impact of blows during a fight, but not pain. But somehow Khaled had clamped down on Tricklock's left hand with his teeth and the pain was intense. Khaled had a two handed grip on Tricklock's arm, and clung like a pit bull. With great difficulty, Tricklock ignored the pain, grabbed Khaled's left hand, and pried it off his own arm twisting against Khaled's joint. He felt Khaled's teeth crunch through bone but ignored the pain. Tricklock now had the terrorist's arm twisted, and he slammed his fist down onto Khaled's elbow. Khaled's elbow joint was not designed to bend backwards, and Tricklock's blow snapped Khaled's left arm. The terrorist screamed, rolled away, scrambled to his feet, and was up and running through the night before Tricklock could tackle him.

Tricklock pursued but soon returned. In the dark, Khaled had too much of a head start. Tricklock quickly freed Simon and then Tanya, and then there were hugs and blubbering all around. Tricklock's hand throbbed, and when he examined it under light he was shocked to see that Khaled had bitten off the little finger of his left hand. No wonder his finger hurt so bad, it was severed at the second knuckle and not cleanly. The stump was jagged and even *looked* incredibly painful. Tricklock talked Tanya through the task of bandaging what remained of his finger while Simon searched the ground for the rest of his dad's pinky. Unfortunately he never found the finger, but he was able to collect his dad's phone and Khaled's Glock.

Tricklock gathered everyone around, "I know you two have been through a scary time, but as soon as we can collect our things I want to leave here and move to the road. Looks like you two took some battle damage, can you travel? Are you both up-too moving right now?"

Simon said, "I'm ready."

Tanya chimed in, "Me too."

Simon exclaimed, "That was awesome dad! In Go tactics, your attack would be said to have demonstrated Kiai, which means fighting spirit."

Simon raised his left palm, "Give me a high four."

Tricklock was amazed, "Simon, that was incredibly inappropriate. I loved that!"

Simon beamed. He was feeling giddy with relief now that his father had returned and saved them. Khaled was on the run and the clamor and stress of the nightmarish confrontation with the terrorist was over.

Tricklock urged them back to reality, "You two can tell me all about your ordeal while we travel. Let's saddle up and get moving."

Tanya said, "Alright, let's put on your harness. I feel like I'm a jockey when I'm riding you. I just need one of those little whips."

"You feel like a jockey because you're on drugs. Now let's get moving."

Khaled ran through the night furious and in pain, but he was not defeated. In fact he was more determined than ever to get Tricklock. His arm radiated extraordinary pain, the American had hyperextended Khaled's left arm and cracked his elbow. He had actually heard a sickening snap, but at least there were no jagged bones poking through the skin—he would be OK. He had also done damage to Tricklock, biting his finger off. He only wished he could have bitten a more vital area. It was time to re-group. A new plan was already coming together in his head. Khaled headed for the old windmill where he had stashed his backpack and spare weapons. This was far from over. So far Tricklock had always been one step ahead. Khaled vowed that this would not continue. He suddenly realized he had been neglecting his prayers. It was a serious mistake. When he arrived at the windmill he oriented himself towards Mecca, prostrated himself, and prayed.

Pecos Wilderness Early Morning Day Five: It was 1:00 a.m. and Tricklock trudged through the night with Tanya on his back; yesterday had been a long day and this one looked to be a repeat. None of his group had slept. Simon took up the rear, his revolver in hand. He was understandably paranoid about attacks. They were all fueled by adrenaline and hope. Tricklock traced his earlier path to the road. He carried Tanya's weight effortlessly. He resolved to walk all night if necessary. When they actually intersected the main gravel road it was like discovering the Holy Grail. The road seemed like the culmination of their arduous quest, but they were not yet out of danger. They paused to rest and refuel with water and food. Tricklock cut their break short and continued on down the road in the direction of civilization. They moved wearily down the gravel road bathed in pale moonlight. They walked for hours and for what felt like many miles. Tricklock felt as if he could carry Tanya all the way into town. He felt tingly all over, a sensation he recognized from his long runs and triathlons. It is called *runner's high* and is caused by the bodies' release of chemical endorphins—nature's biological pain killers. Despite his feeling of invincibility, he took his *runner's high* as a sign that he was nearing the end of his strength.

Although Tricklock felt strong for the moment, Simon was shuffling in a haze of exhaustion, and Tanya's legs were numb from lack of circulation. Tricklock stopped his group on the side of the road. As they rested, they noticed twin orbs of light in the distance. The headlights grew larger as they approached and Tricklock stood in the center of the road and spread his arms, blocking the road. When the vehicle stopped, it turned out to be a fish and game officer. The ranger immediately spared no effort to assist the obviously distressed trio. With the ranger's help Tricklock carefully placed Tanya in the back seat. They were a battered and forlorn band of brothers. Tanya had a fractured leg and was pale and bedraggled, Simon sported a broken nose and black eyes, and Tricklock had a scuffed up face and bandaged hand. They were dirty and blood streaked. Ranger George Sanchez recognized Tricklock. It was a small town, and George even knew Tricklock's father Isaac. George immediately mobilized all the resources at his disposal on behalf of the local hero.

Tricklock provided a brief recap of recent events and asked to be taken to the nearest full service hospital. He also requested that the local police meet them as soon as possible. The ranger finished loading the disheveled wayfarers, gave his superiors a heads up, and headed to the emergency room. He had been out searching for a missing ranger, but this situation obviously took precedence. In the back of the vehicle, Tricklock, Simon, and Tanya finally breathed a sigh of relief. Tricklock was insistent that Tanya immediately get definitive medical care, he had been worried sick about her. Simon's broken nose also needed attention, and Tricklock had minor injuries that needed to be dealt with, including his severed finger. He foresaw that Tanya and maybe Simon would need to spend some time in the hospital, but despite the inevitable objections he planned to leave the hospital as soon as possible.

After Khaled fled from Tricklock, he had unsuccessfully tried to radio Waleed. When Waleed had left he was in terrible physical health. There was no predicting his current life situation. Nonetheless, Khaled headed towards Youssef's last known location which was also Waleed's ultimate destination.

Khaled was desperate. Despite his broken arm, he ran as fast as he could towards his goal. While he ran, his mind seemed abnormally penetrating and lucid. He felt he was being inspired and strengthened by Allah. His thoughts were almost magically coalescing into a concrete plan of action.

As Khaled pushed himself to his limits, time seemed to pass as if he were in a dream, surreal snap shots of disconnected moments. Occasionally he saw things in brutal clarity. Khaled continued to stagger on as if in a trance. When he finally arrived in the vicinity of the knoll where he had sent his soldier, he found Waleed unconscious. Khaled found it impossible to arouse Waleed—he was too far gone. Khaled was amazed that his soldier had made it this far. Waleed would be a martyr. He had bravely sacrificed his life for the cause. Khaled closely examined his surroundings. He saw the charred remains of an abandoned campfire and a curious pile of yellowish gravel. He climbed the gravel mound and peered over the top. He saw that the berm concealed the entrance to an abandoned mine shaft. He edged closer to the brink and tossed in a pebble to determine the depth. The stone clattered and bounced off the slate sides of the shaft. Khaled was surprised to hear urgent pleas emanating from the depths of the pit. He was stunned when he recognized the voice.

Youssef was still alive! Khaled called down to him and they began to talk back and forth. Khaled searched the area and found a fallen tree about 20 feet long. He dragged the tree to the pit and tilted it in. Soon he could hear someone scrabbling up the tree. Youssef emerged filthy and with a ravening thirst. Khaled satisfied Youssef's immediate physical needs before catching him up on recent events. Youssef told of his disastrous confrontation with Tricklock and his son. When asked by Khaled, Youssef denied seeing a woman. Youssef was very lucky, although the mine shaft appeared bottomless, it was not. In fact, the hole was only 20 feet deep and at only 10 feet from the top the shaft started sloping to the bottom. When Youssef fell down the pit he was knocked unconscious but was otherwise unhurt. Until Khaled arrived, Youssef thought he would starve to death at the bottom of the pit.

Youssef was actually starting to recover from his injuries and illness, and although he was still weak he was feeling stronger. Youssef gingerly splinted

Khaled's left arm. Khaled's elbow still hurt terribly, which further fueled his hatred for Tricklock.

Youssef was concerned, "What will we do with Waleed? He is still alive, although barely."

Khaled walked over to Waleed and closely examined him. It was obvious he would not live long. Khaled stood back, drew his pistol and calmly put a bullet into Waleed's head.

"Youssef, push Waleed's body into the hole where it will not be discovered and defiled by infidels. Then conceal all traces of blood."

Youssef experienced shock and disbelief.

Khaled read the expression on Youssef's face and angrily exclaimed, "Waleed was near death and we could not have saved him. He is a martyr to our cause. Now quickly do as I say."

Youssef moved like a zombie, slowly as if he were in a trance. Khaled felt exasperated. After Youssef reluctantly pushed Waleed's body into the mine-shaft, they collected their gear and set off. Khaled had ambitious plans. They had much to do and not a lot of time to do it in.

Chapter 14

SEIZE THE DAY

George sped through the night with his vehicle lights flashing. His three unusual passengers were precious cargo. He drove to the nearest full service hospital, which was in nearby Santa Fe. Tricklock and his companions were weary, but even though it was early morning there were necessary phone calls to be made. Tanya called her boss and briefly explained the events of the past few days. Needless to say, he was thunderstruck and saw Tanya's ordeal through the prism of weeks of riveting stories, follow-up reports, and soaring ratings. She gave him the name of the hospital and mentally prepared to have the tables turned on her. Her station was sure to dispatch a news team. Like it or not she was now part of the story.

Tricklock dreaded the prospect of phoning Simon's mother, but he knew he had to call. When BA answered the phone, she immediately knew that something was wrong.

Tricklock started the conversation, "Sorry to call so late, Simon is perfectly fine, but we had a little situation on our camping trip."

Without delving into the more disturbing details of their ordeal, Tricklock summarized the events of the last few days. He also explained that both he and Simon would probably be tied up with police enquiries for a while. When he put Simon on the phone, his son followed his lead, leaving out details that he knew would freak out his mother and prolong the conversation. He ended by promising to call early the next day and provide a more detailed account of his ordeal.

After Simon hung up, Tricklock laughed and said, "Good job! You were suitably vague and masterfully downplayed the rough bits."

Simon grinned, "That's good for now, but I promised to call her tomorrow. I'm going to have to tell her more details before she sees it on the news."

They arrived at the hospital amid a modest gathering of police and press. It appeared that news of their adventure had already trickled out. Medical professionals quickly trundled off Tanya and Simon to examination rooms. While the nurses attended to their medical needs, Tricklock took the opportunity to make a few crucial phone calls. He had held off making these specific calls during the ride to the hospital, because he didn't want anyone to overhear his conversations. He also had to phone his unit commander to fill him in on the situation. When he was finally finished he allowed a nurse to guide him to a triage examination room. For the time being, they cleaned and bandaged what was left of his severed pinky, but he would need surgery in the next few days. Next came the interminable police interviews and statements—he thought they would never end. The police were especially disappointed that he couldn't shed any light on the missing forest ranger, but if Khaled and his minions were responsible for the ranger, Tricklock had no knowledge of the circumstances.

The hospital admitted Tanya and scheduled her for immediate surgery. Simon soon returned to the waiting room. There was not much the doctors could do for his broken nose and two black eyes. The bridge of his nose was cracked, but it would heal on its own. Tricklock decided that the first thing they needed to do was to get a hotel room. After they caught a few hours' sleep, he would arrange for a tow truck to retrieve his pickup. He would have to replace the components that Youssef had ripped off his engine, but the damage should be easily repaired. The police were helpful and gave them a lift to the closest hotel.

Tricklock and Simon were weary and scruffy. They checked into their room and luxuriated in hot showers and soft beds. At Tricklock's insistence, they rose early and ate in the hotel. They had a busy day ahead of them. Tricklock planned to avoid the press, retrieve his vehicle, get some fresh clothes, and regain his freedom of movement. He started early and talked to a lot of different folks. Word had spread and everyone was very helpful. He hired a local tow truck and explained the situation. He also passed-on the make and model of his truck. The mechanic stocked up on possible engine parts that a vandal could snatch from under the hood to disable that type of engine, and then they headed out.

It was strange to retrace the initial stages of their journey that had begun only a few days before. They passed a camper trailer hooked to an SUV, and Tricklock remembered Tanya's story. He would notify the police so they could check it out; it might be the terrorist command post. When they arrived at his truck, the police were just finishing their sweep for fingerprints and other evidence. Tricklock talked to the officer in charge and explained his intentions. He also told him of his suspicions about the camper they had seen parked off the trail. Tanya had already related her part in the drama and had told of her encounter with the SUV and camper. It should be easy to check the plate number to see if it matched the number that Tanya had jotted down. The police detective released the pickup truck to Tricklock and the police began to leave.

The mechanic raised the hood and soon identified the parts that were missing. He installed the replacements and the truck started right up. There was nothing they could immediately do about the broken window, but at least the truck was running again. The tow truck and driver left with their mission complete and their services no longer needed. When Tricklock drove past the camper trailer it was already surrounded by police cars. The cops were probably running the plate and beginning the process of getting a search warrant. Suddenly, Tricklock and his son were alone in the truck. They locked eyes and both started laughing.

Tricklock said, "It's amazing the difference one day can make. Yesterday we were huddled in the forest being stalked by terrorists, our whole realty was catawampus, and today we're cruising along safe in my truck. It's strange but true. Life is like a roasted chicken."

Simon gawped, "What the heck is a catawampus, and why is life like a roasted chicken?"

"You'll have to google catawampus. I'm tired of giving you vocabulary lessons, but the chicken—now that is blond wisdom my son. Once I brought home one of those rotisserie chickens they sell in grocery stores. It's an easy no-hassle dinner. My girlfriend at the time leaned over and peered down at the crispy fowl sprinkled with lemon pepper. The chicken was nestled in its plastic container with its legs trussed-up and its little wings all shriveled and poking out. If you look at those chickens up close, they do look pretty weird. Anyway, when I joined her at the chicken she said, 'God bless its little heart. Yesterday that chicken was pecking around in the yard minding its own business and wham! Now look at it!'"

Simon nodded his head, "I see it now. She was very wise."

Pecos Wilderness Morning of Day Five: Khaled and Youssef were many miles away, still in the Pecos Wilderness. After pushing Waleed's body into the pit, Youssef and Khaled had trekked to the main road. Occasionally they had rested, but Khaled pushed the pace. Speed was crucial to his plans. Tricklock and his companions had a substantial head start. He was sure that Tricklock would have immediately walked to the road, hoping to flag down a vehicle and get back to town. Once in town Tricklock would inform the authorities as to Khaled's activities. The police would have their descriptions and quickly organize a manhunt, probably using dogs and aircraft. Khaled wanted to be miles away from the forest before the police formed their dragnet.

Sunrise was still a couple of hours away when Khaled and Youssef stumbled onto the gravel road, intersecting it much farther north than they had planned. They turned their weary faces towards civilization and began to walk. They hiked for miles without seeing any people or vehicles. As dawn was breaking, they noticed a truck and camper trailer parked off the road in a small meadow. Lights were on and they could hear voices inside. Khaled and Youssef conferred in whispers. When Khaled outlined his plan, Youssef was disturbed but not surprised. His emotions were numbed by exhaustion and the trauma of the past few days. He was still plagued by the after effects of his illness, injuries, and close brush with death. But those terrible experiences paled in comparison to the emotions he had felt during Khaled's callous execution of their friend Waleed. Khaled was ruthless and truly deserved his fierce reputation.

Youssef knocked on the camper entrance. A young man who looked to be in his early thirties opened the door. Youssef almost vomited when he inhaled the disgusting smells of frying pork sausage. His heart sank when he spied a young woman and young girl in the back of the camper. He was looking at walking corpses. Youssef forced a friendly smile onto his face. He explained that his car had a dead battery and he had no phone reception to call for aid. The young man said he would be glad to help. His name was Sam and he offered to drive his truck to their vehicle and help them start it with jumper cables. Sam gave his wife a peck on the cheek and told her he would be back in a few minutes. The three men got into Sam's truck and drove off. A few hundred yards down the road, Khaled thrust a gun into Sam's face and ordered him to park his truck. Khaled ordered Sam to get out of the vehicle and lay on his belly with his arms outstretched.

Khaled began to question Sam, "Keep your face in the dirt and answer my questions. Why are you out here in the forest?"

When the terrified man began to stammer, Khaled mashed Sam's skull with a large rock. While the American twitched in the dust, Khaled continued to pound the man's head. When Khaled finally stopped, Sam's head looked like a lurid Picasso painting, a cubist masterpiece of violence. Although he knew what to expect, Youssef was still stunned by the sudden brutal murder of the innocent man.

Khaled squatted next to Sam's body and examined the dead man's shattered skull with interest—he absentmindedly stirred the moist brain with a stick, seemingly lost in thought.

After a time he looked up at Youssef and smiled, "I decided I wasn't really in the mood to waste time with this infidel. Let's get moving."

They concealed Sam's body off the road and drove his truck back to the camper. Khaled insisted that they leave no witnesses. Youssef half-heartedly argued for an immediate escape, but Khaled would not be swayed. They arrived at the camper trailer and Khaled ordered Youssef to stay outside as a lookout. Khaled yanked opened the door and brandished his pistol.

Khaled barked, "Get out of the camper! Your husband and child's life depend on your un-questioning obedience!"

The woman was terrified. She clutched her child protectively to her chest and stumbled from the camper. The horrified woman walked ahead of Khaled into the woods. She was confused and in shock and moved like a compliant automaton. Once they were well out of sight of the road, Khaled stopped in a small glade.

Khaled talked softly, "I want to explain what is going on and put your mind at ease."

He smiled and approached the woman, "Sam agreed to help us with an important investigation. My name is Khaled and I'm an FBI agent."

He extended his arm as if to shake her hand, and when the petite woman instinctively lifted her hand in response, Khaled gut punched her so hard he could feel his fist hit her spine. Air whooshed out of the tiny woman's lungs and she folded. Khaled had ruptured internal organs and knocked the breath out of her. Her diaphragm was paralyzed; her efforts to breathe were desperate but futile. Before she could collapse to the ground, Khaled grabbed the helpless woman by the hair, stepped behind her, and violently wrenched her head back. He viciously slit her pale throat with a practiced swipe of his razor sharp knife. He cut hard and deep, making sure to sever her windpipe and both her carotid arteries. Khaled let her collapse to the ground. While his mother gurgled and sprayed her life's blood onto the dirt, the toddler staggered uncomprehendingly over to her side. Khaled speared the top of the girl's skull, wiped his knife clean on the dead child's shirt and afterwards stuffed the dead mother and child under brush and debris.

When Khaled returned to the camper, Youssef told him that he had seen no people or vehicles. Khaled beamed; things were looking up. They washed their faces and straightened their appearance. They ransacked the camper and loaded blankets, food, and water into the bed of the truck which was enclosed by a camper shell. It had been a long day. The two weary men drove away from the camper and headed towards town. Khaled decided it was not safe to return to their camper command post. His first priority was to put some distance between them and this godforsaken forest. Next they needed to find a safe place to catch a few hours of sleep. Without sleep their mental functions and judgment would quickly deteriorate. The need for sleep was maddening, but despite the inconvenience Khaled knew they had to briefly *go to ground*.

Youssef's acquired knowledge of American culture finally paid off. He suggested to Khaled that they head to the local Walmart. He explained that the store chain had a policy of permitting vehicles, campers, and RVs to use their parking lots. Youssef used his smart phone to locate the closest Walmart. It was still early in the morning when they arrived. Khaled parked in the midst of other obvious travelers taking advantage of Walmart's camper policy. They made their beds in the back of the pickup, hidden and sheltered beneath the camper shell. After their recent hardships, even these cramped accommodations seemed luxurious. It was a measure of their suffering of the past few days. They fell asleep almost instantly, safely hidden in plain sight.

A few hours later they awoke, left Walmart, and bought their lunch at a fast food drive through. Khaled was certain that by now the authorities had their descriptions. Tricklock would have assumed that Khaled would rejoin Waleed, not Youssef. Either way they were still two dusky complected, Middle Eastern men plopped in the middle of white America. Luckily, they blended in with the people of New Mexico more easily than they would have in the Northeastern U.S. Here they could both pass for Hispanics at a distance.

Khaled drove past their original camp site near the Tricklock residence. He was looking for something specific and found it when he spied a faint jeep trail relatively close to the ranch. They drove their vehicle off road into the desert. Khaled drove into a dry riverbed and parked parallel to the bank. Scrub sage, mesquite, and evergreens choked the edges of the arroyo and provided good concealment. They camouflaged the vehicle with brush, so it would be invisible from the air, or from casual hikers and passersby. Khaled had a bold plan. While the authorities were just beginning to look for them many miles away in the forest, he would already be stalking Tricklock's parents and if he was lucky, he might get another shot at Tricklock and his son.

Only a few miles away from his parent's home, Tricklock drove his truck with Simon in the passenger seat. It was time to talk serious. Tricklock told

Simon about some of the phone calls he had made and something about his thoughts and plans.

Simon was not enthusiastic, "Why don't you just let the police handle this from here?"

"The police *are* handling it. If they catch Khaled and his partner in the woods it's all over. But I have a sneaky suspicion that the police will come up empty handed. They are not used to going up against someone like Khaled. I think that if he can, Khaled may head for the ranch. The local police can't guard the ranch. Khaled would spot them a mile away and escape to kill us another day, and that's what I don't want. I don't want to have to worry about Khaled coming after us later on down the road. I want to end this threat."

Simon was upset, "What about me?"

"Don't worry." said Tricklock, "I have an important job for you."

While they drove back to their motel Tricklock went over Simon's mission. It was obvious to Simon that his dad was just trying to keep him safe and out of the way. Tricklock wanted Simon to stay with Tanya, keep her company and watch over her. She had been scheduled for surgery early in the morning and afterwards would be recovering in a hospital room. Simon didn't mind. The hotel was easy walking distance from the hospital. He had grown close to Tanya and wanted to see her after her operation. Simon smiled when he realized that Tanya would soon be experiencing the media from a whole different perspective.

Simon would also have to talk to his mother again, and he was not looking forward to that. His dad also warned him to expect newspaper and TV reporters, and recommended that if they cornered him he should refuse to comment.

"When they start asking you questions just pretend you've lost your marbles. Give them that vacant stare you always do and just repeat their questions back to them."

Simon scowled, "Very funny. That's more great advice from father of the year."

"I know what," suggested Tricklock, "when someone asks you a question just fall to the floor and curl into the fetal position. Then twitch and roll your eyes back in your head."

Simon shook his head, "I was thinking I'd wear a cardboard sign saying weasels chewed off my tongue while I lay unconscious in the forest."

Tricklock nodded in appreciation, 'That might work. It happens all the time around here."

At the hotel, Tricklock organized his gear. Soon he would leave for the ranch. While he packed he continued to coach Simon. He warned his son to keep his location at the hotel a secret. As much as possible, he wanted Simon to keep a low profile. He made sure to leave Simon plenty of cash and arranged a schedule to talk on the phone. They embraced before Tricklock left for the ranch. He had confidence in his son, especially after the recent events in the Pecos. Tricklock wanted to make sure the ranch was safe, then he would prepare the ground in case Khaled showed. He doubted that Khaled and Waleed had been able to escape the forest and make their way to the ranch this fast. In fact, the terrorists might not even show up at his dad's house. But Tricklock had a feeling that if Khaled could go there, he would.

Tricklock drove down the ranch driveway but stopped short of the house. He left his vehicle and searched the outlying buildings and the immediate grounds. Then he checked the main residence. The alarm was still set and the house was clear. He went back to his truck and parked it next to the house facing the driveway entrance. He went in the bed of the truck and unlocked the steel crossover tool box. He had some PJ stuff in there that was probably illegal for him to have, but it was going to come in handy, particularly the M119 Whistling Booby Trap Simulators. At the PJ School, they used them during combat tactics training. Each booby trap came with a tripwire, spring, and whistling unit. When a person walked through the tripwire, it set off a piercing whistle that betrayed their presence to one and all. During PJ training, if a student blundered into a wire and set off the whistler, it meant that in real life they would have set off an explosion and been killed. The whistlers were harmless, but they could still act as an effective early warning system.

Tricklock set up some whistlers at strategic access points to the property. He wished he had more. He did have some white smoke grenades. These could conceivably mask his movement if he had to run across an open area while under fire. Tricklock analyzed the layout of the ranch, not from a defensive viewpoint, but from an offensive perspective. He thought he had a decent plan. He heard gravel crunch and looked up to see his father Isaac's truck driving through the gate. The truck parked and an elderly man got out of the vehicle. He walked over to Tricklock and the two shared a quick hug and some back patting. Marvin was one of Isaac's oldest Marine buddies. When Tricklock had talked to his father on the phone and proposed his plan, they both agreed that Alice should stay away until this situation was resolved one way or another. Isaac sent Marvin to help. Marvin was well aware of the dangerous situation.

"How did mom take this whole thing?"

Marvin frowned, "She did not like it at all. I'm not sure what Isaac said to her or how much he told her, but I took the truck and told her I'd be back in a few days. She's pretty much stranded for the time being."

Tricklock smiled when he thought of his free spirited mother, "OK Marine, you ready to kick some ass?"

Marvin smiled, "Show me what you have in mind. Then I'd like a few details about your camping ordeal."

Tricklock outlined his basic plan and showed Marvin his preparations. Tricklock unlocked his father's workshop and they selected various firearms and ammunition. Marvin also had a few tactical suggestions. Tricklock nodded his head in agreement. They planned to set a classic L shaped ambush. In case they did have to change shooting positions, they parked their trucks in strategic locations. They would only have to run half the distance across open areas. If needed, they would have smoke grenades to mask their movements and their truck's wheels to hide behind for cover. Tricklock also drove Isaac's other car from the garage and parked it. He used the car to block the driveway at a narrow choke point so that no one could speed down the driveway and ram their vehicle into the house.

Tricklock surveyed their preparations, "I think we're about as prepared as we can be. Can you think of anything we've failed to take into account?"

Marvin shook his head, "I think we're ready for just about anything."

"Don't say that." replied Tricklock, "I always worry about Murphy's Law. If anything can go wrong it will. This is not your fight. I know you want to help, but I want you to mainly stay in the house and cover me. I may have to retreat there if things go south."

Not far away, Khaled explained his plan to Youssef, "I will stay here at the ranch, but I have another mission for you."

Youssef was becoming used to Khaled's unpredictability, "What would you have me do?"

Khaled would stake out the Tricklock ranch while Youssef would catch a ride into town. Khaled thought it was too risky for Youssef to use their stolen vehicle. The woman with Tricklock was seriously injured. Khaled thought it would be easy to locate her at a local hospital. Once in town, Youssef would find his way to the medical center and pay her a visit. Youssef was nervous and reluctant to kill a helpless woman in her hospital bed, but he knew better than to argue with Khaled. He was beginning to understand the degree of commitment and perseverance that was necessary to prevail in jihad. During the course of this mission his own weaknesses had been revealed, but Khaled had shown him the way. Khaled was truly a great warrior inspired and protected by Allah. Youssef walked to the main road and headed towards town. Before long a vehicle stopped and the driver asked him if he needed a ride. Youssef accepted gratefully. These people in Pecos were very friendly and helpful.

Simon hardly recognized his face in the mirror. His reflection reminded him of an animal and human hybrid, a cross between a man and a raccoon. Both his eyes were blackened, a result of his broken nose. At least his nose wasn't crooked—it was still straight as an arrow. He also had a goodly amount of cuts and scrapes. Actually, he looked kind of hardcore. When he thought about the events of the past few days he could hardly believe any of it had really happened. Now that it was all over, it all seemed surreal. He had some awesome stories to tell. This was national news stuff. He envisioned himself surrounded by beautiful girls, hanging on his every heroic word. This might be the highlight of his life. These opportunities didn't come every day; he planned to make the most of it. On this trip he had also learned that his dad was pretty awesome after all.

Now for the hard stuff, he took a deep breath and dialed his mother. She picked up on the first ring. She was all about details. For the next hour Simon told his story and answered a million questions. When he finally hung up he felt as if his brain was sucked dry. He needed to get out of the room; it was time to visit Tanya, his new best friend. She was awesome and badass. It was too bad that she was too old for him, but she would be the ultimate girlfriend for his dad. In fact, he would point that out to his father the next time they got together. Simon spiffed up as much as was possible given his battered face and headed out the door.

Simon walked the few blocks to the hospital and entered through the main entrance. After enquiring at numerous different information desks he finally obtained a floor and room number. Simon did not have very much experience with hospitals. If all hospitals were like this, he decided that he did not want to get sick. This place was confusing, smelled strange, and was very official and intimidating. He finally located Tanya on the third floor. The nurses at the desk were helpful and pointed out her room. Simon approached the room with trepidation. He was not sure what he would find.

His fears were groundless. When he entered the room Tanya was all smiles and hugs.

"Well look at you Tanya, what a big difference since last night! Amazing! Life is like a roasted chicken."

Tanya squinched her face, "What is that supposed to mean?"

Simon laughed, "Long story."

"It sounds like some of your dad's bizarre wisdom."

"Speaking of my dad, you're not going to believe this."

Simon went on to explain his father's current whereabouts and plans and all that had taken place since he had last seen her. He explained about his grandfather Isaac and his Marine background. And he told how Isaac had sent Marvin, one his Marine buddies, to help his dad.

"My dad also wanted me to give you this gift."

Tanya's eyebrows arched, "This is a strange hospital gift, kind of scary. What do think he's thinking?"

Simon shrugged, "I don't know, but my dad seems to have a way with these things."

Tanya changed the subject, "I'll bet Marvin and Tricklock make a formidable team, especially if they have time to strategize and set up traps. You saw what your father was able to do in the Pecos, and that was alone and on the fly."

"Dad is supposed to be phoning later and I'll get an update, but what about you? What did they do to your leg?"

"Well your father was 100% correct. I now have hardware in my leg. They put some screws and plates in my ankle, but it could have been a lot worse. Although it's a bad fracture, the breaks were pretty straight forward and relatively easy to repair. In fact, I should be outta here in a day or so, but I will probably set off airport metal detectors for a while."

"Maybe we can drive you back to Colorado when you get ready to leave." Simon suggested, "You won't be able to work the gas pedal with your right foot like that."

Tanya changed the subject, "Simon, how would you like to be famous? Don't laugh; there should be a TV crew here from Denver any time now. I've already been approached by other TV news crews, but I want my own station to run this first. Simon this is huge! The video of your father is still national news, and then a terrorist hit squad tries to kill him and his innocent young son on American soil during a camping trip. It's just an amazing story! Think of all the crazy things that happened out there!"

"What should I expect?" Simon asked.

"Well, you will be right here next to me. The reporter, a co-worker of mine, will recap events and then turn the cameras on us and ask questions. This won't be a live broadcast so you don't have to worry about making mistakes."

Simon nodded his head, "I've thought about this. The only reason I'm agreeing to this, is because I think it will help me to hook up with hot chicks."

Simon burst out laughing and Tanya punched his arm.

She was laughing too, "Like father like son."

"Why do you say that?" Simon asked.

"Because, your father didn't waste any time asking me out, he's pretty cheeky actually."

Simon was amazed, "When did all this happen?"

"About five minutes after I met you guys at the trout stream. Of course I immediately accepted."

"Dang, seems like I underestimated the old man again!"

Simon and Tanya both burst out laughing, but in deference to Tanya's casted leg, there was no rolling on the floor.

While Simon chatted with Tanya, oblivious to any danger, Youssef lurked near the hospital entrance. When Youssef saw a TV crew enter the hospital, he knew that they must be on their way to interview the woman. It had been easy to track down her whereabouts. Buzz on the street had been quickly building since the dramatic appearance last night of Tricklock and his two companions. Youssef had spent enough time in America to realize that this was a sensational news story. It should be easy to impersonate a reporter to gain access to the woman. He would help to write the end of this story, but he would make sure there was no happy ending. Surprise America!

Many miles away Khaled was conducting his own surveillance. Khaled watched from a distance as Tricklock moved about the ranch. After a time another truck arrived. By their actions Khaled guessed that the new arrival was Tricklock's father Isaac. When they parked their vehicles in strange places he became alarmed. Did they expect an attack? Were they preparing a trap for him? It did not seem likely, but Khaled had under estimated Tricklock for the last time.

Khaled moved stealthily to the ranch's entrance. He concealed himself in some trees near the ranch gate. When the time was right he planned to enter using the main entrance. He had watched Tricklock's father use the driveway and knew there were no traps. Tricklock had also parked a vehicle to block the narrow road where it wound between two stone walls. Whatever its purpose, the vehicle would provide perfect cover and concealment for Khaled.

Khaled was disappointed and wary. He did not like this situation. He was out numbered, he had a broken arm, and it appeared that he had lost the element of surprise. He prayed to Allah for guidance. Khaled knew that he was sometimes impulsive and reckless, but he was not stupid. He did not believe in suicide missions, at least not where he was concerned. He wanted to complete his mission and escape. He needed to kill Tricklock and return to Afghanistan.

Then he could claim responsibility and gloat at America's weakness and impotence. But as it was, it looked like the smart thing to do would be to abandon this mission.

It was late afternoon and the light would soon begin to fail. Khaled remained hidden, still mulling over his options when he heard a car approaching. As it neared the entrance to the driveway it began to slow. The driver was an elderly woman. Khaled decided to take a chance and stop the car. In order to make the sharp turn into the driveway, the vehicle had to slow almost to a complete stop. Khaled chose that moment to step in front of the vehicle. He pushed out his palm in the international *stop* gesture.

When the stranger leaped in front of her car, Alice instinctively stomped on the brakes. The young man approached the driver's side, and she rolled down the window to talk. Before she could react, the man yanked opened the door and dragged her from the vehicle by her hair. Khaled flung her in the dust and quickly jammed the car in park.

Khaled loomed threateningly over the woman where she lay in the dirt, "What is your name?"

Her voice wavered when she answered, "Alice Tricklock."

Khaled ordered Alice to get up. When she struggled painfully to her feet Khaled punched her hard in the jaw. He heard bone crack and she dropped like a rock. Khaled threw the unconscious woman into the back seat and drove the car a hundred meters down the road. Khaled was certain that no one at the residence could have witnessed the dramatic events at the ranch gate.

Allah had answered his prayers! Khaled now had the edge he needed to prevail on this mission. He removed the woman's shoes and used the shoestrings to securely bind her wrists behind her back; he made sure to tie them painfully tight. Alice slowly regained consciousness. She was groggy and disoriented, and then memory came flooding back. Her jaw throbbed with electric jolts of fire, especially when she tried to talk. She could tell it was fractured. Her wrists were tied together behind her back. She was losing circulation and the hurt was dreadful.

Khaled spoke softly, "This must be very confusing and painful for you. You do not need to know who I am or what this is all about. You just need to do what I tell you. Obey me without question."

Khaled yanked her out of the car. He grabbed her roughly by the chin, causing excruciating stabs of pain to shoot through her jaw.

He locked eyes with her, "Do you understand?"

Alice tried to speak and made a gurgling sound.

"This is what you will do. You are going to walk down your driveway towards your house. I will walk just behind you. I just want to have a pleasant conversation with your husband and your son. Their lives and your own depend on your cooperation and unquestioning obedience."

Khaled pushed Alice in front of him, using her as a shield. Sharp rocks sliced painfully into her bare feet and she stumbled frequently. Khaled forced Alice forward, totally callous towards the elderly woman's physical pain and discomfort. She meant nothing to him. In Khaled's mind she was already dead. Khaled clutched a fistful of Alice's hair and twisted her head back. He gripped a pistol in his right hand and pressed the barrel against her neck. Khaled would use Tricklock's mother to lure him and his father into the open, and then he would kill them all. He would savor and relish the moment when he met Tricklock and his father face to face.

Chapter 15

END GAME MOVES

Youssef watched from a distance. It appeared as though the hospital was letting in reporters but was refusing to let TV cameras inside. He looked at how the journalists dressed and acted. They wore casual clothes, khakis and various types of collared shirts and light jackets. He had cleaned up as best he could in that dead family's camper, but he needed clean clothes. He called a taxi and when it arrived he told the driver to take him to a men's clothing store. Youssef paid the driver and walked inside. He bought a complete set of clothes, including a new pair of shoes. He walked out of the store looking and feeling like a different man—he felt like an aspiring news reporter.

Youssef strolled to a nearby café and sat at a table. On the way in he grabbed a newspaper. He ordered some tea and pastry. He was in no hurry. He wanted to let the real reporters finish their interviews and leave. He did not want a lot of interfering people around when he visited the woman. The newspaper made for interesting reading. Tricklock obviously knew all their names, because Youssef himself had blurted out the information when he had been hanging from the edge of the pit in fear for his life. The police had impounded their camper and vehicles. Youssef also learned that the mysterious woman whom he had never actually met was herself a journalist from Denver. She might have also been following Tricklock; it was very puzzling. There were still unanswered questions.

The newspaper article was sparse on details. He was sure the police knew more but were withholding information for their own reasons. So far there were no descriptions of him and Khaled but they had only escaped the terrible forest last night. What a debacle! Although Khaled deserved his warrior reputation, his planning and preparation for this mission had turned out to be sadly lacking. It seemed that in this case, even The Great Face Eater had made mistakes. Youssef had suffered injury, debilitating illness, and near death in an abandoned mine shaft. He was weak from trudging for days through bleak wilderness, up and down hills, and with very little food. He had endured freezing nights, water parasites, and thin air that made his lungs burn and his heart pound. But worse of all, Khaled had seemingly been out maneuvered at every turn by the American, and this despite being encumbered with his teenage son and a lame female.

Youssef thought back to his training in the al Qaeda camp. At the time he had thought it the most arduous ordeal of his life. Afterwards he had imagined himself to be invincible, a piece of human steel cast into an al Qaeda weapon. He had mastered his rifle and learned hand to hand combat. He learned to make bombs and use explosives. He thought he was prepared for any kind of fight. He was convinced that he and the men around him were smarter, stronger, and braver than their American enemies. He had been taught that the only reason the United States continually bested them in battle was their superior technology and weaponry. He was taught that al Qaeda had two great advantages over the infidels. Their cause was righteous and they had Allah the one true God on their side. Youssef's harrowing experiences over the past few days had shaken his confidence.

When Youssef had given up in the pit, he had waited for death. Then Khaled had miraculously appeared and rescued him. He felt born again. Surely that had been a sign from Allah. Khaled's leadership and unwavering faith in their ultimate success re-energized Youssef. Khaled was ruthless and relentless. Although it had first appeared to Youssef that it was unlikely that he and Khaled would evade capture, Khaled had convinced him that they could still destroy Tricklock and escape the American authorities. They still had access to money and quality travel documents.

After they killed Tricklock they would travel the *Terrorist Underground Railroad* and escape from this godless country.

Youssef settled his bill and left the café. It was time to pay Tanya Brown a visit. He would use his knife to gut her like a fish, smothering her pathetic cries with a pillow. He made enquiries and this time used public transportation to travel to the hospital. Inside the lobby he boldly approached the information desk. Youssef found it remarkably easy to masquerade as a reporter. He quickly obtained the information he sought. The woman behind the counter was very helpful and trusting. She had encountered many other journalists earlier in the day and expected others. When Youssef flashed his college ID as press credentials, the receptionist barely glanced at his photo. She gave him Miss Brown's floor and room number and told him to check in with the shift nurse before visiting with the patient.

Youssef walked to the elevator and punched in the third floor. When he stepped out of the elevator there was no one at the shift desk. He glanced around to see how the room numbers sequenced and walked confidently down the hallway. He paused before the entrance to Tanya's room. He could hear voices; she was not alone. Youssef did not want to bungle this. He might only have one chance to kill Tanya Brown. He walked back to the nurse's station, which was now occupied.

"Excuse me. I'm here to interview Miss Brown. Is she accepting visitors?"

The nurse had been dealing with reporters all day, "I think so. She's just talking to a friend. She's a reporter herself so she's been very accessible to the press. She's in room 300."

Youssef thanked the nurse and walked around the corner back towards room 300. He saw a restroom and entered. He needed a moment to plan and gather his wits. Now that he was so close to his target he was jittery and his hands trembled. Knifing a person to death is a serious thing, especially when the target is a feckless woman. Youssef had never killed up close with a blade. Once again he mentally rehearsed his actions and played out various scenarios. His thoughts were interrupted when someone turned the handle to the locked bathroom door. The unseen person realized the restroom was occupied and moved on. The brief interlude galvanized Youssef. He took a couple of deep breaths and put his right hand in his trouser pocket. He gripped the hard shape of the large folding knife. Feeling confident and purposeful, he opened the bathroom door and strode down the empty corridor towards room 300.

Many miles from the hospital, Tricklock and Marvin fine-tuned their preparations inside Isaac's ranch house. Tricklock had prepared the ground for his hoped-for encounter with Khaled. He had booby trapped many of the approaches to the house. He had also barricaded the driveway from a frontal attack by a speeding car. He had arranged other vehicles in front of the house to provide cover in case he needed to move to one of the out-lying buildings. Tricklock had also upped his weaponry. As a gunsmith and avid practitioner of the shooting sports Isaac naturally had a diverse collection of fine firearms.

Tricklock had his Glock and plenty of loaded magazines, but in a real fight a pistol is only used as a secondary or backup weapon. For his primary weapon Tricklock chose an M-4 rifle. This was Tricklock's pararescue duty rifle, and he knew it like the back of his hand. He had used the M-4 his entire career—it felt like a part of his body. He loaded the rifle with a 30 round magazine and had four spare magazines tucked into belt pouches. For use at closer ranges, he prepped a semi-automatic, 12 gauge shotgun. He loaded the shotgun with buckshot and carried plenty of extra shells.

Tricklock also had the services of Isaac's old Marine buddy Marvin. Tricklock had phoned his father and filled him in on what had happened and told him of his gut feeling that Khaled would show at the ranch. After Tricklock told of his plans, Isaac had made his own arrangements. Isaac insisted that Tricklock needed backup. He sent Marvin who was a trusted Marine buddy who had seen a lot of combat. Tricklock didn't want to put Isaac's friend in mortal danger, but Marvin insisted on helping. Tricklock planned to use him to provide cover fire in case he had to run from place to place. Given the short amount of time he had to work with, Tricklock thought he was as prepared as he could be. Of course this reception party might all be for naught. Khaled might still be trapped in the Pecos Wilderness trying to figure a way out of the forest, or he might be long gone from New Mexico by now. But Tricklock had a hunch that if he could, Khaled would visit the ranch hoping to find him here at his parent's home recovering from his ordeal.

WILLIAM F. SINE

Tricklock saw movement at the front gate. He grabbed his binoculars and focused the lenses. His spirits sank and his heart raced. Khaled had captured his mother! Khaled pressed the barrel of a pistol to Alice's neck and used her as a human shield. His mom showed heart wrenching signs of physical damage and abuse. How had Khaled captured his mother? Khaled moved forward, pushing Alice in front of him. The terrorist stopped behind one of the vehicles that Tricklock had positioned. The car partially shielded Khaled. Only his upper body was visible above the hood. He continued to press the barrel of his gun against Alice's neck. Tricklock opened the front door and stepped onto the deck.

Khaled yelled for both Tricklock and his father to lay down their weapons and approach him with their hands held above their heads. Khaled had obviously mistaken Marvin for Tricklock's dad Isaac. Tricklock feared that as soon as he and Marvin were close enough, Khaled would just shoot them out of hand. Tricklock predicted that Khaled would probably not give him a chance to act or even speak, but nonetheless he knew he had to quickly comply with Khaled's demands. If he did not, he knew that Khaled would hurt his mother to compel his compliance. Khaled was ruthless and would not hesitate. Tricklock had no choice.

Marvin and Tricklock shared a meaningful glance and slowly set down their weapons. The two Americans walked resignedly towards Khaled with their arms raised. When Tricklock and Marvin were about 25 yards from the terrorist, Khaled moved the barrel from Alice's neck and pointed his pistol at Tricklock; he was taking no chances with the American. When Tricklock was 15 yards away, Khaled ordered them to stop. At this close range Khaled could not miss his shot, but Tricklock was still too far away to attempt to charge at the terrorist. Khaled smiled and aimed his gun.

At the hospital, Youssef was also approaching his moment of truth. Youssef slowed his walk as he neared Tanya's hospital room. He carefully opened the door and peeked in. Tanya Brown lay in bed with her eyes closed. She appeared to be alone. The other person he had heard talking earlier must have left. The woman's leg was enclosed in a cast and IV tubing ran from a hanging plastic bag into her left arm. Youssef crept through the doorway and silently purloined a pillow from the empty bed next to Tanya. The woman lay helpless only a few feet away from him. Youssef approached Tanya from her right side. He slid his large folding knife from his pocket and opened the blade. The polished stainless steel gleamed wicked in the fluorescent light of the hospital room. The blade made a faint snick as it locked open. Tanya opened her eyes.

Although she had never laid eyes on Youssef, Tanya immediately knew in her gut that the dusky-skinned man wielding the knife was one of the three assassins that had been hounding them these past days. Youssef tried to push the pillow onto Tanya's face to muffle any screams or cries for help. Easier said than done; Tanya yelled for help while she fought to keep the pillow off her face. Youssef was shocked by the woman's strength. He had not expected such fierce resistance. Tanya screamed and made a lot of noise while she struggled for her life. She wrenched the pillow from Youssef's grasp and chopped at his knife hand all the while calling for help. Youssef stepped back to regroup, searching for an opening. Tanya's right hand scrabbled on her bedside table and suddenly came up thrusting towards Youssef.

A brilliant orange geyser of liquid fire splashed into the center of Youssef's face. Youssef screamed and dropped his blade. The acrid pepper spray, the strange and prescient gift from Tricklock, burned Youssef's face like acid. He writhed on the floor clutching his face in agony. His blind eyes burned like fire and gushed tears. The caustic fumes of the potent spray cauterized his lungs. His chest was a bed of hot coals that burned away his breath.

Simon burst into the room, "Tanya! Are you alright?"

Simon took in the room at a glance, immediately sizing up the situation.

He yelled into the corridor, "Quick! Somebody help!"

Simon grabbed a lamp to use as a weapon and stepped between Tanya and Youssef. He spied Youssef's knife on the floor and kicked it away. The blade skittered across the slick tile floor and into the hallway. Simon's mouth gaped as he recognized the man on the floor—it was Youssef back from the dead. Simon had seen the terrorist fall into the mine, but here he was. Simon felt like he was trapped in a nightmare where it is impossible to kill the pursuing monster. Two orderlies dressed in hospital greens rushed into the room.

Simon blurted, "He tried to murder Tanya! He's one of the men that were trying to kill us in the woods."

Simon rushed over to Tanya who was shaking badly. Two burly orderlies pushed Youssef onto his stomach and held him down. They were used to restraining combative patients and had no trouble subduing the smallish Youssef. More people crowded into the room to help. Someone yelled that the police were on the way. Now more than ever, Tanya and Simon were the focus of intense scrutiny. The killer on the floor had made their abstract stories come to life. Youssef had stopped struggling, but his vision was a smear of blurred color. Apparently he would survive, although he wasn't sure he wanted too. He had failed.

Tricklock stared at Khaled, seemingly mesmerized and powerless to act. He watched as Khaled transitioned from aiming his pistol to squeezing the trigger. Time slowed and Tricklock could see Khaled's finger slowly tensing on the trigger. Then the impossible happened. Khaled's leer disappeared along with his left ear. A split second later Tricklock heard the abrasive crack of a rifle; it was music to his ears. A momentary halo of red mist capped Khaled's head. Blood gushed from the side of the terrorist's skull, and he collapsed to the ground unconscious. Tricklock was moving even before Khaled hit the ground. In moments Tricklock was at his mother's side and guided her over to Marvin.

"Marvin, get mom to the hospital *now*! She's hurt and in shock."

Marvin half carried Alice to one of the parked cars and sped from the ranch. Gravel sprayed from his rear wheels. Tricklock was not sure that Khaled was acting alone, but he suspected that he was. Nonetheless, Tricklock wanted his mother away from the ranch in case one of Khaled's minions was on the property. If Khaled was not acting alone, his partner would probably approach from the flank. Tricklock was taking no chances with his mother's safety.

Tricklock picked up Khaled's gun and tucked it in his waistband. He quickly searched the would-be assassin for other weapons and dragged him to a nearby parked vehicle. If Khaled's partner opened fire, Tricklock could use the car as a defensive barricade. He checked Khaled's pulse; he was still alive. It looked like the bullet had grazed Khaled's left cheek, shearing off his ear in the process. It was hard to know if the bullet had caused serious brain damage. Khaled could have a simple concussion, or he could be in a coma for days. Tricklock turned his attention to the ridge and could barely make out his father walking down the hill towards him. Isaac was almost invisible while he wore his camouflaged ghillie suit. When Tricklock had explained his scheme to entrap Khaled, his father had embellished the plan and insisted on setting up as a designated marksman, commonly referred to as a sniper.

Isaac was a Marine-trained sniper and with his passion for hunting and his profession as a gunsmith, he had maintained and even honed his skills over the years. Isaac had used a Remington 700 bolt action rifle with a Leupold scope. The 308 caliber Remington has been the standard sniper rifle of the American military for decades. Being an accomplished gunsmith, Isaac had enhanced his rifle and even loaded his own match grade cartridges. Isaac had tried to shoot Khaled in the center of his face, but Khaled had shifted position just as Isaac pulled the trigger. The shot had been off by a couple of inches and tore off the terrorist's ear. It was a very fortunate shot. Thank God for hydrostatic shock. Even though the bullet had not made a direct hit, its high velocity had still caused enough damage to cause unconsciousness. Of course, there was no need to let his son Jake in on the details of his sketchy shot. Isaac would forever claim that his shot was intentional and should be immortalized in the annals of famous sniper shots. A little luck now and then never hurt— sometimes it is called destiny.

When Isaac saw that Khaled had captured his wife, he needed to muster all of his great powers of self-control in order to take the shot. In that moment so much had depended on his skill. He never wanted to experience that much pressure ever again. When his son had phoned and explained his plan, Isaac knew he had to help. He had mysteriously cut their vacation short and had insisted that Alice stay put until he called her. He promised to be back in a couple of days. Alice was miffed by Isaac's cryptic behavior. Isaac and Marvin had driven away with the only vehicle, but Alice was not so easily stranded. She rented a car and drove it home. She had no idea she was driving into the middle of a gunfight. It was a close call. Isaac had almost lost her. He knew that in the coming days she would need his help to cope with her traumatic ordeal.

Tricklock called 911 and talked to the dispatcher. In the last couple of days he had provided the New Mexico State Police with a lot of excitement. Police cruisers and an ambulance were soon on the way. When his father arrived they embraced. They would talk later, but for now Tricklock asked his dad to fetch a pair of handcuffs from his workshop. Isaac ambled off to do his son's bidding and to strip off the ghillie suit. Now that his adrenaline was wearing off he was feeling mighty shaky—he was really feeling his age. His thoughts turned to Alice. As soon as the police finished with him he would track her down. As hard as it had been on him, choosing the right moment to shoot, steadying his nerves, controlling his breath and pulling the trigger, it must have been much harder on Alice. She had been a battered and helpless hostage who thought she was about to see her only son gunned down in cold blood.

Tricklock watched his father disappear into his workshop. He was filled with admiration for his dad. The last thing he had expected to see was Khaled holding a gun to his mother's head. His hunch that Khaled would make one last attack on the ranch had played out, although not exactly as he foresaw it. All of his preparations and booby-traps had been useless. As usual, it was the unexpected that had almost ruined the day. He was still puzzled as to how Khaled had managed to take his mother hostage. His father's idea of setting up as a designated marksman had saved the day.

Tricklock heard a faint rustle behind him. Before he could turn towards the sound he was slammed in the back. As he was going down, Tricklock knew that Khaled had attacked him from behind. Khaled had regained consciousness and waited until Tricklock's attention was focused elsewhere. With his good arm Khaled clenched a piece of nearby wood and slowly rose to his feet. Despite his efforts at stealth he was still unsteady and had made a slight noise. Tricklock realized what had just happened, but before he could react Khaled lunged forward and bashed Tricklock with the short piece of discarded plank. The board glanced off Tricklock's back and struck his head. Tricklock staggered. Khaled rammed his shoulder into the center of the American's spine.

The impact rocked Tricklock and he went down with Khaled on top. Tricklock had been taken by surprise and was stunned by the head blow, but he was still conscious. Tricklock struggled to turn into his attacker. Khaled still had the board and managed to club it across Tricklock's forehead. Tricklock felt wood grate against bone and a moment later blood streamed into his eyes. Tricklock grabbed Khaled's wrist and twisted, forcing Khaled to drop the board. Tricklock knew that one of Khaled's arms was injured from their earlier fight in the Pecos. He chopped at Khaled's wounded arm and connected. The terrorist screamed and flinched back.

Momentarily free, Tricklock scrambled to his hands and knees. Dust billowed around him, choking his lungs and obscuring his vision. When Khaled lashed out with his boot, Tricklock did not see the kick coming. Khaled's boot heel thudded into Tricklock's face. Tricklock felt and heard the crunch of his nose breaking. The vicious kick also knocked out some of Tricklock's teeth and he spit them out to stop from choking. He reeled backwards onto his back, his vision dimming at the edges. The kick had done serious damage and he fought to remain conscious.

Khaled knew that Tricklock was badly shaken. He also knew that he was a jiu-jitsu fighter. Khaled knew that in his weakened condition, Tricklock would be functioning on instinct and training. In fact he counted on it. Khaled stomped the American hard in the crotch, and when Tricklock convulsed, Khaled leaped onto the American's chest. Tricklock lay on his back with Khaled on top straddling. If Khaled had been a jiu-jitsu fighter, he would have begun his *ground and pound,* bludgeoning the American into unconsciousness and death.

Khaled was not a jiu-jitsu fighter, and he was not interested in clubbing Tricklock with his fists. He was a practitioner of kina mutai, and he had a more painful and gruesome end planned for this American who had caused him so much grief. Tricklock was in full guard and instinctively pulled Khaled's head down to his chest. This is what a fighter like Tricklock normally did in this situation. By grasping the back of his opponent's neck and torquing his head down, a fighter in guard position can make it extremely difficult for his adversary to rain down effective punches. In this case Khaled had been hoping that Tricklock's training would take over, he wanted the American to pull his head down. Jake Tricklock did not know he fought a practitioner of the martial art of biting and mauling.

When Tricklock pulled down on Khaled's head the terrorist didn't resist. Khaled was in the perfect position to administer a powerful bite. He planned to rip through Tricklock's chest muscles then move to the side of the American's neck where he would use his teeth to tear out the large veins and arteries. Massive blood loss would kill the American in minutes. Khaled hooked his good arm under Tricklock's armpit and grabbed a fistful of fabric. Khaled wanted to hold Tricklock fast. When he began his bite, the American's sole instinct would be to escape. Khaled needed to clamp onto him so that he had plenty of time to bite. Like the Iraqi commando he had killed, Khaled expected Tricklock to be consumed with an overwhelming instinct to get away from the pain and crippling damage.

Tricklock felt Khaled sink his teeth into his chest. The agony was indescribable, like setting fire to a cluster of raw exposed nerves, but Tricklock's instinct was *not* to get away at all costs. His reaction was to stop the bite, and he knew just how to do it. Tricklock forced his hands around Khaled's throat and pressed the tips of his thumbs against the terrorist's voice box. Tricklock squeezed with an iron grip fueled by his excruciating pain. He crushed Khaled's larynx with sickening pops and crackles. When Tricklock's thumbs mangled Khaled's fragile cartilage and vocal cords, the unstoppable natural reflex was for Khaled to open his mouth and hack violently. That immediately put an end to Khaled's biting.

Tricklock lay on his back and held Khaled at arm's length. The terrorist was insane with pain and rage. He struggled to breathe and to free himself from Tricklock's grip. He gnashed his teeth and slavered like a wild animal. Khaled pulled away and lunged for the American's face. Tricklock shoved his thumbs into the sides of Khaled's mouth and ripped outwards. Khaled shrieked and rolled to the side. Tricklock leaped onto Khaled's back and held him down. Khaled's torn cheek flaps fluttered and bled in the dust.

Moments later Isaac arrived with the handcuffs. He had been in his workshop pocketing the cuffs when he heard a commotion outside. When he investigated he was shocked to see his son grappling in the dirt with the terrorist. By the time he reached the fracas, the fight was over and his son crouched on top of the battered would-be killer. Isaac handed his son the Smith and Wesson handcuffs and Tricklock clamped Khaled's wrists behind his back.

In an ironic twist of poetic justice, he inadvertently over-tightened the cuffs, causing Khaled maximum pain and loss of circulation.

Isaac stared pop-eyed at his son, "You look like you've been through a meat grinder! Jesus, I leave for two minutes and you get the shit stomped out of you!"

Tricklock rolled Khaled onto his back, "You were saying?"

Isaac's eyes almost bugged out of his head when he saw the terrorist, "I take it back. Son, you're looking pretty good."

Tricklock laughed, "That's more like it. Now help me find my teeth. I need to rinse them off and put them in a glass of milk."

Isaac shook his head, "There's something you don't hear every day."

Tricklock explained, "Milk preserves knocked out teeth so a dentist can put them back in."

The State Troopers soon arrived and took custody of Khaled. Tricklock was glad the terrorist was still alive. He was sure to be a treasure trove of intelligence. The troopers had also brought along Simon. Simon told him all about the events in Tanya's hospital room. Tricklock was amazed; they had survived so many close calls. The Tricklock clan had powerful guardian angels.

Simon said, "That pepper spray you gave Tanya sure came in handy. How did you know she would need that?"

"I didn't know. If I thought there was a chance one of those guys would show up at the hospital, I never would have left you two. Since she couldn't keep her gun in the hospital, I just thought the spray would give her some peace of mind."

Simon nodded his head, "That was one of the better gifts you've given, much more practical than flowers."

Tricklock shrugged, "Well, flowers are good under the right circumstances."

Simon said, "Yeah, I guess. You know I'm looking at you standing here all covered in blood and grime. You have half a finger, a smashed nose, a boot print on your crotch, bite marks on your chest, and missing teeth. It really makes me realize something."

"What's that?" asked Tricklock.

Simon smiled, "Life is like a roasted chicken."

ABOUT THE AUTHOR

 William F. Sine spent twenty-eight years as a pararescue-man, during which time he participated in high-profile humanitarian and combat rescue missions around the world.

After retiring from the air force as a senior master sergeant in 2003, he became the first civilian to secure a teaching position at the Pararescue and Combat Rescue Officer School in New Mexico.

The recipient of numerous military awards and decorations, including the Distinguished Flying Cross with Valor and the Purple Heart, Sine is also the author of the nonfiction book *Guardian Angel: Life and Death Adventures with Pararescue, the World's Most Powerful Commando Rescue Force* as well as the military thriller novel *Tricklock*.

CPSIA information can be obtained at www.ICGtesting.com
Printed in the USA
LVOW05s0703020115

421158LV00034B/1331/P